Jack Vance

Rhialto the Marvellous

Jack Vance

TALES of the
DYING EARTH
Book IV

Rhialto the Marvellous

Jack Vance (signature)

Spatterlight Press Signature Series, Volume 29

Copyright © 1984, 2005 by Jack Vance

Illustrations copyright © 1979, 1984 by Stephen Fabian

All rights reserved. This book or any portion thereof may not be reproduced or used in any manner whatsoever without the express written permission of the publisher except for the use of brief quotations in a book review.

Published by Spatterlight Press

Cover art by Konstantin Korobov

ISBN 978-1-61947-384-3

Spatterlight Press LLC

340 S. Lemon Ave #1916
Walnut, CA 91789

www.jackvance.com

Contents

Introduction i

Foreword v

   I: The Murthe 1

  II: Fader's Waft 33

 III: Morreion 141

Introduction

> "Now I wonder what it is you find in that dark pool to keep you staring so?" the stranger asked, first of all. "I do not very certainly know," replied Manuel, "but mistily I seem to see drowned there the loves and the desires and the adventures I had when I wore another body than this. For the water of Haranton, I must tell you, is not like the water of other fountains, and curious dreams engender in this pool."
>
> — James Branch Cabell, *Figures of Earth*

Curious dreams engender in Vance's *Dying Earth* tales, just as a curious voice is used to narrate them. That distinctive voice in prose, nearly inimitable, is Jack Vance's and his alone. It is present in his science fiction works in various respective concentrations; to a lesser degree it can be detected, so to speak, in his mystery works. But it is in his works of fantasy, the *Lyonesse* novels and the Dying Earth stories, including *Rhialto the Marvellous*, that it becomes an extract, a distillation. Expressed in this literary voice is story development attuned to irony; is humor, a certain whimsical cynicism — and sometimes outright comedy.

The influence of James Branch Cabell on Vance was noted by Lin Carter; the influence of Clark Ashton Smith seems apparent, at least to me, both in tone and attitude. But over time, Vance developed a luxuriant voice and a tart, comedic approach — part and parcel of one another — that is close to unique. But there's always more to unpack in this gift box: he brought to all his work a gift for ideas, for conceptual daring, that takes him well beyond Cabell.

I recently used the phrase "bravely flowing prolixity" to describe an aspect of H.P. Lovecraft's style. While Vance often uses relatively simple sentence construction, in the sense that a master carpenter's cabinet is simple but exquisitely joined, he sometimes rolls out a *gorgeous* prolixity, a gem-like verbosity, constructed with a craftsmanship that could find comparison in Baroque classical music. It sings in the mind's ear. Indeed, in his time Vance was both a musician and a carpenter — was even a ceramic glazier — and these skills seem to transfer to his writing.

Among my favorites of Vance's Dying Earth fantasies are the picaresque adventures of that cunning wastrel Cugel the Clever, especially *The Eyes of the Overworld*. While Cugel is not a conventionally admirable person, astute readers find they enjoy spending time with him. He's amusing, he's the embodiment of the clever protagonist found in old school fairy tales — often tricking his way out of difficulties — and he makes us smile, even if it's the sly smile of a guilty confederate. In *The Eyes of the Overworld,* Cugel was enslaved by a sorcerer — and finds himself at odds with all sorcerers. But isn't everyone at odds with a sorcerer? When is a genuinely trustworthy worker of magic found on the Dying Earth? Even when sorcerers are partnered, as in *Rhialto the Marvellous*, they enact devious schemes against one another.

Rhialto the Marvelous, a fine work of Dying Earth fantasy in itself, reminds us that we must distrust purely magical creatures as well as human sorcerers. Fanciful beings, exampled by the djinn-like sandestins of *Rhialto,* are devious, peevish, and treacherous, often wittily jeering at the mortals who employ them.

The magician Rhialto is ostensibly a more likable character than Cugel. Despite a heartfelt practicality, Rhialto does seem to have some compassion, and he shows gallantry and restraint with women — to one lady's unspoken frustration, a paradox that is common in Vance — and on the whole he is more sinned against than sinning.

Another influence on Vance's fantasy, in a manner difficult to clearly define, may be the humorist P.G. Wodehouse. If Wodehouse was not an influence, they at least have much in common. The Wodehousian tone of affectionate cynicism can be cited, along with Wodehouse's tendency to tinker into being the maximum possible entertainment value of every passage. Consider this clip from the second part of *Rhialto the Marvellous*:

> Stepping forward, Rhialto addressed the group…
>
> "Creatures, men, half-men and things! I extend to you my good wishes, and my deep sympathy that you are forced to live so intimately in the company of each other.
>
> "Since your intellects are, in the main, of no great complexity, I will be terse. Somewhere in the forest, not too far from yonder tall button-top, is a blue crystal, thus and so, which I wish to possess. All of you are now ordered to search for this crystal. He who finds it and brings it here will be greatly rewarded. To stimulate zeal and expedite the search, I now visit upon each of you a burning sensation, which will be repeated at ever shorter intervals…

Rhialto's address in this passage is casually droll, starting with a blithe insult, as if he's entertaining himself (the creatures he addresses are unlikely to get the joke). He goes on to employ understated but acerbic insult humor regarding the dim intellects of the assemblage, and silkily mentions the onerous and inexorable consequences of slacking on the job. It is the rare reader who won't chuckle at this.

Vance's fantasy is distinct from his science-fiction, with a separate internal logic, but sometimes his science-fiction offers a flavor of fantasy — a particularly clear example can be found in his acclaimed novella *The Dragon Masters*. And in his fantasy we find Vancean modes also found in his science-fiction, as when he's delighting in satirizing the parochial, japing some provincial people's unshakeable exaltation of their own customs:

> The local folk, a small pale people with dark hair and long still eyes, used the word, "Sxysskzyiks" — "The Civilized People" — to describe themselves, and in fact took the sense of the word seriously. Their culture comprised a staggering set of precepts, the mastery of which served as an index to status, so that ambitious persons spent vast energies learning finger-gestures, ear-decoration, the proper knots by which one tied his turban, his sash, his shoe-ribbons; the manner in which one tied the same knots for one's grandfather; the proper and distinctive placement

of pickles on plates of winkles, snails, chestnut stew, fried meats and other foods; the curses specifically appropriate after stepping on a thorn, meeting a ghost, falling from a low ladder, falling from a tree, or any of a hundred other circumstances.

Vance was an able seaman with the Merchant Marine, for a time, and doubtless his visits to far destinations — each culture blessed with its own exaggerated sense of self importance — were grist for the mill of his humor.

I've emphasized the underlying humor in Vance's fantasy, but he never strays far from an atmospheric awareness of life's melancholies, even evoking grim extremes, so that fantasy is grounded by the earthiness of the grave.

In *Rhialto the Marvellous* a tribe of glib, self-justifying anthropophages feast for centuries on thousands of living humans plucked from their suspended animation in a nearby ruin. In another passage Vance describes an enormous battle, conveying it in a tone of sad resignation, and we come away with a sense of its tragic pointlessness, the waste of human potential, though also with a recognition of the courage of its combatants. Not all wars in Vance are depicted as meaningless — his *Lyonesse* books recognize that some nations are worth fighting for — but here we see them from the perspective of a magician who lives century after century, who flits through time and sees, in the big picture, the dismal recurrence of carnage.

The third part of *Rhialto the Marvellous*, centered on the fate of Morreion, a magician marooned on a world at the furthest edge of the universe, is shot through with melancholy but leavened with humor, however tart. Vance is a master of striking this balance. He had a gift for folding the dark in with the bright, for segueing seamlessly from the whimsical to the lugubrious. Yet even the doleful, in Vance, is beautifully wrought, and raptly entertaining.

And so I commend you to this glowing, darkly glimmering clutch of magical journeys with the vainglorious, sardonically amusing, sartorially splendid Rhialto. Keep your eyes open, savor this delicacy, and do not overly trust a sandestin.

— *John Shirley*

Foreword

These are tales of the Twenty-First Aeon, when Earth is old and the sun is about to go out. In Ascolais and Almery, lands to the west of the Falling Wall, live a group of magicians who have formed an association the better to protect their interests. Their number fluctuates, but at this time they are:

Ildefonse, the Preceptor.

Rhialto the Marvellous.

Hurtiancz, short and burly, notorious for his truculent disposition.

Herark the Harbinger, precise and somewhat severe.

Shrue, a diabolist, whose witticisms mystify his associates, and sometimes disturb their sleep of nights.

Gilgad, a small man with large gray eyes in a round gray face, always attired in rose-red garments. His hands are clammy, cold and damp; his touch is avoided by all.

Vermoulian the Dream-walker, a person peculiarly tall and thin, with a stately stride.

Mune the Mage, who speaks minimally and manages a household of four spouses.

Zilifant, robust of body with long brown hair and a flowing beard.

Darvilk the Miaanther, who, for inscrutable purposes, affects a black domino.

Perdustin, a slight blond person without intimates, who enjoys secrecy and mystery, and refuses to reveal his place of abode.

Ao of the Opals, saturnine, with a pointed black beard and a caustic manner.

Eshmiel, who, with a delight almost childish in its purity, uses a bizarre semblance half-white and half-black.

Barbanikos, who is short and squat with a great puff of white hair.

Haze of Wheary Water, a hot-eyed wisp with green skin and orange willow-leaves for hair.

Panderleou, a collector of rare and wonderful artifacts from all the accessible dimensions.

Byzant the Necrope.

Dulce-Lolo, whose semblance is that of a portly epicure.

Tchamast, morose of mood, an avowed ascetic, whose distrust of the female race runs so deep that he will allow only male insects into the precincts of his manse.

Teutch, who seldom speaks with his mouth but uses an unusual sleight to flick words from his finger-tips. As an Elder of the Hub, he has been allowed the control of his private infinity.

Zahoulik-Khuntze, whose iron fingernails and toenails are engraved with curious signs.

Nahourezzin, a savant of Old Romarth.

Zanzel Melancthones.

Hache-Moncour, whose vanities and airs surpass even those of Rhialto.

Magic is a practical science, or, more properly, a craft, since emphasis is placed primarily upon utility, rather than basic understanding. This is only a general statement, since in a field of such profound scope, every practitioner will have his individual style, and during the glorious times of Grand Motholam, many of the magician-philosophers tried to grasp the principles which governed the field.

In the end, these investigators, who included the greatest names in sorcery, learned only enough to realize that full and comprehensive knowledge was impossible. In the first place, a desired effect might be achieved through any number of modes, any of which represented a life-time of study, each deriving its force from a different coercive environment.

The great magicians of Grand Motholam were sufficiently supple that they perceived the limits of human understanding, and spent most of their efforts dealing with practical problems, searching for abstract principles only when all else failed. For this reason, magic retains its distinctly human flavor, even though the activating agents are never human. A casual glance into one of the basic catalogues emphasizes this human orientation; the nomenclature has a quaint and archaic flavor. Looking into (for instance) Chapter Four of Killiclaw's *Primer of Practical Magic*, 'Interpersonal Effectuations', one notices, indited in bright purple ink, such terminology as:

Xarfaggio's Physical Malepsy
Arnhoult's Sequestrious Digitalia
Lutar Brassnose's Twelve-fold Bounty
The Spell of Forlorn Encystment
Tinkler's Old-fashioned Froust
Clambard's Rein of Long Nerves
The Green and Purple Postponement of Joy
Panguire's Triumphs of Discomfort
Lugwiler's Dismal Itch
Khulip's Nasal Enhancement
Radl's Pervasion of the Incorrect Chord

A spell in essence corresponds to a code, or set of instructions, inserted into the sensorium of an entity which is able and not unwilling to alter the environment in accordance with the message conveyed by the spell. These entities are not necessarily 'intelligent', nor even 'sentient', and their conduct, from the tyro's point of view, is unpredictable, capricious and dangerous.

The most pliable and cooperative of these creatures range from the lowly and frail elementals, through the sandestins. More fractious entities are known by the Temuchin as 'daihak', which include 'demons' and 'gods'. A magician's power derives from the abilities of the entities he is able to control. Every magician of consequence employs one or more sandestins. A few arch-magicians of Grand Motholam dared to employ the force of the lesser daihaks. To recite or even to list the names of these magicians is to evoke wonder and awe. Their names tingle with power. Some of Grand Motholam's most notable and dramatic were:

PHANDAAL THE GREAT

AMBERLIN I

AMBERLIN II

DIBARCAS MAIOR (who studied under Phandaal)

ARCH-MAGE MAEL LEL LAIO (he lived in a palace carved from a single moon-stone)

THE VAPURIALS

THE GREEN AND PURPLE COLLEGE

ZINQZIN THE ENCYCLOPAEDIST

KYROL OF PORPHYRHYNCOS

CALANCTUS THE CALM

LLORIO THE SORCERESS

The magicians of the 21st Aeon were, in comparison, a disparate and uncertain group, lacking both grandeur and consistency.

I: The Murthe

1

One cool morning toward the middle of the 21st Aeon, Rhialto sat at breakfast in the east cupola of his manse Falu. On this particular morning the old sun rose behind a curtain of frosty haze, to cast a wan and poignant light across Low Meadow.

For reasons Rhialto could not define, he lacked appetite for his breakfast and gave only desultory attention to a dish of watercress, stewed persimmon and sausage in favor of strong tea and a rusk. Then, despite a dozen tasks awaiting him in his work-room, he sat back in his chair, to gaze absently across the meadow toward Were Wood.

In this mood of abstraction, his perceptions remained strangely sensitive. An insect settled upon the leaf of a nearby aspen tree; Rhialto took careful note of the angle at which it crooked its legs and the myriad red glints in its bulging eyes. Interesting and significant, thought Rhialto.

After absorbing the insect's full import, Rhialto extended his attention to the landscape at large. He contemplated the slope of the meadow as it dropped toward the Ts and the distribution of its herbs. He studied the crooked boles at the edge of the forest, the red rays slanting through the foliage, the indigo and dark green of the shadows. His vision was remarkable for its absolute clarity; his hearing was no less acute... He leaned forward, straining to hear — what? Sighs of inaudible music?

Nothing. Rhialto relaxed, smiling at his own odd fancies, and poured out a final cup of tea... He let it cool untasted. On impulse he rose to his feet and went into the parlour, where he donned a cloak, a hunter's cap, and took up that baton known as 'Malfezar's Woe'. He then summoned Ladanque, his chamberlain and general factotum.

"Ladanque, I will be strolling the forest for a period. Take care that Vat Five retains its roil. If you wish, you may distil the contents of the large blue alembic into a stoppered flask. Use a low heat and avoid breathing the vapor; it will bring a purulent rash to your face."

"Very well, sir. What of the clevenger?"

"Pay it no heed. Do not approach the cage. Remember, its talk of both virgins and wealth is illusory; I doubt if it knows the meaning of either term."

"Just so, sir."

Rhialto departed the manse. He set off across the meadow by a trail which took him to the Ts, over a stone bridge, and into the forest.

The trail, which had been traced by night-creatures from the forest on their way across the meadow, presently disappeared. Rhialto went on, following where the forest aisles led: through glades where candole, red meadow-sweet and white dymphne splotched the grass with colour; past stands of white birches and black aspens; beside ledges of old stone, springs and small streams.

If other creatures walked the woods, none were evident. Entering a little clearing with a single white birch at the center, Rhialto paused to listen… He heard only silence.

A minute passed. Rhialto stood motionless.

Silence. Had it been absolute?

The music, if such it had been, assuredly had evolved in his own brain.

Curious, thought Rhialto.

He came to an open place, where a white birch stood frail against a background of dense black deodars. As he turned away, again he thought to hear music.

Soundless music? An inherent contradiction!

Odd, thought Rhialto, especially since the music seemed to come from outside himself… He thought to hear it again: a flutter of abstract chords, imparting an emotion at once sweet, melancholy, triumphant: definite yet uncertain.

The Murthe

Rhialto gazed in all directions. The music, or whatever it might be, seemed to come from a source near at hand. Prudence urged that he turn in his tracks and hurry back to Falu, never looking over his shoulder... He went forward, and came upon a still pool, dark and deep, reflecting the far bank with the exactness of a mirror. Standing motionless, Rhialto saw reflected the image of a woman, strangely pale, with silver hair bound by a black fillet. She wore a knee-length white kirtle, and went bare-armed and bare-legged.

Rhialto looked up to the far bank. He discovered neither woman, nor man, nor creature of any kind. He dropped his eyes to the surface of the pool, where, as before, the woman stood reflected.

For a long moment Rhialto studied the image. The woman appeared tall, with small breasts and narrow flanks; she seemed fresh and clean-limbed as a girl. Her face, while lacking neither delicacy nor classic proportion, showed a stillness from which all frivolity was absent. Rhialto, whose expertise in the field of calligynics had earned him his cognomen, found her beautiful but severe, and probably unapproachable, especially if she refused to show herself except as a reflection... And perhaps also for other reasons, thought Rhialto, who had conceived an inkling as to the identity of the woman.

Rhialto spoke: "Madame, did you call me here with your music? If so, explain how I can help you, though I promise no definite undertaking."

The woman showed a cool smile not altogether to Rhialto's liking. He bowed stiffly. "If you have nothing to say to me, I will intrude no longer upon your privacy." He performed another curt bow, and as he did so, something thrust him forward so that he plunged into the pool.

The water was extremely cold. Rhialto floundered to the bank and pulled himself ashore. Whoever or whatever had thrust him into the water could not be seen.

Gradually the surface of the pool became smooth. The image of the woman was no longer visible.

Rhialto trudged glumly back to Falu, where he indulged himself in a hot bath and drank verbena tea.

For a period he sat in his work-room, studying various books from the 18th Aeon. The adventure in the forest had not agreed with him. He felt feverish and ringing noises sounded in his ears.

Rhialto at last prepared himself a prophylactic tonic which caused him even greater discomfort. He took to his bed, swallowed a soporific tablet, and at last fell into a troubled sleep.

The indisposition persisted for three days. On the morning of the fourth day Rhialto communicated with the magician Ildefonse, at his manse Boumergarth beside the River Scaum.

Ildefonse felt sufficient concern that he flew at speed to Falu in the smallest of his whirlaways.

In full detail Rhialto described the events which had culminated at the still pool in the forest. "So there you have it. I am anxious to learn your opinion."

Ildefonse looked frowning off toward the forest. Today he used his ordinary semblance: that of a portly middle-aged gentleman with thin blond whiskers, a balding pate, and a manner of jovial innocence. The two magicians sat under the purple plumanthia arbor to the side of Falu. On a nearby table, Ladanque had arranged a service of fancy pastries, three varieties of tea and a decanter of soft white wine. "Extraordinary, certainly," said Ildefonse, "especially when taken with a recent experience of my own."

Rhialto glanced sharply sidelong toward Ildefonse. "You were played a similar trick?"

Ildefonse responded in measured tones: "The answer is both 'yes' and 'no'."

"Interesting," said Rhialto.

Ildefonse selected his words with care. "Before I elaborate, let me ask this: have you ever before heard this, let us say, 'shadow music'?"

"Never."

"And its purport was —?"

"Indescribable. Neither tragic nor gay; sweet, yet wry and bitter."

"Did you perceive a melody, or theme, or even a progression, which might give us a clue?"

"Only a hint. If you will allow me a trifle of preciosity, it filled me with a yearning for the lost and unattainable."

"Aha!" said Ildefonse. "And the woman? Something must have identified her as the Murthe?"

Rhialto considered. "Her pallor and silver hair might have been that of a forest wefkin, in the guise of an antique nymph. Her beauty was real, but I felt no urge to embrace her. I daresay all might have changed upon better acquaintance."

"Hmmf. Your elegant airs, so I suspect, will carry small weight with the Murthe...When did her identity occur to you?"

"I became certain as I slogged home, water squelching in my boots. My mood was glum; perhaps the squalm was starting its work. In any case, woman and music came together in my mind and the name evolved. Once home I instantly read Calanctus and took advice. The squalm apparently was real. Today I was finally able to call on you."

"You should have called before, though I have had similar problems...What is that irksome noise?"

Rhialto looked along the road. "Someone is approaching in a vehicle...It appears to be Zanzel Melancthones."

"And what is that strange bounding thing behind him?"

Rhialto craned his neck. "It is unclear...We shall soon find out."

Along the road, rolling at speed on four tall wheels, came a luxurious double-divan of fifteen golden-ocher cushions. A man-like creature attached by a chain ran behind in the dust.

Rising to his feet, Ildefonse held up his hand. "Halloa, Zanzel! It is I, Ildefonse! Where do you go in such haste? Who is that curious creature coursing so fleetly behind?"

Zanzel brought the vehicle to a halt. "Ildefonse, and dear Rhialto: how good to see you both! I had quite forgotten that this old road passes by Falu, and I discover it now to my pleasure."

"It is our joint good fortune!" declared Ildefonse. "And your captive?"

Zanzel glanced over his shoulder. "We have here an insidiator: that is my reasoned opinion. I am taking him to be executed where his ghost will bring me no bad luck. What of yonder meadow? It is safely clear of my domain."

"And hard on my own," growled Rhialto. "You must find a spot convenient to us both."

"What of me?" cried the captive. "Have I nothing to say in the matter?"

"Well then, convenient to the three of us."

"Just a moment, before you prosecute your duties," said Ildefonse. "Tell me more of this creature."

"There is little to tell. I discovered him by chance when he opened an egg from the wrong end. If you notice, he has six toes, a crested scalp and tufts of feathers growing from his shoulders, all of which puts his origin in the 18th or even the late 17th Aeon. His name, so he avers, is Lehuster."

"Interesting!" declared Ildefonse. "He is, in a sense, a living fossil. Lehuster, are you aware of your distinction?"

Zanzel permitted Lehuster no response. "Good day to you both! Rhialto, you appear somewhat peaked! You must dose yourself with a good posset and rest: that is my prescription."

"Thank you," said Rhialto. "Come past again when your leisure allows and meanwhile remember that my domain extends to yonder ridge. You must execute Lehuster well beyond this point."

"One moment!" cried Lehuster. "Are there no reasonable minds in the 21st Aeon? Have you no interest why I have come forward to these dismal times? I hereby offer to trade my life for important information!"

"Indeed!" said Ildefonse. "What sort of information?"

"I will make my revelations only at a conclave of high magicians, where pledges are a matter of public record and must be honoured."

The short-tempered Zanzel jerked around in his seat. "What! Do you now blacken my reputation as well?"

Ildefonse held up his hand. "Zanzel, I implore your patience! Who knows what this six-fingered rascal has to tell us? Lehuster, what is the thrust of your news?"

"The Murthe is at large among you, with squalms and ensqualmations. I will say no more until my safety is assured."

"Bah!" snorted Zanzel. "You cannot fuddle us with such fol-de-rol. Gentlemen, I bid you good-day; I must be off about my business."

Ildefonse demurred. "This is an extraordinary case! Zanzel, you are well-meaning but unaware of certain facts. As Preceptor, I now must order you to bring Lehuster alive and well to an immediate conclave at Boumergarth, where we will explore all phases of this matter. Rhialto, I trust that you are well enough to be on hand?"

"Absolutely and by all means! The topic is of importance."

The Murthe

"Very well then: all to Boumergarth, in haste!"

Lehuster ventured an objection. "Must I run all the way? I will arrive too fatigued to testify."

Ildefonse said: "To regularize matters, I will assume custody of Lehuster. Zanzel, be good enough to loosen the chain."

"Folly and nonsense!" grumbled Zanzel. "This scoundrel should be executed before he confuses all of us!"

Rhialto, somewhat surprised by Zanzel's vehemence, spoke with decision: "Ildefonse is correct! We must learn what we can."

2

The conclave at Boumergarth, assembled to hear the revelations of Lehuster, attracted only fifteen of the association's membership, which at this time numbered approximately twenty-five. On hand today were Ildefonse, Rhialto, Zanzel, the diabolist Shrue, Hurtiancz, Byzant the Necrope, Teutch who directed the intricacies of a private infinity, Mune the Mage, the cool and clever Perdustin, Tchamast who claimed to know the source of all IOUN stones, Barbanikos, Haze of Wheary Water, Ao of the Opals, Panderleou, whose collection of ultra-world artifacts was envied by all, and Gilgad.

Without ceremony Ildefonse called the conclave to order. "I am disappointed that our full roster has not appeared, since we must consider a matter of extraordinary importance.

"Let me first describe the recent experience of our colleague Rhialto. In barest outline, he was lured into Were Wood by the hint of an imaginary song. After wandering for a period, he met a woman who pushed him into a pool of extremely cold water...Gentlemen, please! I see no occasion for levity! This is a most important affair, and Rhialto's misfortunes are not to be taken lightly! Indeed, for various reasons our speculations lead us to the Murthe." Ildefonse looked from face to face. "Yes, you heard me correctly."

When the mutter of comment had dwindled away, Ildefonse continued his remarks. "In an apparently unrelated circumstance, Zanzel recently made the acquaintance of a certain Lehuster, a denizen of the 18th Aeon. Lehuster, who stands yonder, indicates that he has important news to bring us, and again he mentions the Murthe. He has kindly agreed to share his information with us, and I now call upon Lehuster to step forward and report those facts of which he is cognizant. Lehuster, if you will!"

Lehuster made no move. "I must withhold my testimony until I am guaranteed fairly my life, a bargain which should cause no pain, since I have committed no crime."

Zanzel called out angrily: "You forget that I myself witnessed your conduct!"

"Merely a solecism. Ildefonse, do you then promise to hold my life in security?"

"You have my guaranty! Speak on!"

Zanzel sprang to his feet. "This is preposterous! Must we welcome each scoundrel of time into our midst, to satiate himself on our good things, meanwhile perverting our customs?"

The burly and irascible Hurtiancz spoke. "I endorse the progressive views of Zanzel! Lehuster may be only the first of a horde of deviates, morons, and incorrect thinkers sluiced into our placid region!"

Ildefonse spoke in soothing tones. "If Lehuster's news is truly valuable, we must reluctantly concede him his due. Lehuster, speak! We will overlook your flawed conduct as well as your offensive feathers. I, for one, am anxious to hear your news."

Lehuster advanced to the podium. "I must place my remarks in historical perspective. My personal time is the late First Epoch of the 18th Aeon, at a time well before Grand Motholam, but when the Master Magicians and the Great Witches rivalled each other in power: a case similar to the Eleventh Epoch of the 17th Aeon, when the magicians and the sorceresses each strove to outdo the other, and eventually precipitated the War of the Wizards and Witches.

"The witches won this great war. Many of the wizards became archveults; many others were destroyed and the witches, led by the White Witch Llorio, dominated all.

"For an epoch they lived in glory. Llorio became the Murthe and took up residence in a temple. There, as a living idol, comprised both of organic woman and abstract female force, she was joyfully worshipped by every woman of the human race.

The Murthe

The witches, led by the White Witch Llorio, dominated all.

"Three magicians survived the war: Teus Treviolus, Schliman Shabat and Phunurus the Orfo. They joined in a cabal and after deeds of daring, craft and cunning to tax credibility, they seized the Murthe, compressed her to a poincture, and took her from the temple. The women became distraught; their power waned while that of the magicians revived. For epochs they lived in a taut accommodation; and these were adventurous times!

"Finally the Murthe won free and rallied her witches. But Calanctus the Calm, under whom I served, rose to the challenge. He broke the witches and chased them north to the back of the Great Erm, where to this day a few still crouch in crevices dreading every sound lest it be the footfall of Calanctus.

"As for the Murthe, Calanctus dealt nobly with her and allowed her exile to a far star, then went into seclusion, after first charging me to keep the Murthe under surveillance.

"His orders came too late; she arrived neither at Naos nor at Sadal Suud. I never abandoned the search and recently discovered a trail of time-light* leading to the 21st Aeon; in fact, the terminus is now.

"I am therefore convinced that the Murthe is extant today, and so must be considered a danger of immediacy; indeed, she has already ensqualmed among this present group.

"As for myself, Lehuster the Benefer, I am here for a single purpose: to marshal the magicians into a faithful cabal that they may control the resurgent female force and so maintain placidity. The urgency is great!"

Lehuster went to the side and stood with arms folded: a posture which caused the red feathers growing along his shoulders to project like epaulettes.

Ildefonse cleared his throat. "Lehuster has rendered us a circumstantial account. Zanzel, are you satisfied that Lehuster has fairly won his life and liberty, provided that he agrees to mend his ways?"

"Bah!" muttered Zanzel. "He has produced only hearsay and old scandal. I am not so easily hoodwinked."

---

* time-light: an untranslatable and even incomprehensible concept. In this context, the term implies a track across the chronic continuum, perceptible to an appropriate sensory apparatus.

Ildefonse frowned and pulled at his yellow beard. He turned to Lehuster. "You have heard Zanzel's comment. Can you sustain your remarks?"

"Ensqualmation will prove me out, as you will see, but by then it will be too late."

Vermoulian the Dream-walker chose to address the group. Rising to his feet, he spoke with transparent sincerity. "As I go about my work, I walk through dreams of many sorts. Recently — indeed, only two nights since — I came upon a dream of the type we call the 'intractive' or 'inoptative', in which the walker exerts little control, and even may encounter danger. Oddly enough, the Murthe was a participant in this dream, and so it may well be relevant to the present discussion."

Hurtiancz jumped to his feet and made a gesture of annoyance. "We came here at great inconvenience, to sentence and execute this archveult Lehuster; we do not care to ramble through one of your interminable dreams."

"Hurtiancz, be silent!" snapped Vermoulian with peevish vigor. "I now have the floor, and I shall regale everyone with my account, including as many particulars as I deem necessary."

"I call upon the Preceptor for a ruling!" cried Hurtiancz.

Ildefonse said: "Vermoulian, if your dream is truly germane to the issues, continue, but please speak to the point."

"That goes without saying!" said Vermoulian with dignity. "For the sake of brevity, I will merely state that in attempting to walk that dream identified as AXR-11 GG7, Volume Seven of the Index, I entered a hitherto unclassified dream of the inoptative series. I found myself in a landscape of great charm, where I encountered a group of men, all cultured, artistic and exquisitely refined of manner. Some wore soft silky beards of a chestnut color, while others dressed their hair in tasteful curls, and all were most cordial.

"I will allude only to the salient points of what they told me. All possessions are in common, and greed is unknown. In order that time should be adequate for the enrichment of the personality, toil is kept to a minimum, and shared equally among all. 'Peace' is the watchword; blows are never struck, nor are voices raised in strident anger, nor to call out chiding criticism. Weapons? The concept is a cause for shuddering and shock.

"One of the men became my special friend, and told me much. 'We dine upon nutritious nuts and seeds and ripe juicy fruit; we drink only the purest and most natural water from the springs. At night we sit around the campfire and sing merry little ballads. On special occasions we make a punch called *opo*, from pure fruits, natural honey, and sweet sessamy, and everyone is allowed a good sip.

"'Still, we too know moments of melancholy. Look! Yonder sits noble young Pulmer, who leaps and dances with wonderful grace. Yesterday he tried to leap the brook but fell short into the water; we all rushed to console him, and soon he was happy once more.'

"I asked: 'And the women: where do they keep themselves?'

"'Ah, the women, whom we revere for their kindness, strength, wisdom and patience, as well as for the delicacy of their judgments! Sometimes they even join us at the campfire and then we have some fine romps and games. The women always make sure that no one becomes outrageously foolish, and propriety is never exceeded.'

"'A gracious life! And how do you procreate?'

"'Oh ho ho! We have discovered that if we make ourselves very agreeable, the women sometimes allow us little indulgences… Ah! Now! Be at your best! Here is the Great Lady herself!'

"Across the meadow came Llorio the Murthe: a woman pure and strong; and all the men jumped to their feet and waved their hands and smiled their greetings. She spoke to me: 'Vermoulian, have you come to help us? Splendid! Skills like yours will be needed in our effort! I welcome you into our group!'

"Entranced by her stately grace, I stepped forward to embrace her, in friendship and joy, but as I extended my arms she blew a bubble into my face. Before I could question her, I awoke, anxious and bewildered."

Lehuster said: "I can resolve your bewilderment. You were ensqualmed."

"During a dream?" demanded Vermoulian. "I cannot credit such nonsense."

Ildefonse spoke in a troubled voice: "Lehuster, be good enough to instruct us as to the signs by which ensqualmation may be recognized?"

"Gladly. In the final stages the evidence is obvious: the victim becomes a woman. An early mannerism is the habit of darting the

The Murthe

Lehuster said: "I can resolve your bewilderment. You were ensqualmed."

tongue rapidly in and out of the mouth. Have you not noticed this signal among your comrades?"

"Only in Zanzel himself, but he is one of our most reputable associates. The concept is unthinkable."

"When one deals with the Murthe, the unthinkable becomes the ordinary, and Zanzel's repute carries no more weight than last year's mouse-dropping — if that much."

Zanzel pounded the table. "I am infuriated by the allegation! May I not so much as moisten my lips without incurring a storm of recrimination?"

Again Ildefonse spoke sternly to Lehuster: "It must be said that Zanzel's complaints carry weight. You must either utter an unequivocal accusation, presenting documents and proofs, or else hold your tongue."

Lehuster performed a polite bow. "I will make a terse statement. In essence, the Murthe must be thwarted if we are not to witness the final triumph of the female race. We must form a strong and defiant cabal! The Murthe is not invincible; it is three aeons since she was defeated by Calanctus, and the past is barred to her."

Ildefonse said ponderously: "If your analysis is correct, we must undertake to secure the future against this pangynic nightmare."

"Most urgent is the present! Already the Murthe has been at work!"

"Balderdash, flagrant and wild!" cried Zanzel. "Has Lehuster no conscience whatever?"

"I admit to puzzlement," said Ildefonse. "Why should the Murthe select this time and place for her operations?"

Lehuster said: "Here and now her opposition is negligible. I look around this room; I see fifteen seals dozing on a rock. Pedants like Tchamast; mystics like Ao; buffoons like Hurtiancz and Zanzel. Vermoulian explores unregistered dreams with notepad, calipers and specimen-bottles. Teutch arranges the details of his private infinity. Rhialto exerts his marvels only in the pursuit of pubescent maidens. Still, by ensqualming this group, the Murthe creates a useful company of witches, and so she must be thwarted."

Ildefonse asked: "Lehuster, is this your concept of a 'terse statement' in response to my question? First rumor, then speculation, then scandal and bias?"

"For the sake of clarity perhaps I overshot the mark," said Lehuster. "Also — in all candour — I have forgotten your question."

"You were asked to supply proof in the matter of a certain ensqualmation."

Lehuster looked from face to face. Everywhere tongues darted in and out of mouths. "Alas," said Lehuster. "I fear that I must wait for another occasion to finish my statement."

The room exploded into a confusion of bursting lights and howling sound. When quiet returned, Lehuster was gone.

3

Black night had come to both High and Low Meadows. In the workroom at Falu Ildefonse accepted a half-gill of aquavit from Rhialto, and settled into a slung-leather chair.

For a space the two magicians warily inspected each other; then Ildefonse heaved a deep sigh. "A sad case when old comrades must prove themselves before they sit at ease!"

"First things first," said Rhialto. "I will fling a web around the room, that no one knows our doings... It is done. Now then! I have avoided the squalm; it only remains to prove that you are a whole man."

"Not so fast!" said Ildefonse. "Both must undergo the test; otherwise credibility walks on one leg."

Rhialto gave a sour shrug. "As you wish, though the test lacks dignity."

"No matter; it must be done."

The tests were accomplished; mutual reassurance was achieved. Ildefonse said: "Truth to tell, I felt little concern when I noticed *Calanctus: His Dogma and Dicta* out upon the table."

Rhialto spoke in a confidential manner: "When I met Llorio in the forest, she tried most earnestly to beguile me with her beauty. Gallantry forbids my recitation of details. But I recognized her at once and even the vanity of a Rhialto could not credit her in the role of a heart-sick amourette, and only by thrusting me into the pond and distracting my attention was she able to apply her squalm. I returned to Falu and followed the full therapy as prescribed by Calanctus and the squalm was broken."

Raising his goblet, Ildefonse swallowed the contents at a gulp. "She also appeared before me, though on an elevated level. I encountered her in a waking dream on a wide plain, marked out in a gridwork of distorted and abstract perspectives. She stood at an apparent distance of fifty yards, truly effulgent in her silver-pale beauty, arranged obviously for my benefit. She seemed tall in stature, and towered over me as if I were a child. A psychological ploy, of course, which caused me to smile.

"I called out in a forthright voice: 'Llorio the Murthe, I can see you easily; you need not soar so high.'

"She responded gently enough: 'Ildefonse, my stature need not concern you; my words carry the same import, spoken high or low.'

" 'All very well, but why incur the risk of a vertigo? Your natural proportions are certainly more pleasing to the eye. I can see every pore in your skin. Still, no matter; it is all one with me. Why do you wander into my musing?'

" 'Ildefonse, of all men alive, you are the wisest. The time now is late, but not too late! The female race may still reshape the universe! First, I will lead a sortie to Sadal Suud; among the Seventeen Moons we will renew the human destiny. Your kindly strength, your virtue and grandeur are rich endowments for the role which now you must play.'

"The flavor of these words was not to my liking. I said: 'Llorio, you are a woman of surpassing beauty, though you would seem to lack that provocative warmth which draws man to woman, and adds dimension to the character.'

"The Murthe responded curtly: 'The quality you describe is a kind of lewd obsequiousness which, happily, has now become obsolete. As for the 'surpassing beauty', it is an apotheotic quality generated by the surging music of the female soul, which you, in your crassness, perceive only as a set of pleasing contours.'

"I replied with my usual gusto: 'Crass or not, I am content with what I see, and as for sorties to far places, let us first march in triumph to the bed-chamber at Boumergarth which is close at hand and there test each other's mettle. Come then, diminish your stature so that I may take your hand; you stand at an inconvenient altitude and the bed would collapse under your weight — in fact, under present conditions, our coupling would hardly be noticed by either of us.'

"Llorio said with scorn: 'Ildefonse, you are a disgusting old satyr, and I see that I was mistaken in my appraisal of your worth. Nevertheless, you must serve our cause with full force.'

"In a stately manner she walked away, into the eccentric angles of the perspective, and with every step she seemed to dwindle, either in the distance or in stature. She walked pensively, in a manner which almost might be construed as invitational. I succumbed to impulse and set out after her — first at a dignified saunter, then faster and faster until I galloped on pounding legs and finally dropped in exhaustion to the ground. Llorio turned and spoke: 'See how the grossness of your character has caused you a foolish indignity!'

"She flicked her hand to throw down a squalm which struck me on the forehead. 'I now give you leave to return to your manse.' And with that she was gone.

"I awoke on the couch in my work-room. Instantly I sought out my *Calanctus* and applied his recommended prophylactics in full measure."

"Most odd!" said Rhialto. "I wonder how Calanctus dealt with her."

"Just as we must do, by forming a strong and relentless cabal."

"Just so, but where and how? Zanzel has been ensqualmed, and certainly he is not alone."

"Bring out your farvoyer; let us learn the worst. Some may still be saved."

Rhialto rolled out an ornate old tabouret, waxed so many times as to appear almost black. "Who will you see first?"

"Try the staunch if mysterious Gilgad. He is a man of discrimination and not easily fooled."

"We may still be disappointed," said Rhialto. "When last I looked, a nervous snake might have envied the deft motion of his tongue." He touched one of the scallops which adorned the edge of the tabouret and spoke a cantrap, to evoke the miniature of Gilgad in a construct of his near surroundings.

Gilgad stood in the kitchen of his manse Thrume, berating the cook. Rather than his customary plum-red suit, the new Gilgad wore wide rose-red pantaloons tied at waist and ankle with coquettish black ribbons. Gilgad's black blouse displayed in tasteful embroidery a dozen red and green birds. Gilgad also used a smart new hair-style, with opulent rolls of hair over each ear, a pair of fine ruby hair-pins to hold the coiffure in place, and a costly white plume surmounting all.

Rhialto told Ildefonse: "Gilgad has been quick to accept the dictates of high fashion."

Ildefonse held up his hand. "Listen!"

From the display came Gilgad's thin voice, now raised in anger: "— grime and grit in profusion; it may have served during my previous half-human condition, but now many things have altered and I see the world, including this sordid kitchen, in a new light. Henceforth, I demand full punctilio! All areas and surfaces must be scoured; extreme neatness will prevail! Further! My metamorphosis will seem peculiar to certain among you, and I suppose that you will crack your little jokes. But I have keen ears and have little jokes of my own! Need I mention Kuniy, who hops about his duties on little soft feet with a mouse-tail trailing behind him, squeaking at the sight of a cat?"

Rhialto touched a scallop to remove the image of Gilgad. "Sad. Gilgad was always something of a dandy and, if you recall, his temper was often uncertain, or even acrid. Ensqualmation evidently fails to ennoble its victim. Ah well, so it goes. Who next?"

"Let us investigate Eshmiel, whose loyalty surely remains staunch."

Rhialto touched a scallop and on the tabouret appeared Eshmiel in the dressing room of his manse Sil Soum. Eshmiel's previous guise had been notable for its stark and absolute chiaroscuro, with the right side of his body white and the left side black. His garments had followed a similar scheme, though their cut was often bizarre or even frivolous.*

In squalmation, Eshmiel had not discarded his taste for striking contrast, but now he seemed to be wavering between such themes as blue and purple, yellow and orange, pink and umber: these being the colors adorning the mannequins ranged around the room. As Rhialto and Ildefonse watched, Eshmiel marched back and forth, inspecting

---

* Eshmiel's more thoughtful associates often speculated that Eshmiel used this means to symbolize the Grand Polarities permeating the universe, while at the same time asserting the infinite variety to be derived from the apparent simplicity. These persons considered Eshmiel's message profound but optimistic, though Eshmiel himself refused to issue an analysis.

first one, then another, but finding nothing suitable to his needs, which caused him an obvious vexation.

Ildefonse sighed heavily. "Eshmiel is clearly gone. Let us grit our teeth and investigate the cases first of Hurtiancz and then Dulce-Lolo."

Magician after magician appeared on the tabouret, and in the end no doubt remained but that ensqualmation had infected all.

Rhialto spoke gloomily: "Not one of the group showed so much as a twitch of distress! All wallowed in the squalming as if it were a boon! Would you and I react in the same way?"

Ildefonse winced and pulled at his blond beard. "It makes the blood to run cold."

"So now we are alone," said Rhialto. "The decisions are ours to make."

"They are not simple," said Ildefonse after reflection. "We have come under attack: do we retaliate? If so: how? Or even: why? The world is moribund."

"But I am not! I am Rhialto, and such treatment offends me!"

Ildefonse nodded thoughtfully. "That is an important point. I, with equal vehemence, am Ildefonse!"

"More, you are Ildefonse the Preceptor! And now you must use your legitimate powers."

Ildefonse inspected Rhialto through blue eyes blandly half-closed. "Agreed! I nominate you to enforce my edicts!"

Rhialto ignored the pleasantry. "I am thinking of IOUN stones."

Ildefonse sat up in his chair. "What is your exact meaning?"

"You must decree confiscation from the ensqualmated witches of all IOUN stones, on grounds of policy. Then we will work a time-stasis and send sandestins out to gather the stones."

"All very well, but our comrades often conceal their treasures with ingenious care."

"I must confess to a whimsical little recreation — a kind of intellectual game, as it were. Over the years I have ascertained the hiding-place of every IOUN stone current among the association. You keep yours, for instance, in the water reservoir of the convenience at the back of your work-room."

"That, Rhialto, is an ignoble body of knowledge. Still, at this point, we cannot gag at trifles. I hereby confiscate all IOUN stones in the

RHIALTO THE MARVELLOUS

custody of our bewitched former comrades. Now, if you will impact the continuum with a spell, I will call in my sandestins Osherl, Ssisk and Walfing."

"My creatures Topo and Bellume are also available for duty."

The confiscation went with an almost excessive facility. Ildefonse declared: "We have struck an important blow. Our position is now clear; our challenge is bold and direct!"

Rhialto frowningly considered the stones. "We have struck a blow; we have issued a challenge: what now?"

Ildefonse blew out his cheeks. "The prudent course is to hide until the Murthe goes away."

Rhialto gave a sour grunt. "Should she find us and pull us squeaking from our holes, all dignity is lost. Surely this is not the way of Calanctus."

"Let us then discover the way of Calanctus," said Ildefonse. "Bring out Poggiore's *Absolutes*; he devotes an entire chapter to the Murthe. Fetch also *The Decretals* of Calanctus, and, if you have it, *Calanctus: His Means and Modes*."

4

Dawn was still to come. The sky over Wilda Water showed a flush of plum, aquamarine and dark rose. Rhialto slammed shut the iron covers of the *Decretals*. "I find no help. Calanctus describes the persistent female genius, but he is not explicit in his remedies."

Ildefonse, looking through *The Doctrines of Calanctus*, said: "I find here an interesting passage. Calanctus likens a woman to the Ciaeic Ocean which absorbs the long and full thrust of the Antipodal Current as it sweeps around Cape Spang, but only while the weather holds fair. If the wind shifts but a trifle, this apparently placid ocean hurls an abrupt flood ten or even twenty feet high back around the cape, engulfing all before it. When stasis is restored and the pressure relieved, the Ciaeic is as before, placidly accepting the current. Do you concur with this interpretation of the female geist?"

"Not on all counts," said Rhialto. "At times Calanctus verges upon the hyperbolic. This might be regarded as a typical case, especially since he provides no program for holding off or even diverting the Ciaeic flood."

"He seems to suggest that one does not strive, ordinarily, to control this surge but, rather, rides over it in a staunch ship of high freeboard."

Rhialto shrugged. "Perhaps so. As always, I am impatient with obscure symbolism. The analogy assists us not at all."

Ildefonse ruminated. "It suggests that rather than meeting the Murthe power against power, we must slide across and over the gush of her hoarded energy, until at last she has spent herself and we, like stout ships, float secure and dry."

"Again, a pretty image, but limited. The Murthe displays a protean power."

Ildefonse stroked his beard and looked pensively off into space. "Indeed, one inevitably starts to wonder whether this fervor, cleverness and durability might also govern her — or, so to speak, might tend to influence her conduct in, let us say, the realm of —"

"I understand the gist of your speculation," said Rhialto. "It is most likely nuncupatory."

Ildefonse gave his head a wistful shake. "Sometimes one's thoughts go where they will."

A golden insect darted out of the shadows, circled the lamp and flew back into the darkness. Rhialto instantly became alert. "Someone has entered Falu, and now waits in the parlour." He went to the door and called out sharply: "Who is there? Speak, or dance the tarantella on feet of fire."

"Hold hard your spell!" spoke a voice. "It is I, Lehuster!"

"In that case, come forward."

Into the work-room came Lehuster, soiled and limping, his shoulder feathers bedraggled, in a state of obvious fatigue. He carried a sack which he gratefully dropped upon the leather-slung couch under the window.

Ildefonse surveyed him with frowning disfavor. "Well then, Lehuster, you are here at last! A dozen times during the night we might have used your counsel, but you were nowhere to be found. What, then, is your report?"

Rhialto handed Lehuster a tot of aquavit. "This will alleviate your fatigue; drink and then speak freely."

Lehuster consumed the liquid at a gulp. "Aha! A tipple of rare quality!...Well then, I have little enough to tell you, though I have spent a most toilsome night, performing necessary tasks. All are ensqualmed, save only yourselves. The Murthe, however, believes that she controls the entire association."

"What?" cried Rhialto. "Does she take us so lightly?"

"No great matter." Lehuster held out the empty goblet. "If you please! A bird flies erratically on one wing...Further, the Murthe appropriated all IOUN stones to her personal use —"

"Not so!" said Ildefonse with a chuckle. "We cleverly took them first."

"You seized a clutch of glass baubles. The Murthe took the true stones, including those owned by you and Rhialto, and left brummagem in their place."

Rhialto ran to the basket where the presumptive IOUN stones reposed. He groaned. "The mischievous vixen has robbed us in cold blood!"

Lehuster gestured to the sack he had tossed upon the couch. "On this occasion, we have bested her. Yonder are the stones! I seized them while she bathed. I suggest that you send a sandestin to replace them with the false stones. If you hurry, there is still time; the Murthe dallies at her toilette. Meanwhile hide the true stones in some extra-dimensional cubby-hole, so that they may not be taken from you again."

Rhialto summoned his sandestin Bellume and issued an appropriate instruction.

Ildefonse turned to Lehuster: "By what means did Calanctus confound this dire and frightening female?"

"Mystery still shrouds the occasion," said Lehuster. "Calanctus apparently used an intense personal force and so kept Llorio at bay."

"Hmmf. We must learn more of Calanctus. The chronicles make no mention of his death; he may still be extant, perhaps in the Land of Cutz!"

"Such questions also trouble the Murthe," said Lehuster. "We may well be able to confuse her and induce her retreat."

"How so?"

"There is no time to lose. You and Rhialto must create an ideal semblance in the shape of Calanctus, and here, at least, I can be of assistance. The creation need not be permanent, but it must be sufficiently vital so that Llorio is persuaded that once again she pits herself against Calanctus."

Ildefonse pulled doubtfully at his beard. "That is a major undertaking."

"With scant time for its execution! Remember, by winning the IOUN stones you have defied the Murthe with a challenge which she cannot ignore!"

Rhialto jumped to his feet. "Quickly then! Let us do as Lehuster suggests! Time is short."

"Hmmf," growled Ildefonse. "I do not fear this misguided harridan. Is there no easier way?"

"Yes! Flight to a far dimension!"

"You know me better than that!" declared Ildefonse. "To work! We will send this witch squealing and leaping with skirts held high as she bounds over the brambles!"

"That shall be our slogan," declared Lehuster. "To work!"

The semblance of Calanctus took form on the work table: first an armature of silver and tantalum wires built upon an articulated spinal truss, then a shadowy sheathing of tentative concepts, then the skull and sensorium, into which were inserted all the works of Calanctus, and a hundred other tracts, including catalogues, compendia, pantologies and universal syntheses, until Lehuster counselled a stop. "Already he knows twenty times as much as the first Calanctus! I wonder if he can organize such a mass?"

The muscles were stretched and drawn taut; the skin was applied, along with a thick pelt of dark short hair over the scalp and down the forehead. Lehuster worked long and hard at the features, adjusting the jut of the jaw, the thrust of the short straight nose, the breadth of the forehead, the exact shape and curve of eyebrows and hair-line.

The ears were affixed and the auditory channels adjusted. Lehuster spoke in an even voice: "You are Calanctus, first hero of the 18th Aeon."

The semblance of Calanctus took form on the work table...

The Murthe

The eyes opened and gazed thoughtfully at Lehuster.

"I am your friend," said Lehuster. "Calanctus, arise! Go sit in yonder chair."

The Calanctus-form rose from the table with only a trifling effort, swung his strong legs to the floor and went to sit in the chair.

Lehuster turned to Rhialto and Ildefonse. "It would be better if now you stepped into the parlor for a few minutes. I must instill memories and associations into this mind; he must be vivid with life."

"A full lifetime of memories in so short a time?" demanded Ildefonse. "Impossible!"

"Not so, in a time-compression! I will also teach him music and poetry; he must be passionate as well as vivid. My instrument is this bit of dry flower-petal; its perfume works magic."

Somewhat reluctantly Ildefonse and Rhialto went to the parlor, where they watched morning come full to Low Meadow.

Lehuster called them to the work-room. "There sits Calanctus. His mind is rich with knowledge; he is perhaps even broader in his concepts than his namesake. Calanctus, this is Rhialto and this is Ildefonse; they are your friends."

Calanctus looked from one to the other with mild blue eyes. "I am glad to hear that! From what I have learned, the world is sorely in need of amity."

Lehuster said aside: "He is Calanctus, but with a difference, or even a certain lack. I have given him a quart of my blood, but perhaps it is not enough... Still, we shall see."

Ildefonse asked: "What of power? Can he enforce his commands?"

Lehuster looked toward the neo-Calanctus. "I have loaded his sensorium with IOUN stones. Since he has never known harm he is easy and gentle despite his innate force."

"What does he know of the Murthe?"

"All there is to be known. He shows no emotion."

Rhialto and Ildefonse regarded their creation with skepticism. "So far Calanctus seems still an abstraction, without over-much volition," said Rhialto. "Can we not give him a more visceral identification with the real Calanctus?"

Lehuster hesitated. "Yes. It is a scarab which Calanctus always wore on his wrist. Dress him now in apparel, then I will give him the scarab."

Ten minutes later Rhialto and Ildefonse entered the parlour with Calanctus, who now wore a black helmet, a breast-plate of polished black metal, a black cape, black breeches and black boots, with silver buckles and accoutrements.

Lehuster nodded. "He is as he should be. Calanctus, hold out your arm! I will give you a scarab worn by the first Calanctus, whose identity you must assume. This bracelet is yours. Wear it always around your right wrist."

Calanctus said: "I feel the surge of power. I am strong! I am Calanctus!"

Rhialto asked: "Are you strong enough to accept the sleight of magic? The ordinary man must study forty years even to become an apprentice."

"I have the power to accept magic."

"Come then! You shall ingest the *Encyclopedia*, then the Three Books of Phandaal, and if then you are neither dead nor mad I will pronounce you a man strong beyond any of my experience. Come! Back to the work-room."

Ildefonse remained in the parlour…Minutes passed. He heard a queer choking outcry, quickly quelled.

Calanctus returned to the parlour with firm steps. Rhialto, coming after, walked on sagging knees with a green pallor on his face.

Calanctus spoke somberly to Ildefonse: "I have accepted magic. My mind reels with spells; they are wild, but still I control their veering forces. The scarab gave me the strength."

Lehuster spoke. "The time is near. Witches gather on the meadow: Zanzel, Ao of the Opals, Barbanikos, and others. They are fretful and agitated…In fact, Zanzel approaches."

Rhialto looked to Ildefonse. "Shall we use the opportunity?"

"We would be fools if we did not!"

"My thoughts precisely. If you will take yourself to the side arbor…"

Rhialto went out on the front terrace, where he met Zanzel, who lodged an emphatic protest in the matter of the missing IOUN stones.

"Quite right!" said Rhialto. "It was a dastardly act, done at the behest of Ildefonse. Come to the side arbor and I will redress the wrong."

"I feel the surge of power. I am strong! I am Calanctus!"

Zanzel walked to the side arbor where Ildefonse desensitized her with the Spell of Internal Solitude. Ladanque, Rhialto's chamberlain, lifted Zanzel to a barrow and wheeled her to the gardener's shed.

Rhialto, emboldened by his success, stepped to the front terrace and signaled to Barbanikos, who, following Rhialto into the side arbor, met a similar disposition.

So it went with Ao of the Opals, Dulce-Lolo, Hurtiancz and others, until the only witches remaining upon the meadow were the absent-minded Vermoulian and Tchamast the Didactor, both of whom ignored Rhialto's signal.

Llorio the Murthe dropped down upon the meadow in a whirl of white cloud-spume… She wore an ankle-length white gown, silver sandals, a silver belt and a black fillet to confine her hair. She put a question to Vermoulian, who pointed toward Rhialto, at the front of Falu.

Llorio slowly approached. Ildefonse, stepping from the arbor, bravely directed a double spell of Internal Solitude against her; it bounced back and, striking Ildefonse, sent him sprawling.

Llorio the Murthe halted. "Rhialto! You have mistreated my coterie! You have stolen my magic stones, and so now you must come to Sadal Suud not as a witch, but as a servant of menial sort, and this shall be your punishment. Ildefonse will fare no better."

From Falu came Calanctus. He halted. Llorio's taut jaw sagged; her mouth fell open.

Llorio spoke in a gasping voice: "How are you here? How did you evade the triangle? How…" The voice seemed to catch in her throat; in consternation she stared into the face of Calanctus. She found her voice. "Why do you look at me like that? Faithless I have not been; I now depart for Sadal Suud! Here I do only what must be done and it is you who are faithless!"

"I also did what must be done, and so it must be done again, for you have ensqualmated men to be your witches; so you have broken the Great Law, which ordains that man shall be man and woman shall be woman."

"When Necessity meets Law, then Law gives way: so you spoke in your Decretals!"

"No matter. Go you shall to Sadal Suud! Go now, go alone, without the ensqualmations."

Llorio said: "It is all one; a sorry band they are, either as wizards or witches, and in candour I wanted them only for entourage."

"Go then, Murthe!"

Llorio instead looked at Calanctus with a peculiar expression mingled of puzzlement and dissatisfaction on her face. She made no move to depart, which would seem to be both a taunt and a provocation. "The aeons have not dealt kindly with you; now you stand like a man of dough! Remember how you threatened to deal with me should we meet again?" She took another step forward, and showed a cool smile. "Are you afraid of my strength? So it must be! Where now are your erotic boasts and predictions?"

"I am a man of peace. I carry concord in my soul rather than attack and subjugation. I threaten naught; I promise hope."

Llorio came a step closer and peered into his face. "Ah!" she cried softly. "You are an empty façade, no more, and not Calanctus! Are you then so ready to taste death's sweetness?"

"I am Calanctus."

Llorio spoke a spell of twisting and torsion, but Calanctus fended it away with a gesture, and called a spell in turn of compressions from seven directions, which caught the Murthe unready and sent her reeling to her knees. Calanctus bent in compassion to lift her erect; she flared into blue flame and Calanctus held her around the waist with charred arms.

Llorio pushed him back, her face contorted. "You are not Calanctus; you are milk where he is blood!"

Even as she spoke the scarab in the bracelet brushed her face; she screamed and from her throat erupted a great spell — an explosion of power too strong for the tissues of her body, so that blood spurted from her mouth and nose. She reeled back to support herself against a tree, while Calanctus toppled slowly to lie broken and torn on his back.

Panting in emotion, Llorio stood looking down at the toppled hulk. From the nostrils issued a lazy filament of black smoke, coiling and swirling above the corpse.

Moving like a man entranced, Lehuster stepped slowly into the smoke. The air shook to a rumble of sound; a sultry yellow glare flashed like lightning; in the place of Lehuster stood a man of massive body, his skin glowing with internal light. He wore short black pantaloons and sandals, with legs and chest bare; his hair was black, his face square, with a stern nose and jutting jaw. He bent over the corpse and taking the scarab clasped it to his own wrist.

The new Calanctus spoke to Llorio: "My trouble has gone for nought! I came to this time as Lehuster, thus to leave sleeping old pains and old rages; now these hopes are forlorn, and all is as before. I am I, and once more we stand at odds!"

Llorio stood silent, her chest heaving.

Calanctus spoke on: "What of your other spells, to batter and break, or to beguile men's dreams and soften resolve? If so, try them on me, since I am not the poor mild Calanctus who carried the hopes of all of us, and who met so rude a destiny."

"Hope?" cried Llorio. "When the world is done and I have been thwarted? What remains? Nothing. Neither hope nor honor nor anguish nor pain! All is gone! Ashes blow across the desert. All has been lost, or forgotten; the best and the dearest are gone. Who are these creatures who stand here so foolishly? Ildefonse? Rhialto? Vapid ghosts, mowing with round mouths! Hope! Nothing remains. All is gone, all is done; even death is in the past."

So cried out Llorio, from the passion of despair, the blood still dripping from her nose. Calanctus stood quietly, waiting till her passion spent itself.

"To Sadal Suud I will go. I have failed; I stand at bay, surrounded by the enemies of my race."

Calanctus, reaching forward, touched her face. "Call me enemy as you like! Still, I love your dear features; I treasure your virtues and your peculiar faults; and I would not have them changed save in the direction of kindliness."

Llorio took a step backward. "I concede nothing; I will change nothing."

"Ah well, it was only an idle thought. What is this blood?"

"My brain is bleeding; I used all my power to destroy this poor futile corpse. I too am dying; I taste the savor of death. Calanctus, you have won your victory at last!"

"As usual, you overshoot the mark. I have won no victory; you are not dying nor need you go off to Sadal Suud, which is a steaming quagmire infested by owls, gnats and rodents: quite unsuitable for one of your delicacy. Who would do the laundry?"

"You will allow me neither death, nor yet refuge on a new world! Is this not defeat piled on defeat?"

"Words only. Come now; take my hand and we will call a truce."

"Never!" cried Llorio. "This symbolizes the ultimate conquest, to which I will never surrender!"

"I will gladly put by the symbol for the reality. Then you shall see whether or not I am able to make good my boasts."

"Never! I submit my person to no man's pleasure."

"Then will you not at least come away with me, so that we may drink wine on the terrace of my air-castle, and look across the panorama, and speak as the words idly come to mind?"

"Never!"

"One moment!" called Ildefonse. "Before you go, be good enough to desqualmate this coterie of witches, and so spare us the effort!"

"Bah, it is no great task," said Calanctus. "Evoke the Second Retrotropic, followed by a stabilizing fixture: a matter of minutes."

"Precisely so," said Ildefonse. "This, essentially, was my plan."

Rhialto turned to Ladanque. "Bring out the witches. Rank them on the meadow."

"And the corpse?"

Rhialto spoke a spell of dissolution; the dead thing collapsed into dust.

Llorio hesitated, looking first north, then south, as if in indecision; then, turning, she walked pensively across the meadow. Calanctus followed; the two halted and stood facing each other. First Llorio spoke, then Calanctus, then Llorio; then they both looked together toward the east, and then they were gone.

II: Fader's Waft

1

By day the sun cast a wan maroon gloom across the land; by night all was dark and still, with only a few pale stars to post the old constellations. Time went at a languid pace, without purpose or urgency, and folk made few long-range plans.

Grand Motholam was three aeons gone; the great masters of magic were extinct, each having suffered a more or less undignified demise: through the treachery of a trusted confidante; or during an amorous befuddlement; or by the machinations of a secret cabal; or through some unexpected and horrifying disaster.

The magicians of this, the 21st Aeon, for the most part resided in the quiet river valleys of Almery and Ascolais, though a few recluses kept to the Land of Cutz in the north, or the Land of the Falling Wall, or even the Steppes of Shwang in the distant east.

By reason of special factors (which lie beyond the scope of this present exposition) the magicians of the day were a various lot; gathered in colloquy, they seemed an assembly of rare and wonderful birds, each most mindful of his own plumage. While, on the whole, lacking the flamboyant magnificence of Grand Motholam, they were no less capricious and self-willed, and only after a number of unhappy incidents were they persuaded to regulate themselves by a code of conduct. This code, known as 'the Monstrament', or, less formally, 'the Blue Principles', was engraved upon a blue prism, which was housed in a secret place. The association included the most notable magicians of the region. By unanimous acclaim, Ildefonse was proclaimed Preceptor, and invested with large powers.

Ildefonse resided at Boumergarth, an ancient castle of four towers on the banks of the River Scaum. He had been chosen Preceptor not only for his dedication to the Blue Principles, but also for his equable temperament, which at times seemed almost bland. His tolerance was proverbial; at one turn he might be found chuckling to the lewd jokes of Dulce-Lolo; the next might find him engrossed in the opinions of the ascetic Tchamast, whose suspicions of the female sex ran deep.

Ildefonse ordinarily appeared as a jovial sage with twinkling blue eyes, a bald pate and a straggling blond beard: a semblance which tended to engender trust, frequently to private advantage, and the use of the word 'ingenuous', when applied to Ildefonse, was probably incorrect.

At this juncture the magicians subscribing to the Blue Principles numbered twenty-two.* Despite the clear advantages of orderly conduct, certain agile intelligences could not resist the thrill of the illicit and played mischievous tricks, on one occasion performing a most serious transgression against the Blue Principles.

The case involved Rhialto, sometimes known as 'the Marvellous'. He resided at Falu, not far from Wilda Water, in a district of low hills and dim forests at the eastern verge of Ascolais.

Among his fellows Rhialto, for whatever justification, was considered somewhat supercilious and enjoyed no wide popularity. His natural semblance was that of a proud and distinguished grandee, with short black hair, austere features, and a manner of careless ease. Rhialto was not without vanity, which, when taken with his aloof manner, often exasperated his fellows. And certain among them pointedly turned away when Rhialto appeared at a gathering, to Rhialto's sublime indifference.

Hache-Moncour was one of the few who cultivated Rhialto. He had contrived for himself the semblance of a Ctharion nature-god, with bronze curls and exquisite features, flawed (in the opinion of some) by a fulsome richness of mouth and eyes perhaps a trifle too round and limpid. Motivated, perhaps, by envy, at times he seemed almost to emulate Rhialto's mannerisms.

In Hache-Moncour's original condition, he had formed a number of fidgeting habits. When absorbed in thought, he squinted and pulled at

---

* See Foreword.

his ears; when perplexed, he scratched vigorously under his arms. Such habits, which he found hard to abandon, marred the careless aplomb toward which he so earnestly worked. He suspected Rhialto of smiling at his lapses, which honed the edge of his envy, and so the mischiefs began.

After a banquet at the hall of Mune the Mage, the magicians prepared to depart. Making their way into the foyer, they took up their cloaks and hats. Rhialto, always punctilious in his courtesies, extended to Hurtiancz first his cloak, then his hat. Hurtiancz, whose heavy-featured head rested directly upon his squat shoulders, acknowledged the service with a grunt. Hache-Moncour, standing nearby, saw his opportunity and cast a spell which enlarged Hurtiancz's hat by several sizes, so that when the irascible magician clapped the hat on his head, it dropped in back almost to his shoulders, while in front only the bulbous tip of his nose remained visible.

Hurtiancz tore the hat from his head and studied it from all angles, but Hache-Moncour had removed the spell and nothing seemed out of order. Once again Hurtiancz tried the hat on his head, and now it fit properly.

Even then all might have been ignored had not Hache-Moncour made a pictorial imprint of the scene, which he subsequently circulated among the magicians and other persons of the local nobility whose good opinion Hurtiancz wished to cultivate. The picture showed Hurtiancz with only the red lump of his nose in sight and Rhialto in the background wearing a smile of cool amusement.

Only Rhialto failed to receive a copy of the picture and no one thought to mention it to him, least of all Hurtiancz, whose outrage knew no bounds, and who now could hardly speak calmly when Rhialto's name was mentioned.

Hache-Moncour was delighted by the success of his prank. Any tarnishing of Rhialto's repute could only serve to enhance his own; additionally, he discovered a malicious pleasure in Rhialto's discomfiture.

Hache-Moncour thereupon initiated a whole series of intrigues, which at last became for Hache-Moncour something of an obsession, and his goal became the full and utter humiliation of the proud Rhialto.

Hache-Moncour worked with consummate subtlety, so that Rhialto at first noticed nothing. The plots were for the most part paltry, but always carried a sting.

Upon learning that Rhialto was refurbishing the guest-rooms at Falu, Hache-Moncour purloined a prized gem from Ao of the Opals and arranged that it should hang from the drop-chain of the commode in the new lavatory at Falu.

In due course, Ao learned of the use to which his magnificent two-inch tear-drop opal had been put, and his rancor, like that of Hurtiancz, approached the violence of a shivering fit. Despite all, Ao was constrained by Article Four of the Blue Principles, and so kept his resentment within check.

On another occasion, during Rhialto's experiments with bubbles of luminous plasm, Hache-Moncour caused such a bubble to settle into a unique harquisade tree which Zilifant had imported from Canopus and thereupon had nurtured by day and by night with intense solicitude. Once within the tree, the plasm exploded, pulverizing the brittle glass foliage and permeating Zilifant's premises with a vile and persistent odor.

Zilifant instantly complained to Rhialto in a voice croaking and creaking under the weight of anger. Rhialto responded with cool logic, citing six definite reasons why none of his plasms were responsible for the damage, and, while expressing regret, refused to make restitution of any sort. Zilifant's convictions were quietly reinforced by Hache-Moncour, who stated that Rhialto had boastfully announced his intention of using the harquisade tree as a target. "Further," said Hache-Moncour, "Rhialto went on to say, and here I quote, 'Zilifant constantly exudes such a personal chife into the air that the stench of the plasm may well be redundant.'"

And so it went. Gilgad owned a pet simiode, of which he was inordinately fond. At twilight Hache-Moncour, wearing a black domino, a black cloak and a black hat identical to the garments worn by Rhialto, captured the beast and dragged it away at the end of a chain to Falu. Here Hache-Moncour beat the beast well and tied it on a short scope between a pair of chastity-plants, which caused the beast an additional affliction.

Gilgad, taking information from peasants, followed the trail to Falu. He released the simiode, listened to its howling complaints, then confronted Rhialto with the evidence of his guilt.

Rhialto crisply denied all knowledge of the deed, but Gilgad, waxing passionate, would not be convinced. He cried out: "Boodis identifies you explicitly! He claims that you made terrifying threats; that you declared: 'I am Rhialto, and if you think you have been beaten soundly, wait only until I refresh myself!' Is that not an attitude of merciless cruelty?"

Rhialto said: "You must decide whom you will believe: me or that repulsive beast." He gave a disdainful bow, and returning into Falu, closed the door. Gilgad cried out a final complaint, then wheeled Boodis home in a barrow padded with silken cushions. Thereafter, among his detractors, Rhialto could confidently include Gilgad.

On another occasion, Rhialto, acting in all innocence, was played false by the ordinary fluxions of circumstance, and once again became the target of recrimination. Initially, Hache-Moncour played no part in the affair, but later made large of it, to compound its effect.

The episode began on a level of pleasant anticipation. The ranking nobleman of the region was Duke Tambasco, a person of impeccable dignity and ancient lineage. Each year, to celebrate the sun's gallant efforts to survive, Duke Tambasco sponsored a Grand Ball at his palace Quanorq. The guest-list was most select, and on this occasion included Ildefonse, Rhialto and Byzant the Necrope.

Ildefonse and Byzant met at Boumergarth, and over tots of Ildefonse's best hyperglossom each congratulated the other on his splendid appearance, and made lewd wagers as to who would score the most notable triumphs among the beauties at the ball.

For the occasion Ildefonse chose to appear as a stalwart young bravo with golden curls falling past his ears, a fine golden mustache, and a manner both hearty and large. To complement the thrust of the image, he wore a suit of green velvet, a dark green and gold sash, and a dashing wide-brimmed hat with a white plume.

Byzant, planning with equal care, chose the semblance of a graceful young aesthete, sensitive to nuance and vulnerable to the most fugitive breath of beauty. He joined emerald-green eyes, copper-red ringlets and a marmoreal complexion into a juxtaposition calculated to excite the ardor of the most beautiful women at the ball. "I will seek out the most ravishing of all!" he told Ildefonse. "I will fascinate her with my appearance and captivate her with my soul; she will fall into an amorous swoon which I will shamelessly exploit."

"I see but a single flaw in your argument," chuckled Ildefonse. "When you discover this creature of superb attraction, she will already be on my arm and oblivious to all else."

"Ildefonse, you have always been a braggart in connection with your conquests!" cried Byzant. "At Quanorq we shall judge by performance alone, and then we shall see who is the true adept!"

"So it shall be!"

After a final tot of the hyperglossom, the two gallants set off to Falu, where to their astonishment they found that Rhialto had totally forgotten the occasion.

Ildefonse and Byzant were impatient, and would allow Rhialto no time to make preparations, so Rhialto merely pulled a tasseled cap over his black hair and declared himself ready to depart.

Byzant stood back in surprise. "But you have made no preparations! You are not arrayed in splendid garments! You have neither laved your feet nor scented your hair!"

"No matter," said Rhialto. "I will seclude myself in the shadows and envy you your successes. At least I shall enjoy the music and the spectacle."

Byzant chuckled complacently. "No matter, Rhialto; it is time that you had some wind taken from your sails. Tonight Ildefonse and I are primed and ready; you will be entitled to watch our superb talents used to absolutely compelling effect!"

"Byzant speaks with exact accuracy," declared Ildefonse. "You have had your share of triumphs; tonight you are fated to stand aside and watch while a pair of experts do what is needful to bring the loveliest of the lovely to their knees!"

"If it must be, so it must be," said Rhialto. "My concern now is for the heart-sick victims of your craft. Have you no pity?"

"None whatever!" declared Ildefonse. "We wage our amorous campaigns with full force; we give no quarter and accept no paroles!"

Rhialto gave his head a rueful shake. "A tragedy that I was not reminded of the ball in time!"

"Come now, Rhialto!" chuckled Byzant. "You must take the bad with the good; whimpering avails nothing."

Ildefonse cried out. "Meanwhile, time advances! Shall we depart?"

Arriving at Quanorq the three paid their respects to Duke Tambasco and congratulated him upon the magnificence of his arrangements: compliments which the duke acknowledged with a formal bow, and the three magicians made way for others.

For a period the three wandered here and there, and indeed on this occasion Duke Tambasco had outdone himself. Grandees and their charming ladies crowded the halls and galleries, and at four buffets choice viands and fine liquors were deployed in profusion.

The three magicians at last repaired to the foyer of the great ballroom where, stationing themselves to the side, they took note of the beautiful ladies as they passed and discussed the merits and distinguishing characteristics of each. In due course they decided that, while many comely maidens were in evidence, none could match the agonizingly exquisite beauty of the Lady Shaunica of Lake Island.

Ildefonse presently puffed out his fine blond mustaches and went his way. Byzant also took his leave of Rhialto, who went to sit in a shadowed alcove to the side.

Ildefonse found the first opportunity to exert his expertise. Advancing upon the Lady Shaunica he performed a sweeping salute and offered to escort her through the measures of a pavane. "I am profoundly skillful in the execution of this particular dance," he assured her. "I with my bold flourishes and you with your gracious beauty make a notable pair; we shall be the focus of all eyes! Then, after the dance, I will escort you to the buffet. We will take a goblet or two of wine and you will discover that I am a person of remarkable parts! More than this, I now declare that I am prepared to offer you my fullest esteem!"

"That is most gracious of you," said the Lady Shaunica. "I am profoundly moved. However, at this juncture, I have no taste for dancing, and I dare drink no more wine for fear of becoming coarse, which would certainly arouse your disapproval."

Ildefonse performed a punctilious bow and prepared to assert his charm even more explicitly, but when he looked up, Lady Shaunica already had made her departure.

Ildefonse gave a grunt of annoyance, pulled at his mustaches, and strode off to seek a maiden of more malleable tendency.

By chance, the Lady Shaunica almost immediately encountered Byzant. To attract her attention and possibly win her admiration, Byzant addressed her with a quatrain in an archaic language known as Old Naotic, but the Lady Shaunica was only startled and bewildered.

Byzant smilingly translated the lyric and explained certain irregularities of the Naotic philology. "But after all," said Byzant, "these concepts need not intrude into the rapport between us. I sense that you feel its warm languor as strongly as I!"

"Perhaps not quite so strongly," said the Lady Shaunica. "But then I am insensitive to such influences, and in fact I feel no rapport whatever."

"It will come, it will come!" Byzant assured her. "I own a rare perception in that I can see souls in all their shimmering color. Yours and mine waver in the same noble radiances! Come, let us stroll out on the terrace! I will impart to you a secret." He reached to take her hand.

The Lady Shaunica, somewhat puzzled by Byzant's effusiveness, drew back. "Truly, I do not care to hear secrets upon such short acquaintance."

"It is not so much a secret as an impartment! And what, after all, is duration? I have known you no more than half an hour, but already I have composed two lyrics and an ode to your beauty! Come! Out on the terrace! Away and beyond! Into the star-light, under the trees; we shall discard our garments and stride with the wild innocence of sylvan divinities!"

Lady Shaunica drew back still another step. "Thank you, but I am somewhat self-conscious. Suppose we ran so briskly that we could not find our way back to the palace, and in the morning the peasants found us running naked along the road? What could we tell them? Your proposal lacks appeal."

Byzant threw high his arms and, rolling back his eyes, clutched at his red curls, hoping that the Lady Shaunica would recognize his agony of spirit and take pity, but she had already slipped away. Byzant went angrily to the buffet, where he drank several goblets of strong wine.

A few moments later the Lady Shaunica, passing through the foyer, chanced upon one of her acquaintances, the Lady Dualtimetta. During their conversation the Lady Shaunica chanced to glance into a nearby alcove, where Rhialto sat alone on a couch of maroon brocade. She whispered to the Lady Dualtimetta: "Look yonder into the alcove: who is that who sits so quietly alone?"

The Lady Dualtimetta turned her head to look. "I have heard his name; it is Rhialto, and sometimes 'Rhialto the Marvellous'. Do you think him elegant? I myself find him austere and even daunting!"

"Truly? Surely not daunting; is he not a man?"

"Naturally! But why does he sit apart as if he disdained everyone at Quanorq?"

"Everyone?" mused the Lady Shaunica as if to herself.

The Lady Dualtimetta moved away. "My dear, excuse me; now I must hurry; I have an important part in the pageant." She went her way.

The Lady Shaunica hesitated, then, smiling as if at some private amusement, went slowly to the alcove. "Sir, may I join you here in the shadows?"

Rhialto rose to his feet. "Lady Shaunica, you are well aware that you may join me wherever you wish."

"Thank you." She seated herself on the couch and Rhialto resumed his own place. Still smiling her secret half-smile she asked: "Do you wonder why I come to sit with you?"

"The question had not occurred to me." Rhialto considered a moment. "I might guess that you intend to meet a friend in the foyer, and here is a convenient place to wait."

"That is a genteel reply," said the Lady Shaunica. "In sheer truth, I wonder why a person such as yourself sits aloof in the shadows. Have you been dazed by tragic news? Are you disdainful of all others at Quanorq, and their pitiful attempts to put forward an appealing image?"

Rhialto smiled his own wry half-smile. "I have suffered no tragic shocks. As for the appealing image of the Lady Shaunica, it is enhanced by a luminous intelligence of equal charm."

"Then you have arranged a rendezvous of your own?"

"None whatever."

"Still, you sit alone and speak to no one."

"My motives are complex. What of yours? You sit here in the shadows as well."

The Lady Shaunica laughed. "I ride like a feather on wafts of caprice. Perhaps I am piqued by your restraint, or distance, or indifference, or whatever it may be. Every other gallant has dropped upon me like a vulture on a corpse." She turned him a sidelong glance. "Your conduct therefore becomes provocative, and now you have the truth."

Rhialto was silent a moment, then said: "There are many exchanges to be made between us — if our acquaintance is to persist."

The Lady Shaunica made a flippant gesture. "I have no strong objections."

Rhialto looked across the foyer. "I might then suggest that we discover a place where we can converse with greater privacy. We sit here like birds on a fence."

"A solution is at hand," said the Lady Shaunica. "The duke has allowed me a suite of apartments for the duration of my visit. I will order in a collation and a bottle or two of Maynesse, and we will continue our talk in dignity and seclusion."

"The proposal is flawless," said Rhialto. He rose and, taking the Lady Shaunica's hands, drew her to her feet. "Do I still seem as if dazed by tragic news?"

"No, but let me ask you this: why are you known as 'Rhialto the Marvellous'?"

"It seems to be an old joke," said Rhialto. "I have never been able to trace the source."

As the two walked arm in arm along the main gallery they passed Ildefonse and Byzant standing disconsolately under a marble statue. Rhialto accorded them a polite nod, and made a secret sign of more complicated significance, to the effect that they might feel free to return home without him.

The Lady Shaunica, pressing close to his side, giggled. "What a pair of unlikely comrades! The first a roisterer with mustaches a foot long, the second a poet with the eyes of a sick lizard. Do you know them?"

"Only slightly. In any case it is you who interests me and all your warm sensitivities which to my delight you are allowing me to share."

The Lady Shaunica pressed even more closely against him. "I begin to suspect the source of your soubriquet."

Ildefonse and Byzant, biting their lips in vexation, returned to the foyer, where Ildefonse finally made the acquaintance of a portly matron wearing a lace cap and smelling strongly of musk. She took Ildefonse off to the ball-room, where they danced three galops, a triple-polka and a kind of a strutting cake-walk where Ildefonse, in order to dance correctly, was obliged to raise one leg high in the air, jerk his elbows, throw back his head, then repeat the evolution with all briskness, using the other leg.

As for Byzant, Duke Tambasco introduced him to a tall poetess with coarse yellow hair worn in loose lank strands. Thinking to recognize a temperament similar to her own, she took him into the garden where, behind a clump of hydrangeas, she recited an ode of twenty-nine stanzas.

Eventually both Ildefonse and Byzant won free, but now the night was waning and the ball was at an end. In sour spirits they returned to their domiciles, and each, through some illogical transfer of emotion, blamed Rhialto for his lack of success.

2

Rhialto at last became impatient with the plague of ill feeling directed his way for no very clear reason, and kept to himself at Falu.

After a period, solitude began to pall. Rhialto summoned his major-domo. "Frole, I will be absent from Falu for a time, and you will be left in charge. Here —" he handed Frole a paper "— is a list of instructions. See that you follow them in precise detail. Upon my return I wish to find everything in exact and meticulous order. I specifically forbid that you entertain parties of guests or relatives on, in or near the premises. Also, I warn that if you meddle with the objects in the work-rooms, you do so at risk of your life, or worse. Am I clear?"

"Absolutely and in all respects," said Frole. "How long will you be gone, and how many persons constitute a party?"

"To the first question: an indefinite period. To the second, I will only rephrase my instruction: entertain no persons whatever at Falu during my absence. I expect to find meticulous order upon my return. You may now be off about your duties. I will leave in due course."

Rhialto took himself to the Sousanese Coast, in the remote far corner of South Almery, where the air was mild and the vegetation grew in a profusion of muted colors, and in the case of certain forest trees, to prodigious heights. The local folk, a small pale people with dark hair and long still eyes, used the word 'Sxyzyskzyiks'—"The Civilized People"—to describe themselves, and in fact took the sense of the word seriously. Their culture comprised a staggering set of precepts, the mastery of which served as an index to status, so that ambitious persons spent vast energies learning finger-gestures, ear-decoration, the proper knots by which one tied his turban, his sash, his shoe-ribbons; the manner in which one tied the same knots for one's grandfather; the proper and distinctive placement of pickles on plates of winkles, snails, chestnut stew, fried meats and other foods; the curses specifically appropriate after stepping on a thorn, meeting a ghost, falling from a low ladder, falling from a tree, or any of a hundred other circumstances.

Rhialto took lodging at a tranquil hostelry, and was housed in a pair of airy rooms built on stilts out over the sea. The chairs, bed, table and chest were constructed of varnished black camphor-wood; the floor was muffled from the wash of the sea among the stilts by a rug of pale green matting. Rhialto took meals of ten courses in an arbor beside the water, illuminated at night by the glow of candle-wood sticks.

Slow days passed, ending in sunsets of tragic glory; at night the few stars still extant reflected from the surface of the sea, and the music of curve-necked lutes could be heard from up and down the beach. Rhialto's tensions eased and the exasperations of the Scaum Valley seemed far away. Dressed native-style in a white kirtle, sandals and a loose turban with dangling tassels, Rhialto strolled the beaches, looked through the village bazaars for rare sea-shells, sat under the arbor drinking fruit toddy, watching the slender maidens pass by.

One day at idle whim Rhialto built a sand-castle on the beach. In order to amaze the local children he first made it proof against the assaults of wind and wave, then gave the structure a population of minuscules, accoutered as Zahariots of the Fourteenth Aeon. Each day a force of knights and soldiers marched out to drill upon the beach, then for a period engaged in mock-combat amid shrill yells and cries. Foraging parties hunted crab, gathered sea-grapes and mussels

Fader's Waft

One day at idle whim Rhialto built a sand-castle on the beach.

from the rocks, and meanwhile the children watched in delighted wonder.

One day a band of young hooligans came down the beach with terriers, which they set upon the castle troops.

Rhialto, watching from a distance, worked a charm and up from a court-yard flew a squadron of elite warriors mounted on hummingbirds. They projected volley after volley of fire-darts to send the curs howling down the beach. The warriors then wheeled back upon the youths who, with buttocks aflame, were likewise persuaded to retreat.

When the cringing group returned somewhat later with persons of authority, they found only a wind-blown heap of sand and Rhialto lounging somnolently in the shade of the nearby arbor.

The episode aroused a flurry of wonder and Rhialto for a time became the object of doubt, but along the Sousanese Coast sensation quickly became flat, and before long all was as before.

Meanwhile, in the Valley of the Scaum, Hache-Moncour made capital of Rhialto's absence. At his suggestion, Ildefonse convened a 'Conclave of Reverence', to honor the achievements of the Great Phandaal, the intrepid genius of Grand Motholam who had systematized the control of sandestins. After the group assembled, Hache-Moncour diverted the discussion and guided it by subtle means to the subject of Rhialto and his purported misdeeds.

Hache-Moncour spoke out with vehemence: "Personally, I count Rhialto among my intimates, and I would not think of mentioning his name, except, where possible, for the sake of vindication, and, where impossible, to plead the mitigating circumstances when the inevitable penalties are assessed."

"That is most generous of you," said Ildefonse. "Am I then to take it that Rhialto and his conduct is to become a formal topic of discussion?"

"I fail to see why not," growled Gilgad. "His deeds have been meretricious."

"Come, come!" cried Hache-Moncour. "Do not skulk and whimper; either make your charges or I, speaking as Rhialto's defender, will demand a vote of approbation for Rhialto the Marvellous!"

Gilgad leapt to his feet. "What? You accuse me of skulking? Me, Gilgad, who worked ten spells against Keino the Sea-demon?"

Fader's Waft

"It is only a matter of form," said Hache-Moncour. "In defending Rhialto, I am obliged to use extravagant terms. If I hurl unforgivable insults or reveal secret disgraces, you must regard them as the words of Rhialto, not those of your comrade Hache-Moncour, who only hopes to exert a moderating influence. Well then: since Gilgad is too cowardly to place a formal complaint, who chooses to do so?"

"Bah!" cried Gilgad furiously. "Even in the role of Rhialto's spokesman, you use slurs and insults with a certain lewd gusto. To set the record straight, I formally accuse Rhialto of impropriety and the beating of a simiode, and I move that he be called to account."

Ildefonse suggested: "In the interest of both brevity and elegance, let us allow 'impropriety' to include the 'beating'. Are you agreed?"

Gilgad grudgingly acquiesced to the change.

Ildefonse called out: "Are there seconds to the motion?"

Hache-Moncour looked around the circle of faces. "What a group of pusillanimous nail-biters! If necessary, as Rhialto's surrogate, I will second the motion myself, if only to defeat with finality this example of childish spite!"

"Silence!" thundered Zilifant. "I second the motion!"

"Very good," said Ildefonse. "The floor is open for discussion."

"I move that we dismiss the motion out of hand as a pack of nonsense," said Hache-Moncour. "Even though Rhialto boasts of his success at the Grand Ball, and laughingly describes Ildefonse's antics with a fat matron and Byzant's comic efforts to seduce a raw-boned poetess in a blonde wig."

"Your motion is denied," said Ildefonse through gritted teeth. "Let the charges be heard, in full detail!"

"I see that my intercession is useless," said Hache-Moncour. "I therefore will step aside from my post and voice my own complaints, so that when the final fines and confiscations are levied, I will receive my fair share of the booty."

Here was a new thought, which occupied the assemblage for several minutes, and some went so far as to inscribe lists of items now owned by Rhialto which might better serve their own needs.

Ao of the Opals spoke ponderously: "Rhialto's offenses unfortunately are many! They include deeds and attitudes which, while hard to define, are nonetheless as poignant as a knife in the ribs. I include in this category such attributes as avarice, arrogance, and ostentatious vulgarity."

"The charges would seem to be impalpable," intoned Ildefonse. "Nevertheless, in justice, they must be reckoned into the final account."

Zilifant raised his finger dramatically high: "With brutal malice Rhialto destroyed my prized harquisade from Canopus, the last to be found on this moribund world! When I explained as much to Rhialto, first, with mendacity dripping from his tongue, he denied the deed, then declared: 'Look yonder to Were Wood and its darkling oaks! When the sun goes out they will fare no better and no worse than your alien dendron.' Is that not a travesty upon ordinary decency?"

Hache-Moncour gave his head a sad shake. "I am at a loss for words. I would render an apology in Rhialto's name, were I not convinced that Rhialto would make a flippant mockery of my efforts. Still, can you not extend mercy to this misguided man?"

"Certainly," said Zilifant. "To the precise measure in which he befriended my harquisade. I declare Rhialto guilty of a felony!"

Again Hache-Moncour shook his head. "I find it hard to credit."

Zilifant swung about in a passion. "Have a care! Even in your quixotic advocacy of this scoundrel, I will not have my veracity assailed!"

"You misunderstood me!" stated Hache-Moncour. "I then spoke for myself, in wonder at Rhialto's callous acts."

"Ah, then! We are agreed."

Others of the group cited grievances which Ildefonse noted upon a bill of particulars. At last all had declared themselves, and Ildefonse, in looking down the list, frowned in perplexity. "Amazing how one like Rhialto could live so long among us and never be exposed! Hache-Moncour, do you have anything more to say?"

"Merely a *pro-forma* appeal for mercy."

"The appeal has been heard," said Ildefonse. "We shall now vote. Those who endorse Rhialto's conduct and find him blameless, raise their hands."

Not a hand could be seen.

"Those convinced of Rhialto's guilt?"

All hands were raised.

Ildefonse cleared his throat. "It now becomes my duty to assess the penalty. I must say that Rhialto's absence makes our sad task somewhat easier. Are there any suggestions?"

Byzant said: "I feel that each of us, in the order that we sit at the table, starting with myself, shall be numerated. We will then go to Falu and there, in order of number, select among Rhialto's goods until no one wishes to make a further choice."

Ao of the Opals concurred. "The idea is essentially sound. But the numeration must be made by lot, with a monitor against all spells of temporal stasis."

The system suggested by Ao was eventually put into effect, and all repaired to Falu. Frole the major-domo stepped forward and in an authoritative voice inquired what might be the business of so large a company. "You must know that Rhialto is absent! Come again when he can receive you with suitable ceremony."

Ildefonse began a legalistic declamation but Gilgad, impatient with words, cast a spell of inanition upon Frole, and the magicians, entering Falu, set about enforcing the penalties which had been levied at the conclave.

The irascible Hurtiancz was especially anxious to find Rhialto's IOUN stones, and sought everywhere, to no avail. A document indited in blue ink on blue paper and cased in a frame of blue gold hung on the wall; certain that he had discovered Rhialto's secret hiding place, Hurtiancz impatiently tore the document from the wall and threw it aside, to reveal only the vacant wall, and it was Ildefonse himself who discovered the IOUN stones where they hung among the crystals of a chandelier.

The fine at last was levied in total degree, though not to the satisfaction of those who had been allotted high numbers, nor those who had been slow in pre-empting goods without reference to the numbers. Ildefonse used all his influence to dampen the claims and accusations, meanwhile defending his own retention of the IOUN stones, by reason of service and selfless rectitude.

At last the magicians went their ways, satisfied that justice had been done.

3

In due season Rhialto returned to Falu. His first intimation that all was not as it should be was the sight of Frole standing stiff before the doorway, frozen in a posture of admonition; then, entering the manse, Rhialto took wrathful note of the depredation.

Returning to the doorway, Rhialto dissolved the spell which had held Frole immobile through night and day, rain and shine.

Frole took a cup of tea and a slice of currant cake, after which he was able to report to Rhialto those circumstances which had come under his purview.

Rhialto grimly restored order to the premises, then made an inventory of his losses and damages. They reduced his powers to a low level.

For a period Rhialto paced back and forth beside Wilda Water. At last, with no better program suggesting itself, he donned a pair of old air-boots which had been left behind and made his way to Boumergarth.

Pryffwyd, Ildefonse's chamberlain, met him at the door.

"Your wishes, sir?"

"You may inform Ildefonse that Rhialto is here to consult with him."

"Sir, Lord Ildefonse is preoccupied with matters of importance and will be unable to receive visitors today or at any time in the near future."

Rhialto brought forth a small red disk and, clasping it between his hands, began to chant a set of rhythmic syllables. In sudden concern Pryffwyd asked: "What are you doing?"

"Pryffwyd, your vision is dim; you do not recognize me for Rhialto. I am working to place your eyeballs at the end of foot-long stalks. You will soon be able to see in all directions at once."

Pryffwyd's voice instantly changed. "Ah! The noble Lord Rhialto! I now see you perfectly in every phase! This way, if you will! Lord Ildefonse is meditating in the herb-garden."

Rhialto found Ildefonse dozing in the slanting red rays of the afternoon sunlight. Rhialto clapped his hands together. "Ildefonse, rouse from your torpor! Vile deeds have been done at Falu; I am anxious to hear your explanation."

Fader's Waft

Ildefonse turned a glance of reproach upon Pryffwyd, who merely bowed and asked: "Will there be anything else, sir?"

Ildefonse sighed. "You may serve refreshments, of a light nature, as Rhialto's business will not take us long and he will very shortly be leaving."

"To the contrary!" said Rhialto. "I will be here for an indefinite period. Pryffwyd, serve the best your pantry affords!"

Ildefonse heaved himself up in his chair. "Rhialto, you are taking a high-handed line with my chamberlain and, since we have gone so far, with my refreshments as well!"

"No matter. Explain why you robbed me of my goods. My man Frole tells me that you marched in the forefront of the thieves."

Ildefonse pounded the table with his fist. "Specious and egregious! Frole has misrepresented the facts!"

"How do you explain these remarkable events, which of course I intend to place before the Adjudicator*?"

Ildefonse blinked and blew out his cheeks. "That of course is at your option. Still, you should be aware that legality was observed in every bound and degree. You were charged with certain offenses, the evidence was closely examined and your guilt was ascertained only after diligent deliberation. Through the efforts of myself and Hache-Moncour, the penalty became a small and largely symbolic levy upon your goods."

"'Symbolic'?" cried Rhialto. "You picked me clean!"

Ildefonse pursed his lips. "I concede that at times I noticed a certain lack of restraint, at which I personally protested."

---

* The Monstrament, placed in a crypt at Fader's Waft, drew its coercive force from the 'Adjudicator', ensconced in his 'Blue Egg': a shell opaque to distracting influences. The Adjudicator was Sarsem, a sandestin trained in the interpretation of the Monstrament. Sarsem's judgments were swift and stern, and enforced by the Wiih, a mindless creature from the ninth dimension.

When applying to the Adjudicator for justice, the plaintiff was well advised to come with a clear conscience. Sarsem felt an almost human impatience with his cramped seclusion inside the egg; at times he refused to limit his verdict to the issue at hand, and examined the conduct both of plaintiff and defendant for offenses against the Monstrament, and distributed his penalties with even-handed liberality.

Rhialto, leaning back in his chair, drew a deep sigh of dumbfounded wonder. He considered Ildefonse down the length of his aristocratic nose. In a gentle voice he asked: "The charges were brought by whom?"

Ildefonse frowned thoughtfully. "By many. Gilgad declared that you had beaten his pet simiode."

"Aha. Continue."

"Zilifant charged that your reckless deployment of plasms had destroyed his fine harquisade tree."

"And further?"

"The complaints are too numerous to mention. Almost everyone — save myself and the loyal Hache-Moncour — preferred charges. Then, the conclave of your peers with near-unanimity adjudged you guilty on all counts."

"And who robbed me of my IOUN stones?"

"As a matter of fact, I myself took them into protective custody."

"This trial was conducted by exact legal process?"

Ildefonse took occasion to drink down a goblet of the wine which Pryffwyd had served. "Ah yes, your question! It pertained, I believe, to legality. In response, I will say that the trial, while somewhat informal, was conducted by appropriate and practical means."

"In full accordance with the terms of the Monstrament?"

"Yes, of course. Is that not the proper way? Now then —"

"Why was I not notified and allowed an opportunity for rebuttal?"

"I believe that the subject might well have been discussed," said Ildefonse. "As I recall, no one wished to disturb you on your holiday, especially since your guilt was generally conceded."

Rhialto rose to his feet. "Shall we now visit Fader's Waft?"

Ildefonse raised his hand in a bluff gesture. "Seat yourself, Rhialto! Here comes Pryffwyd with further refreshment; let us drink wine and consider this matter dispassionately; is not that the better way, after all?"

"When I have been vilified, slandered and robbed, by those who had previously shone upon me the sweetest rays of their undying friendship? I had never —"

Ildefonse broke into the flow of Rhialto's remarks. "Yes, yes; perhaps there were procedural errors, but never forget, the findings might have gone worse but for the efforts of myself and Hache-Moncour."

"Indeed?" asked Rhialto coldly. "You are familiar with the Blue Principles?"

"I am generally aware of the important passages," declared Ildefonse bluffly. "As for the more abstruse sections, I may be a trifle dim, but these in any event do not apply."

"Indeed?" Rhialto brought out a torn blue document. "I will read from Paragraph C, of the 'Precursive Manifesto':

> The Monstrament, like a perdurable edifice, depends on integrated blocks of wisdom, each supporting others with bonds of equal strength. He who maximizes the solemnity of certain passages and demeans another as trivial or paltry for the sake of his special pleading is guilty of subversion and submulgery, and shall be punished as directed by Schedule B, Section 3.

Ildefonse blinked. "My present remarks are truly no more than badinage."

"In that case, why did you not testify that at the time Gilgad's beast was abused, you and I were walking beside the River Scaum?"

"That is a good question. In sheer point of fact, I acted on grounds of procedural effect."

"How so?"

"Simple enough! The question: 'Did you walk with Rhialto by the River Scaum at the exact time Gilgad's simiode was beaten?' was never asked. By the rules of jurisprudence I could not properly introduce such evidence. Secondly, you already had been convicted on a number of other counts, and my remarks would only have caused confusion."

"Should not truth be known? Did you not ask yourself who in fact had beaten the beast, and why he identified himself as 'Rhialto'?"

Ildefonse cleared his throat. "Under the circumstances, as I have explained them, such questions are nuncupatory."

Rhialto consulted the torn copy of the Blue Principles. "Paragraph K of Section 2 would seem to describe your act as 'enhanced dereliction'. A harsh penalty — possibly too harsh — is specified, but the Adjudicator will read justice as it is written and apply the strictures to calm and thorough effect."

Ildefonse held up his hands. "Will you take so trivial an affair to Fader's Waft? The consequences are beyond calculation!"

"I will cite a third offense. In the looting of Falu, my copy of the Blue Principles was seized, torn and hurled to the ground. In this deed, which is precisely proscribed under Paragraph A: 'Treasonable Acts', all conspirators share the guilt, and all must pay the penalty. This is far from a 'trivial affair'! I thought that you might share my indignation, and work for restitution and punishment of the guilty, but —"

"Your hopes have been validated!" cried Ildefonse. "I was on the verge of convoking a new conclave, to review the findings of the last session, which now seem to have been guided by emotion. Have patience! The Adjudicator need not be distracted from his passivity."

"Convene the conclave as of this instant! Declare at the outset that I am innocent of all charges, that I have suffered inexcusable wrongs, that I demand not only restitution but multiple damages —"

Ildefonse cried out in shock. "That is an irrational penalty!"

Rhialto said stonily: "As Preceptor this is your decision to make. Otherwise the Adjudicator must assess the penalties."

Ildefonse sighed. "I will call the conclave."

"Announce that only two issues will be considered: first, restitution and the imposition of fines, ranging from three-fold to five-fold, and I will hear neither bluster nor obfuscation; and secondly, identification of the malefactor."

Ildefonse grumbled something under his breath, but Rhialto paid no heed. "Convoke the conclave! Accept no excuses! All must be present, as I am an exasperated man!"

Ildefonse put on an air of forlorn good cheer. "All may yet be well. First I will communicate with your only true ally, other than myself."

"You refer to whom?"

"Hache-Moncour, naturally! We will take his advice at once."

Ildefonse went to a table, where he placed the semblance of Hache-Moncour's face over a pair of orifices shaped to represent an ear and a mouth. "Hache-Moncour, Ildefonse speaks into your ear! I bring significant news! Speak with your mouth!"

"Ildefonse, I speak! What is your news?"

"Rhialto the Marvellous has come to Boumergarth! His mood is one of doubt and malaise. He feels that the conclave made several legalistic mistakes which tend to vitiate its findings; indeed, he demands triple damages from all parties concerned. Otherwise he threatens to take his case to the Adjudicator."

"A great mistake," said the mouth. "An act of reckless despair."

"So I have advised him, but Rhialto is an obstinate man."

The mouth spoke: "Can you not reason with him? Is he quite inflexible?"

"He yields by not so much as the twitch of an eyelash, and only speaks in tedious repetition of the Monstrament and the imposition of penalties. He seems obsessively convinced that a malefactor —"

Rhialto called out: "Speak more tersely, if you will; my time is valuable! Merely convene the conclave; you need not describe my troubled spirit in such sardonic detail."

Ildefonse angrily threw nineteen semblances down upon his communication device. He put a clamp upon the mouth to impede protests and questions, then, speaking out into nineteen ears at once, he ordered an immediate conclave at Boumergarth.

4

The magicians one by one took their places in the Grand Saloon. Hache-Moncour was the last to arrive. Before seating himself he spoke a few quiet words to Herark the Harbinger, with whom he was on good terms.

Rhialto, leaning against a wood-paneled wall to the side, somberly watched the arrival of his erstwhile colleagues. None save Hache-Moncour, who gave him a polite bow, so much as looked in his direction.

Ildefonse convened the meeting in his usual manner, then glanced sidelong towards Rhialto, who maintained his silence. Ildefonse coughed and cleared his throat. "I will come directly to the point. Rhialto claims an unjust confiscation of his property. He demands restitution and punitive damages; failing satisfaction, he states that he will take his case to the Adjudicator. There, in a nut-shell, is the gist of our business today."

Gilgad sprang to his feet, face purple with rage. "Rhialto's posture is grotesque! How can he deny his crime? He beat poor Boodis and tethered him among nettles: a vile and heartless act! I declared as much before; I do so now, and will never revoke the charge!"

"I did not beat your beast," said Rhialto.

"Ha ha! Easy for you to say! Can you prove as much?"

"Certainly. I was walking with Ildefonse beside the River Scaum at the time of the incident."

Gilgad whirled upon Ildefonse. "Is this true?"

Ildefonse made a sour face. "It is true, in every particular."

"Then why did you not say so before?"

"I did not want to confuse a case already turbulent with emotion."

"Most peculiar." With a set face Gilgad resumed his seat, but Zilifant immediately sprang erect. "Nonetheless and undeniably, Rhialto destroyed my harquisade tree with his floating plasm and left a horrid stench about the premises; further, so the rumor goes, he boasted of his accuracy, and imputed the source of the odor to me, Zilifant!"

"I did nothing of the sort," said Rhialto.

"Bah! The evidence is clear, straightforward and unambiguous!"

"Is it, indeed? Mune the Mage and Perdustin were both present at Falu during the experiment. They saw me create four lumes of plasm. One drifted through my delicate silvanissa tendrils, doing no harm. Mune walked through another and failed to complain of odor. We watched all four lumes dwindle to sparks and die. None escaped; none departed the area adjacent to Falu."

Zilifant looked uncertainly from Mune the Mage to Perdustin. "Are these allegations accurate?"

"In a word: yes," said Mune the Mage.

"Why did you not so inform me?"

"Since Rhialto was guilty of other offenses, it seemed unimportant."

"Not to me," said Rhialto.

"Possibly not to you."

"Who informed you of my boasts and insults?"

Zilifant glanced uncertainly toward Hache-Moncour. "I am not sure that I remember properly."

Rhialto turned back to Ildefonse. "What are these other crimes of which I am guilty?"

Fader's Waft

Hurtiancz responded to the challenge. "You cast a spell upon my hat! You sent out mocking pictures!"

"I did nothing of the sort."

"I suppose you can prove otherwise."

"What does the pattern of events suggest? Clearly, the act was performed by the same person who beat Gilgad's beast and vandalized Zilifant's tree. That person was not I."

Hurtiancz uttered a sour grunt. "So much seems to the point. I retract the charge."

Rhialto stepped forward. "Now then: what other crimes have I committed?"

No one spoke.

"In that case, I must now place counter-charges. I accuse the members of this association, singly and jointly, with the exception of myself, of several felonies."

Rhialto presented a tablet to Ildefonse. "There-on I detail the charges. Preceptor, be good enough to read them off."

With a grimace of distaste Ildefonse took the tablet. "Rhialto, are you sure that you wish to go so far? Mistakes have been made; so much we acknowledge! Let us all, yourself included, make a virtue of humility, and proceed with renewed faith into the future! Each of your comrades will advise and assist you in every convenient way, and soon your situation will repair itself! Rhialto, is not this the better way?"

Rhialto enthusiastically clapped his hands together. "Ildefonse, as always, your wisdom is profound! Why, indeed, should we undergo the sordid excesses of a full-blown legal action? Each member of this group need only tender his apology, restore my goods along with triple damages, and we will return to the old footing. Hache-Moncour, why do you not set the example?"

"Gladly," declared Hache-Moncour. "However, I would thereby compromise the others of the group. Whatever my personal concepts, I must await a vote."

Rhialto asked: "Hurtiancz, what of you? Do you care to come forward and apologize?"

Hurtiancz shouted something incomprehensible.

Rhialto turned to Ildefonse: "What of yourself?"

Ildefonse cleared his throat. "I will now read the bill of accusations brought by Rhialto against this association. In detail the charges occupy eighteen pages. I will first read the 'Topic Headings':

    Title One: Trespass.

    Title Two: Larceny, Grand.

    Title Three: Larceny, Petty.

    Title Four: Vandalism.

    Title Five: Assault, upon the person of Frole.

    Title Six: Slander.

    Title Seven: Dishonour to the Monstrament, including wilful mutilation and casting down of a certified copy thereof.

    Title Eight: Conspiracy to commit the above crimes.

    Title Nine: Wilful Retention of stolen property.

    Title Ten: Failure to abide by the Blue Principles, as propounded in the Monstrament.

Ildefonse put the tablet down upon his desk. "I will read the full charges presently, but at this moment, let me ask this: your topics and titles — are they not excessive to the case?"

Rhialto shrugged. "They describe most of the crimes involved, but not all."

"How so? The list seems all-inclusive."

"Have you forgotten the basic mystery? Who sent the pictures which mocked Hurtiancz? Who hung the opal on the drop-chain and thereby offended Ao? Who beat Gilgad's beast? Who destroyed Zilifant's tree? Do not these mysteries cry out for a solution?"

"They are cryptic indeed," admitted Ildefonse. "Of course sheer coincidence might be at work — no? You reject this theory? Well, perhaps so. Still, the questions are not included on your bill of accusations, and so lack immediate relevance."

"As you like," said Rhialto. "I suggest that you appoint a committee composed of Hurtiancz, Ao, Gilgad and Zilifant to pursue the matter."

"All in good time. I will now read the 'Bill of Accusations' in full."

"There is no need to do so," said Rhialto. "The association is well aware of the charges. I myself am not inflexible; three avenues, at least, are open. First, the group by acclamation may yield the damages I seek; secondly, the Preceptor, using his executive powers, may impose the specified levies; or thirdly, we will present the bill to the Adjudicator, for his judgment by the exact schedules of the Monstrament. Ildefonse, will you kindly ascertain which avenue is most congenial to this group?"

Ildefonse gave a guttural grunt. "What must be, must be. I move that we accept Rhialto's demands, even though a few minor hardships may be encountered. Is there a second?"

"Hold!" Barbanikos leapt to his feet, his great plume of white hair waving like a flame. "I must point out that the penalties invoked against Rhialto were partly in censure of his odious personality, so that in no way can he demand full restitution, let alone damages!"

"Hear, hear!" cried Haze of Wheary Water and others.

Thus encouraged, Barbanikos continued: "Any sensitive person would have recognized the reprimand for what it was; he would have returned meekly to the group, anxious only to vindicate himself. Instead, what do we have? A surly visage, a hectoring manner, slurs and threats! Is this appropriate conduct for a person who has just been decisively chastised by his peers?"

Barbanikos paused to refresh himself with a sip of tonic, then proceeded.

"Rhialto has learned nothing! He shows the same impudence as before! Therefore I earnestly recommend that Rhialto's tantrums be ignored. If they proceed, I suggest that he be turned out of doors by the footmen. Rhialto, I say this to you and no more: take care! Be ruled by prudence! You will be the happier man for it! That is my first remark. Now, as for my second —"

Ildefonse interrupted. "Yes, most interesting! Barbanikos, thank you for your incisive opinions."

Barbanikos reluctantly resumed his seat. Ildefonse asked: "Once again: is there a second to my motion?"

"I second the motion," said Rhialto. "Let us now see who votes for and who votes against the Blue Principles."

Hache-Moncour stepped forward. "There is still another point to be considered. In our discussion we have made frequent references to the Monstrament. May I ask as to who can furnish the group a full, undamaged and authentic text? Ildefonse, you naturally include such a document among your references?"

Ildefonse groaned toward the ceiling. "I would not know where to look. Rhialto, however, has brought here, as an exhibit, such a document."

"Unfortunately, Rhialto's exhibit, whatever it purports to be, is torn and no longer valuable. We must insist upon absolute authenticity: in this case, the Perciplex itself. Put Rhialto's damaged scrap out of mind. We will study the Monstrament at Fader's Waft; then and only then will we be able to vote with conviction."

Ildefonse said: "Do you put that in the form of a motion?"

"I do."

Herark the Harbinger called out: "I second the motion!"

The vote was carried almost unanimously, the only silent voices being those of Ildefonse and Rhialto.

Herark rose to his feet. "The hour is late; our time is short! Each of us must resolve to visit Fader's Waft and study the Perciplex at his earliest convenience. Then, when Ildefonse ascertains that all have done their duty, he shall reconvene the conclave and we will once more consider this affair, in a more conciliatory atmosphere, or so I trust."

Rhialto uttered a grim laugh and stepped up on the dais beside Ildefonse. "Any who wish may go to Fader's Waft and test Hache-Moncour's didactic theories at their leisure. I am going now to consult the Adjudicator. Let no one think to test his magic against me! I did not leave all my spells at Falu, and I am protected in dimension."

Byzant the Necrope took exception to the remark. "Rhialto, you are contentious! Must the Adjudicator be troubled by every trifling snit and swivet? Be large, Rhialto!"

"Good advice!" declared Rhialto. "I shall solicit mercy for you at Fader's Waft. Ildefonse, the 'Bill of Accusations', if you please! The Adjudicator will also need this list of names."

Fader's Waft

Hache-Moncour spoke politely: "Since Rhialto is determined, I must warn him of the dangers he will incur at Fader's Waft. They are large indeed!"

"How so?" asked Ildefonse. "Where and how does Rhialto face danger?"

"Is it not clear? The Monstrament states that any person who presents an altered or damaged copy of the Blue Principles in the effort to prove a case at law is guilty of a Schedule H crime and must be expunged. Rhialto, I reluctantly must declare, has today committed such a crime which vitiates his entire case. He will go before the Adjudicator at peril to his life."

Rhialto frowned down at his copy of the Monstrament. "I see no such interdict here. Please indicate the passage which you are citing."

Hache-Moncour took a quick step backward. "If I did so, I would then become guilty of the identical crime we are now discussing. The passage perhaps has been elided by the damage."

"Most peculiar," said Rhialto.

Herark spoke out. "Rhialto, your accusations have been voided by this new crime, and your claims must now be abandoned. Ildefonse, I move that the meeting be adjourned."

"Not so fast," said Ildefonse. "We are suddenly faced with a most complex matter. I suggest that, in view of Hache-Moncour's exposition, we send a committee to Fader's Waft, consisting, let us say, of myself, Eshmiel, Barbanikos, and perhaps Hache-Moncour, there to study the Monstrament quietly and carefully, without reference to our little troubles."

"I will meet you there," said Rhialto. "Even if Hache-Moncour's recollection is correct, which I doubt, I have not quoted from the damaged Monstrament and so am innocent."

"Not so!" declared Hache-Moncour. "You just now examined your spurious document and used it to dispute my statement. Your crime takes precedence and you will be expunged before uttering the first of your charges, which thereupon become moot. Return at this instant to Falu! We will ascribe your conduct to mental disorder."

Ildefonse spoke wearily: "This advice, no matter how well-meant, clearly lacks persuasion. Therefore, as Preceptor, I rule that all present shall go now to Fader's Waft, there to inspect the Monstrament. Our purposes are informational only; we will not disturb the Adjudicator. Come, then! All to Fader's Waft! We will ride in my commodious whirlaway."

5

Ildefonse's majestic whirlaway flew southward, into a region of low rolling hills at the southern edge of Ascolais. Certain of the magicians strolled the upper promenade, intent upon the far vistas of air and cloud; others kept to the lower deck that they might overlook the lands below; still others preferred the leather-cushioned comfort of the saloon.

The time was close upon evening; the near-horizontal light spread odd patterns of red and black shadow across the landscape; Fader's Waft, a hillock somewhat higher and more massive than its fellows, loomed ahead.

The whirlaway settled upon the summit, which, exposed to the draughts of Fader the west wind, was bare and stony. Alighting from the vehicle, the magicians marched across a circular terrace to a six-sided structure roofed with tiles of blue gold.

Rhialto had visited Fader's Waft on a single other occasion, for reasons of simple curiosity. The west wind Fader flapped his cloak as he approached the fane; entering the vestibule he waited for his eyes to adapt to the gloom, then stepped forward into the central chamber.

A pedestal supported the Egg: a spheroid three feet across the widest diameter. A window at one end displayed the Perciplex, a blue prism four inches tall, inwardly engraved with the text of the Monstrament. Through the window the Perciplex projected an image of the Monstrament in legible characters upon a vertical dolomite slab, and so charged with magic was the Perciplex that should an earthquake or other shock cause it to topple, it must right itself immediately, so that it should never present a faulty image, or one which might be misconstrued, to the viewer.

So it had been; so it was now.

※

Fader's Waft

Ildefonse led the way across the terrace, with Hache-Moncour, erect and controlled in his movements on one side, and on the other Hurtiancz in full gesticulation. Behind came the others in a hurrying clot, with Rhialto sauntering disdainfully alone at the rear.

Into the vestibule marched the group, and into the central chamber. Rhialto at the rear heard Hache-Moncour's voice raised in sudden shock and dismay, followed by a mingling of other astonished voices.

Pressing forward, Rhialto saw all as he remembered from his previous visit: pedestal supporting Judicial Egg, Perciplex glowing blue, and the projection of the Monstrament upon the dolomite slab. Today, however, there was a noteworthy difference: the text of the Monstrament appeared in reverse, or mirror-image, upon the dolomite slab.

Rhialto felt a sudden flicker across his consciousness, and almost instantly he heard Ildefonse's roar of protest. "Impropriety, bad faith! The monitor shows a hiatus*! Who would so dare to work a spell on us?"

"This is an outrage!" declared Hache-Moncour. "Whoever is the guilty party, let him step forward and explain his conduct!"

No one replied to the challenge, but Mune the Mage cried out in wonder: "The Monstrament! Was it not in reverse? It now seems in correct condition!"

"Odd!" said Ildefonse. "Most odd!"

Hache-Moncour looked angrily around the company. "These sly tricks are intolerable! They besmirch the dignity of us all! In due course I will personally investigate the case, but as of now our business is the tragic determination of Rhialto's guilt. Let us study the Monstrament."

Rhialto spoke in a voice of icy politeness: "Are you not ignoring a most remarkable fact? The Monstrament was projected in reverse."

Hache-Moncour looked back and forth between Rhialto and the Monstrament in puzzled inquiry. "It seems now as steadfast as ever! I suspect that your eyes played you false; entering darkness from the daylight is often confusing. Now then! With true sorrow I call attention to this passage in Section 3, Paragraph D, which reads —"

---

* hiatus: The Spell of Temporal Stasis, affecting all save he who works the spell. All others are frozen into immotility. Magicians bitterly resent being placed in hiatus by other magicians; too many untoward events take place under these conditions and many carry monitors to warn when a hiatus has occurred.

"One moment," said Ildefonse. "I too saw the reverse projection. Am I also confused?"

Hache-Moncour gave a light laugh. "Such little errors betoken neither degeneracy nor turpitude; perhaps for your lunch you enjoyed a surfeit of plum-pickle, or took a mug too many of your excellent sub-cellar ale! Ha ho! Dyspepsia is the plight of many strong men! Shall we proceed with our business?"

"By no means!" declared Ildefonse in brusque tones. "We shall return to Boumergarth for a fuller investigation of what at every turn becomes a more mystifying situation."

Amid a subdued murmur of conversation, the magicians departed the fane. Rhialto, who had paused to inspect the Egg, held Ildefonse back until they were alone. "You may be interested to learn that this is not even the authentic Perciplex. It is a forgery."

"What!" cried Ildefonse. "Surely you are mistaken!"

"Look for yourself. This prism is too small for the housing. The workmanship is crude. Most significant of all, the true Perciplex could never project in reverse. Watch now! I will shake the Egg and topple the prism. The true Perciplex will right itself."

Rhialto jarred the Egg with such effect that the Perciplex fell to its side, in which position it remained.

Ildefonse faced the Egg. "Adjudicator! Speak! It is Ildefonse the Preceptor who commands!"

No reply was audible.

Once again Ildefonse called out: "Adjudicator! Sarsem! I charge you: speak!"

Again, silence.

Ildefonse turned away. "Back to Boumergarth. The mystery is compounded. It is no longer trivial."

"Never was it trivial," said Rhialto.

"No matter," said Ildefonse curtly. "The affair, now that it concerns me, has taken on a new and large dimension. To Boumergarth!"

6

Assembling again in the Grand Hall, the magicians set up a colloquy of many voices. Ildefonse for a time listened to the somewhat formless interchanges without comment, darting his pale blue eyes from face to face and giving an occasional tug to his untidy beard.

The discussions began to grow heated. Vehement in his wrath was Haze of Wheary Water: a hot-eyed little wefkin who affected a green pelt and a thatch of yellow willow-leaves in the place of hair. Moving with irregular starts and jerks, he asserted his opinions with ever-increasing agitation. "Willy-nilly, backwards, forwards, the Blue is the Blue! As Hache-Moncour averred, the text condemns Rhialto's conduct out of hand, and that is all we care about. I will gladly stand on my head to read such news, or look through a mirror, or peek from behind my handkerchief!" And Haze spoke on, ever more fervently, until the company began to fear that he might injure himself in a paroxysm, or even blurt out some terrible all-inclusive curse to disable everyone. Ildefonse finally invoked the Spell of Soft Silence, so that while Haze ranted as before, his voice no longer could be heard, not even by himself, and presently he returned to his place.

The corpulent and loose-featured Dulce-Lolo analyzed the peculiar reversal of the projection. "I suspect that Sarsem the Adjudicator became careless and allowed the Perciplex to project in reverse, then, observing our consternation, he brought a hiatus upon us and turned the Perciplex to its proper position."

Ildefonse stepped ponderously up on the dais. "I must make an important announcement. The prism you saw tonight is false: a fraud, a forgery. The question of reversal is irrelevant."

Darvilk the Miaanther, normally taciturn, emitted an angry cry. "Then why did you, in full and pompous authority, dragoon us and march us lock-step to Fader's Waft, if only to inspect what you claim to be a falsity?"

Shrue spoke out. "The Miaanther's question strikes the nail! Ildefonse, your conduct merits a reproach."

Ildefonse held his arms high. "The group is not addressing itself to the issue! I repeat again: the Monstrament, the basis of our association, is missing from the Judicial Egg! We are left without law; we are naked as the Egg itself to that faceless shape which walks among us! We cannot dare the duration of a day without undertaking strategies of protection."

Hache-Moncour said with a gentle smile: "Ildefonse, dear friend! Must you cry cataclysm in such wild despair? Our association is based on the wisdom of its members!"

Vermoulian the Dream-walker said: "I predict a simple explanation to the apparent mystery. Sarsem may have removed the Perciplex for cleaning and left a simulacrum temporarily in place."

"This must indeed be the explanation," said Hache-Moncour. "Meanwhile, the simulacrum can be used at need."

"Precisely so!" cried Hurtiancz. "And never forget that, in making use of this version, simulacrum though it may be, we shackle the animal ferocity of Rhialto, and quell his insensate demands."

Ildefonse struck his gavel upon the podium. "Hurtiancz, your remarks are out of order. If you recall, Rhialto staunchly defended his conduct, and where this was impossible, he simply denied it."

Hurtiancz muttered: "I only give tongue to the consensus."

"Your remarks are not appropriate at this time. Rhialto, you have spoken no word: what is your opinion?"

"I am not yet ready to speak."

"Shrue, what of you?"

"Only this: lacking the true Monstrament, all issues of legality must be held in abeyance. Practically, the 'status quo' must be considered as definite and final."

"Nahourezzin: what are your thoughts?"

Nahourezzin, known in Old Romarth as 'the Striped Sadwan', already was pondering the possible courses of the future. "If the Perciplex is indeed gone, then, using the simulacrum as a basis, we must create a new Monstrament, to be known as the Orange Principles."

"Or the Lime-green," suggested Dulce-Lolo. "Or even the Rose-purple, to suggest both splendour and pomp."

"The suggestion lacks merit," said Ildefonse. "Why create a new document of some unfamiliar colour, when the Blue Principle has served us staunchly and well? Rhialto's document, though slightly torn, will suffice for the nonce."

Hurtiancz again bounded out to claim the floor. "If we accept Rhialto's document, then his charges prevail! With a new Perciplex based upon the simulacrum, all previous claims, including Rhialto's demand for triple damages, are repudiated, and Rhialto willy-nilly must pay the penalty for his mischiefs."

"An important point!" cried Tchamast. "Hurtiancz has slashed a clear avenue through this jungle of verbiage; he has clamped his admirable teeth deep into the very gist of the matter." Here Tchamast made reference to the exquisitely shaped rubies which replaced Hurtiancz's original complement of teeth; and Hurtiancz bowed in acknowledgment of the compliment.

Vermoulian the Dream-walker, a person tall and thin as a wand, with a high crest of glossy black hair like the dorsal fin of a sail-fish, was not known for his loquacity. His prominent eyes tended to gaze unfocused past the bony jut of his nose, and were often obscured by a nictitating membrane which conceivably served a useful purpose during his dream-walking. In the punitive phase of the proceedings against Rhialto, he had acquired a very fine glossolary, which, translating as it did the most corrupt gibberish into clear common speech, served him well in the course of his vocation. In any event, and for whatever reason, Vermoulian now thrust himself erect and spoke in a voice dry and precise: "I put the thesis of Hurtiancz into the form of a motion!"

"That is not regular procedure," declared Ildefonse. "Our task at hand is to learn the whereabouts of the Blue Perciplex! We must not be diverted!"

Hache-Moncour stepped forward. "I endorse the views of Ildefonse! I now undertake to make a full, thorough and exhaustive investigation into this deplorable matter, and let the chips fall where they may! In the meantime, our normal business may well proceed, and I suggest to the Preceptor that, in view of my undertaking, Vermoulian's motion now be ruled in order."

Rhialto glanced toward Ildefonse. He raised his hand to his mouth as if to stifle a yawn, making a secret sign in the process. Ildefonse gave a wince of distaste, but nevertheless invoked the Spell of Temporal Stasis.

7

Rhialto and Ildefonse inspected the chamber where their associates sat or stood poised in frozen postures.

"This is a nuisance," grumbled Ildefonse. "Everyone in the group carries a monitor, that he may not be swindled by his friends. Now each of these monitors must be searched out and justified if the deception is to succeed."

"No great matter. I have evolved a new technique which easily befuddles the monitors. I need only a pair of quampics and a red-eyed bifaulgulate sandestin."

Ildefonse brought forth an object of eccentric shape derived from a fulgurite. From the opening peered a small face with eyes as red as currants. "This is Osherl," said Ildefonse. "He is not altogether bifaulgulate, but he is clever and swift, if sometimes a trifle moody. His indenture runs to five points."

"The count is far too high," said Osherl. "Somewhere a mistake has been made."

"I believe the count to be valid and just," said Ildefonse. "Still, in due course I will check my records."

Rhialto spoke to Osherl: "You are anxious to reduce your indenture?"

"Naturally."

"A simple 'yes' or 'no' will suffice."

"Whatever you like; it is all one with me."

Rhialto went on: "Today Ildefonse and I are in a lenient mood. For a few trifling tasks we will mark you down a full point —"

"What?" roared Ildefonse. "Rhialto, you distribute points among my sandestins with a lavish hand!"

"In a good cause," said Rhialto. "Remember, I intend to impose triple damages, with total confiscation in at least one case. I will here and now stipulate that your seizure of my IOUN stones was in the nature of a safeguard, and not subject to the punitive provisions which otherwise might be applied."

Ildefonse spoke more equably: "That is taken for granted. Deal with Osherl as you will."

Osherl said persuasively: "A single point is of no great account —"

Rhialto turned to Ildefonse. "Osherl seems tired and languid. Let us use a more zestful sandestin."

"Perhaps I spoke in haste," said Osherl. "What are your requirements?"

"First, visit each of the persons caught in the stasis, and use these quampics to adjust each monitor so that it will fail to register this particular stasis."

"That is no great work." A gray shadow flitted about the room. "It is done, and I have won an entire point."

"Not so," said Rhialto. "The point is yours after all the tasks have been accomplished."

Osherl gave a sour grunt. "I suspected something of the sort."

"Nevertheless, you have made a good start," said Ildefonse. "Do you see how nicely things go when one is amiable?"

"They only go nicely when you are generous with your points," said Osherl. "What now?"

"Now you will go to each magician in turn," said Rhialto. "With great care remove the dust, chaff and small bits of detritus from the boots of each person present including Ildefonse and myself. Place the yield from each pair of boots in a separate bottle, identified properly with the name of the magician."

"I know none of your names," grumbled Osherl. "You all look alike to me."

"Place the yield in a series of labeled bottles. I will name off the names. First is Herark the Harbinger… Ao of the Opals… Perdustin… Dulce-Lolo… Shrue…" Rhialto named off each of the magicians, and instantly a glass bottle containing dust and trash in greater or lesser quantity appeared on the table.

"Again, no great matter," said Osherl. "What now?"

"The next task may or may not take you afield," said Rhialto. "In any case, do not dally nor loiter along the way, as important consequences rest upon our findings."

"To a dung-beetle, a pile of brontotaubus droppings is a matter of prime significance," said Osherl.

Rhialto knit his brows. "Ildefonse and I are both perplexed by the allusion. Do you care to explain?"

"The concept is abstract," said Osherl. "What is the task?"

"The Adjudicator at Fader's Waft, whom we know as Sarsem, is absent from his post. Bring him here for consultation."

"For a single point? The balance becomes uneven."

"How so? I ask you to locate only one sandestin."

"The process is tedious. I must go first to La, there pull on what might be called the tails of ten thousand sandestins, then listen for the characteristic exclamations of Sarsem."

"No matter," said Ildefonse. "An entire point is an item to be cherished; you will have earned it well and honestly."

Rhialto added: "I will say this: if our business goes well, you will not have cause to complain. Mind, I promise nothing!"

"Very well. But you must dissolve the Stasis; I ride the flux of time as a sailor sails on the wind."

"A final word! Time is of the essence! For you, a second differs little from a century; we are more sensitive in this regard. Be quick!"

Rhialto cried: "Wait! We must hide the bottles of dust. Hurtiancz has the eyes of a hawk, and he might wonder to find a bottle of dust labeled with his name. Under the shelf with the lot!…Good. Ildefonse, remember! We must terminate this colloquy with dispatch!"

"Just so! Are you ready?"

"Not quite! There is one last bit of business!" Rhialto repossessed the glossolary which Vermoulian had obtained at Falu; then Rhialto and Ildefonse, working together and chuckling like schoolboys, fashioned a simulation of the glossolary, changing the vocabulary so that it yielded not clear and precise language but absurdities, insults and sheer nonsense. This new and faulty glossolary was then restored into Vermoulian's keeping. "Now I am ready!" said Rhialto.

Ildefonse lifted the spell and the conference proceeded as if it had never been interrupted.

Hache-Moncour's words hung in the air: "— of my undertaking, Vermoulian's motion may now be ruled in order."

Rhialto jumped up. "I move that the meeting be adjourned until such time as Hache-Moncour completes his investigation. Then we will have full information on which to base our findings."

Vermoulian gave a croak of protest; Ildefonse quickly declared:

Fader's Waft

"Vermoulian seconds the motion; are all in favor? No one seems opposed; the motion is carried and the meeting is adjourned until Hache-Moncour reports his findings. The lights are about to go out and I am off to take my rest. To all: good night."

Casting dark looks toward Rhialto, the magicians departed Boumergarth and went their various ways.

8

Rhialto and Ildefonse repaired to the small study. Ildefonse set out double spy-guards and for a period the two sat drinking wine with their feet raised to the flicker of the fire.

"A dreary business," said Ildefonse at last. "It leaves an evil savor worthy of an archveult! Let us hope we can find guidance in the dust of your bottles or from the testimony of Sarsem. If not, we have no basis for action."

Rhialto gripped the arms of his chair. "Shall we study the bottles? Or would you prefer to take your rest?"

Ildefonse heaved himself to his feet. "I know no fatigue! To the work-room! We shall study each grain of dust under the pantavist: up, down, back, forth — until finally it cries out its tale! Then we drive home the nail with Sarsem's testimony!"

The two went to the work-room. "Now!" declared Ildefonse. "Let us look to your famous bottles!" He examined the contents of several. "From such nondescript sifts I expect nothing of value."

"That remains to be seen," said Rhialto. "We shall need your best macrotic enlarging pantavist, and then your latest edition of *Characteristic Stuffs: Dusts and Microvies of the Latter Aeons.*"

"I have anticipated you," said Ildefonse. "All is here to hand. I will also order up a classificator, to make our work less tedious."

"Excellent."

The inquiry proceeded with easy efficiency. One at a time the bottles were emptied and their contents examined, identified, graded, and classified.

By middle morning the work was through, and the two tired magicians went out upon the terrace to take rest and nourishment.

In the opinion of Ildefonse, the work had yielded little of significance, and his mood was glum. He said at last: "In the main, we are faced with ambiguities. We neither prove nor disprove; the 'Extraordinarys' are too many: specifically, the dusts of Vermoulian, Hurtiancz, Hache-Moncour, Dulce-Lolo and Byzant. Additionally, the 'Extraordinarys' may simply be special cases of the 'Ordinarys', while the 'Ordinarys' may be associated with cryptic deeds beyond our detection."

Rhialto nodded. "Your indications are accurate! Still I do not share your pessimism. Each 'Extraordinary' tells its own tale, except in one case."

"Aha! You are referring to Vermoulian, since the dust from his boots is unique in shape, color and complexity, and different from everything classified in the catalogue."

Rhialto, smiling, shook his head. "I am not referring to Vermoulian. In his case we would seem to be investigating dream-dust, scuffed up from one or another of his dream-landscapes. The catalogues are understandably noncommittal. As for Hurtiancz, he uses medicinal powder to relieve a fungoid infection of the toes, and we can confidently place him on the 'Ordinary' list. Byzant's dust is in the main a powder of phosphatic calcars, evidently deriving from his field of interest, which again the catalogue prefers to ignore. In regard to Dulce-Lolo's amazing many-colored particles, I recall that his part in a recent 'Charade of Folly' required that he paint each of his feet to represent a grotesque face."

Ildefonse stared at Rhialto in wonder. "What purpose could possibly be served by this conduct?"

"I gather that Dulce-Lolo's role in the Pageant was thereby enhanced. Reclining on his back, he kicked his feet on high, meanwhile reciting a dialogue in two voices, falsetto and bass. Particles of the pigment evidently were trapped in his boots, and I must consider him, at least from our immediate perspective, as an 'Ordinary'."

"And what of Hache-Moncour?"

"His dust, while 'Extraordinary', may or may not be instructive. We lack a critical item of information, to this effect: is Hache-Moncour an amateur of caverns and underground chambers?"

Ildefonse tugged at his beard. "Not to my knowledge, but this means

Fader's Waft

little. I did not realize until last week, for instance, that Zahoulik-Khuntze is an Elder at the Hub and Controller of his own distinct infinity."

"Odd but interesting! Back to Hache-Moncour, his boots were rife with a singular dust, discovered only in a few underground places of the world."

"Ha hm. The fact might mean much or nothing."

"Nevertheless, my suspicions incline toward Hache-Moncour."

Ildefonse gave a non-committal grunt. "For proof we must await Sarsem, and hear his story."

"That goes without saying. Osherl will report at the earliest possible instant?"

"So I would expect." Ildefonse glanced thoughtfully toward the work-room. "Excuse me a moment."

Ildefonse left the terrace and almost immediately sounds of contention came from the direction of the work-room. Ildefonse presently returned to the terrace, followed by Osherl and a second sandestin using the guise of a gaunt blue bird-like creature, some six feet in height.

Ildefonse spoke in scathing tones: "Behold these two creatures! They can roam the chronoplex as easily as you or I can walk around the table; yet neither has the wit to announce his presence upon arrival. I found Osherl asleep in his fulgurite and Sarsem perched in the rafters."

"You demean our intellects," snapped Osherl. "Persons of your ilk are unpredictable; they must be dealt with on the basis of exactitude. I have learned never to act without explicit instructions. If I were to do otherwise, your complaints would rasp even more stridently upon my attention. You sent me on a mission from the work-room; with mission accomplished I returned to the work-room. If you wished me to disturb you at your vulgar ingestions you should have made this clear."

Ildefonse puffed out his cheeks. "I detect more than a trace of insolence in these rejoinders!"

"No matter," said Rhialto. "He has brought Sarsem, and this was the requirement. In the main, Osherl, you have done well!"

"And my indenture point?"

"Much depends upon Sarsem's testimony. Sarsem, will you sit?"

"In this guise, I find it more convenient to stand."

Sarsem became a naked young epicene in an integument of lavender scales...

"Then why not alter to human form and join us in comfort at the table?"

"That is a good idea." Sarsem became a naked young epicene in an integument of lavender scales with puffs of purple hair like pom-pons growing down his back. He seated himself at the table but declined refreshment. "This human semblance, though typical, is after all, only a guise. If I were to put such things inside myself, I might well become uneasy."

"As you like. Now to business. Where is the Blue Perciplex which you were required to guard?"

Sarsem asked cautiously: "You refer to the blue prism reposing on the pedestal? You will find such an object as safe as ever in its accustomed place."

"And why have you deserted your post?"

"Simplicity itself! One of your ilk delivered a new and official Perciplex to replace the obsolete version, which had lost its effect."

Rhialto gave a hollow laugh. "And how do you know this for a fact?"

"Through the assertion of your representative." Sarsem sprawled back in the chair. "As I now reflect on the matter, what with the sun's death only a jerk and a tinkle away, a new Perciplex seems a pointless refinement."

"So then: what next?"

"I pointed out the burden of guarding two sacred objects, rather than one. The new, so I was told, would occupy the place of the old, and your representative would take the old to a place of reverent safety. Meanwhile, my services were no longer required."

Rhialto leaned forward. "No doubt indenture points were discussed?"

"I recall some such discussion."

"To what number and to what degree?"

"An appreciable proportion: in fact, all."

"How is this possible when your chug* resides in my work-room?"

---

* chug: a semi-intelligent sub-type of sandestin, which by a system too intricate to be presently detailed, works to control the sandestins. Even use of the word 'chug' is repellent to the sandestin.

Sarsem scowled. "That is as may be."

Upon sudden thought Ildefonse lurched to his feet and departed the terrace. A moment later he returned, and threw himself down in his chair. With a bleak expression he said to Rhialto: "Sarsem's chug is gone. Have you ever heard the like?"

Rhialto reflected. "When might this event have taken place?"

"Evidently during the temporal stasis: when else?" Ildefonse turned upon Sarsem. "We have been victimized together! The reduction of your indenture points was unauthorized! You are the victim of a cruel joke! The reduction is null and void, and we have lost the Perciplex! Sarsem, I cannot commend your performance."

"Ha ha!" cried Sarsem, waving a pale lavender forefinger upon which glinted a silver fingernail. "There is more to come! I am not quite the fool you take me for!"

"How so, and in what regard?"

"I am that rare individual who can instantly scrutinize all sides of a situation! Without reference to my motives, I decided to retain the old Perciplex within the scope of my vigilance."

"Ha, ha, hah! Bravo, Sarsem!"

"Thereupon, your representative —"

"Speak less loosely, Sarsem. The person was not my representative."

"While this person was temporarily distracted, I laid the old prism safely aside. This person, whose good faith you decry, still cannot be deemed irresponsible."

"Why do you say that?"

"Because, like myself, he worried about the safety of the old Perciplex and would not rest until he learned where I had placed it."

Rhialto groaned. "Within the confines of a cavern?"

"Yes, how did you know?"

"We are not without resources. In effect you yielded up the Perciplex to the criminal!"

"Not at all. I placed the prism in a place well-known to me, accessible only by a small and narrow fissure. For double security I reverted the object to the Sixteenth Aeon."

"And how do you know that the criminal himself has not reverted to this era and taken the Perciplex for his own?"

"Can he walk the length of a fissure into which you cannot even thrust your hand? Especially while I keep the opening under survey from then till now, as you might scan the surface of the table? Nothing has come or gone. Ergo, by the rotes of rationality, the Perciplex reposes in its subterranean place, as secure as ever."

Rhialto rose to his feet. "Come: once more back to Fader's Waft! You shall grope down the fissure into the Sixteenth Aeon and reclaim the Perciplex. Ildefonse, are you ready? Summon your small air-carriage."

9

Rhialto, Ildefonse and Sarsem stood disconsolate on the summit of Fader's Waft. Sarsem spoke in a troubled voice. "A most confusing dilemma! I searched the fissure without success; I guarantee that the Perciplex did not leave by this route. I admit to perplexity."

Rhialto suggested: "There may be another route into the cavern; what of that?"

"The idea is plausible," admitted Sarsem. "I will make a survey across the Aeons."

Sarsem presently returned to make his report. "The cave opened to the valley for a brief period during the Sixteenth Aeon. The entrance is not evident now. This is good news, since if I am a trifle nonplussed, our antagonist must be crazy with bafflement."

"Not necessarily true," intoned Rhialto.

Sarsem peered here and there. "In the Sixteenth Aeon, so I recall, three black crags rose yonder, and a river swung into the valley from the east... Fader's Waft at that time was a tall peak defying the storms... Now I am straight. We must drop down into yonder valley."

Sarsem led the way down a barren slope into a gulch choked with tumbled stones.

"Much has changed," said Sarsem. "A crag the shape of a skatler horn rose yonder and another there, and another there, where you now see rounded hummocks. Perhaps among these rocks... Here is the place, though the entrance is tumbled over with detritus. Stand aside; I will skew the latifers, so as to allow access."

Sarsem caused a pulse to shiver along the hillside, whisking away the overburden and revealing an aperture leading into the mountain.

The three marched forward. Ildefonse sent a flux of light into the passage, and started forward, but Rhialto held him back. "One moment!" He indicated a double line of footprints in the fine sand which covered the floor of the cavern. "Sarsem, did you leave these marks?"

"Not I! When I left the cavern, the sand showed a smooth surface."

"Then I deduce that someone has entered the cave after you departed. This person might well have been Hache-Moncour, to judge by the evidence of his boots."

Sarsem drifted into the cavern, making no marks upon the sand. He returned almost at once. "The Perciplex is not where I placed it."

Rhialto and Ildefonse stood stiff with disappointment. "This is dismal news," said Ildefonse. "You have not dealt well with your assigned duty."

"More to the point," said Rhialto, "where now is the Perciplex? In the past, or in the present, or has it been destroyed?"

"Who could be reckless enough to destroy the Blue?" muttered Ildefonse. "Not even an archveult. I believe that the Perciplex is somewhere extant."

"I am inclined to agree," said Rhialto. "Sarsem, in regard to these footprints: from their direction it seems that they were formed before the cavern's mouth was covered — which is to say, the Sixteenth Aeon."

"True. I can also say this: if they were made by someone hoping to find the Perciplex, he failed. The tracks enter the cave, pass the niche where I concealed the prism, continue into the central cavern, wander this way and that in a random pattern, then depart with long strides denoting angry failure. The Perciplex was taken from the cavern prior to the footprints."

Rhialto turned to Ildefonse. "If you recall, Hache-Moncour came to Boumergarth with the subterranean dust still clinging to his boots. Unless he found the Perciplex immediately upon leaving the cave, he failed in his mission."

"Convincing!" said Ildefonse. "Who then took the Perciplex?"

Rhialto said sternly: "Sarsem, your conduct has been less than wise. Need I remind you of this?"

"You need say nothing! In sheer disgust, discharge me from my indenture! The humiliation will be an overwhelming punishment."

"We are not so cruel," said Ildefonse. "We prefer that you make amends by retrieving the Perciplex for us."

Sarsem's lavender face fell. "I must fail you still a second time. I cannot return to the Sixteenth Aeon, because, in effect, I am already there."

"What?" Ildefonse raised high his bristling yellow eyebrows. "I cannot understand."

"No matter," said Sarsem. "The restraints are definite."

"Hmmf," grunted Ildefonse. "We are faced with a problem."

"I observe the single solution," stated Rhialto. "The Preceptor must step back into the Sixteenth Aeon to recover the Perciplex. Ildefonse, prepare yourself! And then —"

"Hold!" cried Ildefonse. "Have you put aside that rationality which once marked your thinking? I cannot possibly leave while turmoil threatens the association! With your keen eyes and rare intelligence, you are the man to recover what is lost! Sarsem, do you not support this point of view?"

"At the moment my thoughts run shallow," said Sarsem. "However, this much is clear: whoever most anxiously wants to restore the old Perciplex to its place will be he who retrieves it from the past."

Rhialto sighed. "Poor Sarsem is by almost any standard feeble-minded; still in this case he has deftly stripped the issue to its naked essentials. If I must go, I must."

The three returned to Boumergarth. Rhialto made careful preparations, packing in his wallet the glossolary, proliferant coins, a catalogue of simple spells, and Osherl enclosed in a walnut shell.

Ildefonse extended his unqualified assurances. "It is, after all, a simple and pleasant adventure," he told Rhialto. "You will find yourself in the Land of Shir-Shan, which at this time is considered the center of the universe. The Grand Gazetteer lists only six magicians currently active, the nearest far to the north, in the present Land of Cutz. A flying creature known as the 'dyvolt' rules the skies; it resembles a pelgrane with a long nasal horn and uses the common language. You should recognize three rules of genteel conduct: the sash is tied to the left; only acrobats, actors and sausage-makers wear yellow; grapes are eaten with a knife and fork."

Rhialto drew back in annoyance. "I do not plan so much as a single meal in Shir-Shan. Perhaps, after all, it would be better if you went."

"Impossible! You are the man for the job! You need only step back, secure the Perciplex, then return to the present. So then, Rhialto! Are you ready?"

"Not quite! How, in fact, do I return to the present?"

"A good question!" Ildefonse turned to Sarsem. "What, exactly, is the procedure?"

"That is out of my province," said Sarsem. "I can project Rhialto any number of aeons into the past, but thereafter he must make his own arrangements."

"Rhialto, do not be impatient!" said Ildefonse. "Sarsem, answer! How then does Rhialto make his return?"

"I suppose that he must rely upon Osherl."

"Good enough!" said Ildefonse. "Osherl can be trusted in this regard, or I am much mistaken."

So went the preparations. Rhialto made himself ready, not neglecting to change his yellow sash tied on the right for a black sash of good quality tied on the left. Osherl disposed himself within the walnut shell, and the two were reverted into the past.

10

Rhialto stood in warm sunlight of a complicated colour: a peach-pink orange suffused with rose and white-rose. He found himself in a valley surrounded by sharp peaks rising a mile into the air. That peak which he would later know as Fader's Waft stood highest of all, with the summit hidden in a tuft of white cloud.

The prospect was at once grand and serene. The valley seemed empty of habitation, although Rhialto noted plantations of melon and blue vines heavy with purple grapes along the valley and up the mountain-side.

To Rhialto's satisfaction, the landmarks cited by Sarsem, an outcrop of glistening black stone flanked by three cypress saplings, were plainly visible, although 'sapling' seemed an inexact description of the gnarled and massive trees in question. Still, Rhialto confidently set off toward the site of the cave.

By Sarsem's best calculations, the time was immediately subsequent to his own visit. Ildefonse had tried to elicit the exact measure of this interval: "A second? A minute? An hour?"

Rhialto's attention had been distracted by Osherl in the matter of indenture points, and he had heard only a phrase or two of Sarsem's response: "—accuracy of high degree!" and "—occasionally a curious kinking and backlash in the inter-aeon sutures—"

Ildefonse had put another inquiry and again Osherl's attempts to secure advantage had diverted Rhialto's attention, and he had only heard Sarsem discussing what seemed to be mathematical theory with Ildefonse: "—often closer than the thousandth part of one percent, plus or minus, which must be reckoned excellent."

Rhialto turned to join the conversation, but the avaricious Osherl placed a new demand, and Rhialto only heard Ildefonse's reference to "—five aeons: an unwieldy period!" Sarsem's response had only been that peculiarly supple shrug characteristic of his sort.

The entrance to the cave was now close at hand. Sarsem had been inexact in his instructions; rather than a barely perceptible crevice behind the first of the gabbro crags, Rhialto found a square opening five feet wide and taller than himself decorated with a careful pattern of pink shells, and a path of crushed white marl.

Rhialto uttered a hiss of vexation. Something was clearly amiss. He advanced up the path to the opening and looked into the cave. Here, at least, Sarsem had spoken accurately: to the right, immediately within the opening and something above the height of his head, a small pocket opened into the stone, and into this pocket Sarsem had placed the Perciplex.

The pocket was now empty, not altogether to Rhialto's surprise. An indefinable odor suggesting organic processes hung in the air; the cave seemed to be inhabited.

Rhialto retreated from the cave entrance and went to sit on a ledge of rock. Across the valley an old man came down the mountainside: a person small and slight, with a great ruff of white hair and a narrow blue face which seemed mostly nose. He wore a garment of black and white stripes and sandals with toes of exaggerated length, with a black sash about his waist tied on the left, in a manner which Rhialto considered absurd and unbecoming, but which evidently found favor with the pace-setters of the day.

Jumping down from the fence, Rhialto approached the old man, and a touch of the finger was enough to activate the glossolary.

The old man noticed Rhialto's approach, but paid no heed and continued on his way, skipping and trotting with light-footed agility. Rhialto called out: "Sir, stop to rest a moment! You move at speed! At your age a man should be kind to himself!"

The old man paused. "No danger there! If all were equally kind I should live the life of a magnate!"

"That is the usual concept. Still, we must do as best we can! What brings you out here among these lonely mountain crags?"

"Simply put, I would rather be here than out on the plain, where confusion reigns supreme. And yourself? From a distant land, so I perceive, from the rather awkward knot by which you tie your sash."

"Fashions differ," said Rhialto. "I am in fact a scholar, sent here to retrieve an important historical object."

The old man looked suspiciously sidewise at Rhialto. "Are you in earnest? I know of nothing within a hundred miles which answers that description — save perhaps the skeleton of my double-headed goat."

"I refer to a blue prism which was left in yonder cave for safe-keeping, but which is not there now."

The old man made a negative sign. "My knowledge of prisms, historical or otherwise, is small. For a fact, I recall the cave before the twastics took up residence, when nothing could be seen but a crevice into the rocks."

"How long ago might this be?"

The old man pulled at his nose. "Let me calculate… It was while Nedde still supplied my barley… Garler had not yet taken his third wife. Still, he had already built his new barn… I would estimate a period of thirty-one years."

Rhialto gritted his teeth. "These twastics: what of them?"

"Most have returned to Canopus; the climate suits them better. Still, the two yonder are decent in their habits and settle their debts in good time, which is more than I can say of my own son-in-law, though to be sure I would not choose a twastic as spouse to my daughter...I hear them now; they are returning from a function at their social club."

A tinkling sound reached Rhialto's ears, as if from the vibration of many small bells. Up the valley road came a pair of twenty-legged creatures eight feet long and four feet high, with large round heads studded with stalks, knobs and tufts, fulfilling functions not immediately apparent. Their caudal segments rose and curled forward in an elegant spiral, and each boasted an iron gong dangling from the tip. Smaller bells and vibrilators hung in gala style from the elbows of each leg. The first wore a robe of dark green velvet; the second a similar robe of cherry-rose plush.

"Yonder go the twastics," said the old man. "As for the contents of the cavern, they can answer your questions better than I."

Rhialto watched the tinkling creatures askance. "All very well, but how should I address them?"

"They are easy in this regard; a simple 'Sir' or 'Your Honor' suffices."

Returning across the valley, Rhialto was able to intercept the twastics before they entered the cavern. He called out: "Sirs! May I put a question? I am here on an important historical mission!"

The twastic wearing the dark green robe responded in a somewhat sibilant voice, using sounds created by a rapid clicking of the mandibles. "This is not our customary time for business. If you wish to order any of our service gungeons, be advised that the minimum shipment is one gross."

"I am interested in another matter. You have inhabited this cavern for about thirty years, so I understand."

"You have been gossiping with Tiffet, who is more garrulous than he should be. Still, your figures are correct."

"When you first arrived, did you find a blue crystal placed in a niche above the entrance? I would appreciate candor in this regard."

"There is no reason why you should not have it. I myself discovered the blue crystal, and cast it away immediately. On Canopus, blue is considered an unfavorable colour."

Rhialto clapped a hand to his forehead. "And then: what next?"

"You must ask Tiffet. He found the trinket in the rubbish." The twastics entered the cavern and disappeared into the darkness.

Rhialto hastened back across the valley and managed to overtake Tiffet.

"Wait, sir!" called Rhialto. "Another historical question or two!"

Tiffet halted. "What now?"

"As you know, I have come far in search of an important blue prism. The twastics threw it from the cave and it seems that you rescued it from the rubbish heap. Where is it now? Produce it and I will make you a rich man."

Tiffet blinked and pulled at his nose. "A blue prism? True. I had quite forgotten it. Quite so! I took it from the rubbish heap and put it on my mantel-piece. Not a week later the taxers came from the King of all Kings, and they took the blue jewel in payment of my taxes and even rescinded the standard beating with staves, for which I was grateful."

"And the blue prism?"

"It was taken to the Royal Treasury at Vasques Tohor, or so I suppose. And now, sir, I must be on my way. Tonight we eat squash soup with cheese and I must be nimble if I am to get my share."

Rhialto once more went to sit on the stone fence and watched as Tiffet hobbled briskly around the mountain. Reaching into his pouch, Rhialto brought out the walnut-shell from which stepped Osherl, now, by reason of some obscure whim, wearing a fox's mask.

The pink mouth spoke: "Well then, Rhialto! You are ready to return with the Perciplex?"

Rhialto thought to perceive a subtly mocking flavor to the question. He said coldly: "May I ask the source of your amusement?"

"It is nothing, Rhialto; I am naturally light-hearted."

"Try as I may, I find nothing amusing in this present situation, and in fact I wish to speak with Sarsem."

"As you wish."

Sarsem appeared across the road, still using the guise of an epicene youth clad in lavender scales. "Rhialto, you wish to confer with me?"

"I am displeased with your work," said Rhialto. "You missed the target date by something over thirty years."

"Only thirty years in five aeons? Such accuracy is far better than adequate."

"Not for my purposes. The Perciplex is not in the cave. Certain merchandisers from Canopus threw it aside. You were required to guard the Perciplex and it is now lost."

Sarsem thought a moment, then said: "I failed in my duty. No more need be said."

"Except this: by reason of your failure, you now must help me find the Perciplex."

Sarsem became argumentative. "Rhialto, you are illogical! I failed in my duty, true. Still, there is no linkage between this idea and the unrelated concept of my attempting to find the missing article. I hope you perceive your mistake, which is of a fundamental nature."

"The linkage is indirect, but real. By failing in your duty, you have incurred a severe penalty. This penalty may be partially expiated by your help in recovering the prism."

Sarsem reflected a moment, then said: "I am unconvinced; somewhere I smell sophistry at work. For instance, who will apply the penalty? You are five aeons gone and no longer even real."

"Ildefonse is my stout ally; he will protect my interests."

Sarsem gave that curious croak which, among creatures of his ilk, indicated amusement. "Rhialto, your innocence is droll. Have you not recognized that Ildefonse is the leader of the cabal against you?"

"Not so!" declared Rhialto. "You refer to an occasion when he jocularly availed himself of my IOUN stones."

Sarsem looked at Osherl. "What is the truth of this?"

Osherl considered. "As of now, Ildefonse breathes fire against Hache-Moncour."

Sarsem scratched his violet nose with a silver fingernail. "Ah well, on the slight chance that Rhialto is correct, I would not have him accusing me of falsity. Rhialto, take this pleurmalion; it will show a blue spot in the sky directly above the Perciplex. Remember, in case of any inquiry — for instance, from Hache-Moncour — it came through Osherl, and not through me. Am I clear on this?"

"Certainly. Hache-Moncour has filled your mind with foolishness. If you decide to share his destiny in the hope of gaining indenture points, you will have the Wiih to deal with."

Sarsem gave a small squeak of consternation, then cried out with somewhat hollow bravado: "You have over-spoken yourself! Trouble me no further; I am bored with the Perciplex; the present version will serve until the sun goes out. As for you, Ildefonse will never notice when you fail to return. Already Hache-Moncour eclipses him in power."

"And when in fact I return with the Perciplex, what then of Hache-Moncour?"

Sarsem chuckled. "Rhialto, have I not made myself clear? Find the Perciplex as you like, glory in your achievement, then settle yourself to enjoy the radiance of the Sixteenth Aeon, even though you will never revenge yourself against your enemies."

"What of Osherl?" asked Rhialto idly. "Will he not take me back to Boumergarth?"

"Ask him yourself."

"Well, Osherl? Are you too defiant and treasonable?"

"Rhialto, I believe that you will enjoy your life in this halcyon aeon. And so that you may start your new life free of fretful oddments and petty details, you may now finalize my indenture."

Rhialto smiled that aloof, almost sinister, smile which so often had annoyed his adversaries. From his wallet darted a black- and red-striped object like a long thin snake. "Chug!" screamed Sarsem in horror. The chug wound itself around Osherl, darted its head into one of the fox-ears, emerged from the other and tied itself in a knot across Osherl's head. Osherl was then dragged to a nearby tree and suspended by the rope through the ears to dangle three feet off the ground.

Rhialto turned to Sarsem: "Eventually I will deal with Osherl as he deserves. Meanwhile, he will assist me to his best abilities. Osherl, am I right in this? Or shall we take further steps?"

Osherl's fox-mask licked its chops nervously. "Rhialto, this is a poor response to my light-hearted badinage, and unworthy threats now hang in the air."

"I never make threats," said Rhialto. "In all candour, I am dumbfounded by Sarsem's recklessness. He totally misjudges the wrath of Ildefonse and myself. His treachery will cost him an awful price. That is not a threat; it is a statement of certainty."

Sarsem, smiling a glazed and insincere smile, faded from sight. Osherl kicked and thrashed his legs to set himself swinging. He cried out: "Your allegations have been too much for poor Sarsem! It would have been far more graceful if—"

"Silence!" Rhialto took up the pleurmalion. "I am interested only in the Perciplex!" He searched around the sky through the tube, but the surrounding mountain-sides blocked most of the view.

Rhialto affected his boots with the Spell of Lightsome Striding, which allowed him to walk through the air, high or low, at his pleasure. Osherl looked on with growing disquiet. At last he called out: "What of me? How long must I dangle here for birds to roost upon?"

Rhialto feigned surprise. "I had already forgotten you... I will say this. It is not pleasant to be betrayed by one's associates."

"Naturally not!" cried Osherl with enthusiasm. "How could you so mistake my little joke?"

"Very well, Osherl, I accept your explanation. Perhaps you can be of some slight assistance, after all, such as facilitating our return to Boumergarth."

"Naturally! It goes without saying!"

"Then we will resume as before." The chug dropped Osherl to the ground and returned to Rhialto's wallet. Osherl grimaced, but without further words returned to the walnut shell.

Rhialto jumped into the air; climbing to a height of twenty feet, he set off down the valley on long stately bounds, and Fader's Waft was left behind.

11

The valley opened upon a plain of far distances, distinguished principally by clouds of dust and smoke lowering over the northern horizon. Closer at hand, where the hills first began to swell up from the plain, Rhialto saw a number of small farmsteads each with its small white silo, round white barn, and orchard of globular blue trees. A mile or so to the west, a village of round pink houses enjoyed the shade of a hundred tall parasol palms. Details of the landscape beyond were blurs of delicate colour, until, at the horizon, curtains of dust and smoke rose ominously high.

Rhialto alighted upon a ledge of rock and bringing out the

pleurmalion scrutinized the sky. To his gratification, he discovered a dark blue spot on the sapphire vault of the northern sky, in the general direction of the smoke and dust.

Rhialto replaced the tube in his pouch, and now, a hundred yards down the slope, he noticed three young girls picking berries from a thicket. They wore black vests over striped blouses, black pantaloons tied at the knee with black ribbons, black stockings and black shoes tied with white puffs at the ankles. Their faces were round; straight black hair was cut square across their foreheads. Rhialto thought them not ill-favored, somewhat in the manner of odd little dolls.

Rhialto approached at a dignified pace, and halted at a distance of ten yards. Always disposed to create a favorable impression before members of the female sex, so long as they were of an age and degree of vitality to notice, Rhialto leaned an arm against a stump, disposed his cloak so that it hung in a casual yet dramatic style.

The girls, preoccupied with their chatter, failed to notice his presence. Rhialto spoke in melodious tones: "Young creatures, allow me to intrude upon your attention, at least for a moment. I am surprised to find so much fresh young beauty wasted upon work so dull, and among brambles so sharp."

The girls looked up slack-jawed, then uttered small squeaks of terror, and stood paralyzed, too frightened to run.

Rhialto frowned. "Why do you tremble? Do I seem such a monster of evil?"

One of the girls managed to quaver: "Sir Ghoul, your ugliness is inspiring! Pray give us our lives so that we may appall others with the tale!"

Rhialto spoke coldly. "I am neither ghoul nor demon, and your horror is not at all flattering."

The girl was emboldened to ask: "In that case, what manner of strange thing might you be?"

A second girl spoke in an awed voice: "He is a Pooner, or perhaps a Bohul, and we are as good as dead!"

Rhialto controlled his irritation. "What foolish talk is this? I am only a traveler from a far land, neither Pooner nor Bohul, and I intend you no harm. Have you never seen a stranger before?"

"Certainly, but never one so dour, meanwhile wearing so comical a hat."

Rhialto nodded crisply. "I do not care to modify my face, but I will gladly hear your advice as to a more fashionable hat."

The first girl said: "This year everyone is wearing a clever felt 'souppot' — so are they called — and magenta is the only suitable color. A single blue ear-flap suffices for modesty, and a caste-sign of glazed faience is considered somewhat dashing."

Rhialto squeezed the walnut shell. "Osherl, procure me a hat of this description. You may also set out a table with a collation of foods tempting to the ordinary tastes of today."

The hat appeared. Rhialto tossed his old hat behind a bush and donned the faddish new article, and the girls clapped their hands in approval.

Meanwhile Osherl had arranged a table laden with dainties on a nearby area.

Rhialto waved the girls forward. "Even the most brittle personalities relax at the sight of viands such as these, and pretty little courtesies and signs of favor, otherwise unthinkable, are sometimes rendered almost automatically — especially in the presence of these fine pastries, piled high with creams and sweet jellies. My dear young ladies, I invite you to partake."

The most cautious of the girls said: "And then, what will you demand of us?"

Another said chidingly: "Tish tush! The gentleman has freely invited us to share his repast; we should respond with equal freedom!"

The third gave a merry laugh. "Dine first and worry later! After all, he can enforce his wishes upon us as he chooses, without the formality of feeding us first, so that worry leads nowhere."

"Perhaps you are right," said the first girl. "For a fact, in his new hat he is less ugly than before, and indeed I am most partial to this thrasher pâté, come what may."

Rhialto said with dignity: "You may enjoy your meal without qualms."

The girls advanced upon the table and, discovering no peculiar conduct on the part of Rhialto, devoured the viands with zest.

Rhialto pointed across the plain. "What are those curious clouds in the sky?"

The girls turned to look as if they had not previously noticed. "That is the direction of Vasques Tohor. The dust doubtless results from the war now being fought."

Rhialto frowned across the plain. "What war is this?"

The girls laughed at Rhialto's ignorance. "It was launched by the Bohulic Dukes of East Attuck; they brought their battle-gangs down in great numbers and threw them without remorse against Vasques Tohor, but they can never prevail against the King of all Kings and his Thousand Knights."

"Very likely not," said Rhialto. "Still, from curiosity I will wander northward and see for myself. I now bid you farewell."

The girls slowly returned to the thicket, but their enthusiasm for berry-picking was gone, and they worked with laggard fingers, watching over their shoulders at the tall form of Rhialto as he sauntered off to the north.

Rhialto proceeded half a mile, then climbed into the air and ran through the sky toward Vasques Tohor.

By the time he arrived on the scene, the battle had been decided. The Bohul battle-gangs, with their memrils and rumbling war-wagons, had done the unthinkable; on the Finneian Plain east of Vasques Tohor the Twenty Potences of the Last Kingdom had been destroyed; Vasques Tohor could no longer be denied to the Bohul Dukes.

The tragic peach-rose light of late afternoon illuminated a clutter of smoke, dust, toppled machines and broken corpses. Legions of long pedigree and many honors had been smashed; their standards and uniforms bedizened the field with color. The Thousand Knights, riding half-living half-metal flyers from Canopus, had thrown themselves against the Bohul war-wagons, but for the most part had been destroyed by fire-rays before they could do damage in return.

The war-wagons now commanded the plain: grim, dismal vehicles rearing sixty feet into the air, armed with both Red Ruin and barb-drivers. On the first tier and wherever they could cling rode assault troops from East Attuck. These were not pretty troops; they were neither handsome, nor clean-limbed nor even dauntless. Rather they

Fader's Waft

were surly veterans of many types and conditions, with only dirt, sweat and foul language in common. At first glance they seemed no more than a rabble, lacking both discipline and morale. Some were old, bearded and pallid; others were bald and fat, or bandy-legged, or thin as weasels. All were unkempt, with faces more petulant than ferocious. Their uniforms were improvised; some wore skull-caps, others leather battle-caps with ear-flaps, others tufted barb-catchers adorned with scalps cut from the blond young heads of the Thousand Knights. Such were the troops which had defeated the Twenty Legions, skulking, hiding, striking, feigning death, striking again, screaming in pain but never fear; the Iron Dukes had long before sated them full with fright.

To the side of the war-wagons stalked rows of memrils: gracile creatures apparently all legs and arms of brown chitin, with small triangular heads raised twenty feet above the ground; it was said that the magician Pikarkas, himself reportedly half-insect, had contrived the memrils from ever more prodigious versions of the executioner beetle.

Tam Tol, King of the Final Kingdom, had stood all day on the parapets of Vasques Tohor, overlooking the Finneian Plain. He watched his elite Knights on their flyers darting down upon the war-wagons; he saw them consumed by Red Ruin. His Twenty Legions, led by the Indomitables, deployed under their ancient standards. They were guarded from above by squadrons of black air-lions, each twenty feet long, armed with fire, gas-jet and fearful sounds.

Tam Tol stood immobile as the Bohul battle-gangs, cursing and sweating, cut down his brave noblemen, and stood long after all hope was gone, heedless of calls and urgencies. His courtiers one by one moved away, to leave Tam Tol at last standing alone, either too numb or too proud to flee.

Behind the parapets mobs ranged the city, gathering all portable wealth, then, departing by the Sunset Gates, made for the sacred city Luid Shug, fifty miles to the west across the Joheim Valley.

Rhialto, running through the sky, halted and surveyed the sky through the pleurmalion. The dark blue spot hung over the western sector of the city; Rhialto proceeded slowly in this direction at a loss for a means to locate the Perciplex quickly and deftly among so much confusion. He became aware of Tam Tol standing alone on the

He watched his elite Knights on their flyers darting down...

parapets: even as he watched, a barb from the turret of a war-wagon struck up through the afternoon sunlight and Tam Tol, struck in the forehead, fell slowly and soundlessly down the face of the parapets to the ground.

The noise from the Finneian Plain dwindled to a whispering murmur. All flyers had departed the air and Rhialto ran on soft plunging steps a mile closer to the dying city. Halting, he used the pleurmalion once more, and discovered, somewhat to his relief, that the blue sky-spot no longer hovered over the city, but out over the Joheim Valley, where the Perciplex was now evidently included in the loot of someone in the column of refugees.

Rhialto ran through the air to station himself directly below the blue spot, merely to discover a new frustration: the individual with the Perciplex could not be isolated in the crowds of trudging bodies and pale faces.

The sun sank into a flux of color, and the blue spot no longer could be seen on the night sky. Rhialto turned away in vexation. He ran south through the twilight, beyond the Joheim Valley and across a wide meandering river. He descended at the outskirts of a town: Vils of the Ten Steeples, and took lodging for the night at a small inn at the back of a garden of rose-trees.

In the common room the conversation dealt with the war and the power of the Bohul battle-gangs. Speculation and rumor were rife, and all marvelled, with gloomy shakes of the head, at the fateful passing of the Last Kingdom.

Rhialto sat at the back of the room, listening but contributing nothing to the conversation, and presently he went quietly off to his chamber.

12

Rhialto breakfasted upon melon and fried clam dumplings in rose syrup. He settled his account and, departing the town, returned to the north.

A human river still flowed across the Joheim Valley. Multitudes had already arrived before the holy city, only to be denied entry, and their encampment spread like a crust away from the city walls. Above hung the blue spot.

Luid Shug had been ordained a holy place during an early era of the aeon by the legendary Goulkoud the God-friend. Coming upon the crater of a small dead volcano, Goulkoud had been seized by twenty paroxysms of enlightenment, during which he stipulated the form and placement of twenty temples in symmetry around the central volcanic neck. Prebendary structures, baths, fountains and hostels for pilgrims occupied the floor of the crater; a narrow boulevard encircled the rim. Around the outside periphery stood twenty enormous god-effigies in twenty niches cut into the crater walls, each corresponding to one of the temples within the city.

Rhialto descended to the ground. Somewhere among the host huddled before the city was the Perciplex, but the sky-spot seemed to wander, despite Rhialto's best efforts to bring it directly overhead, in which effort he was sorely hampered by the crowds.

At the center of the city, atop the old volcanic neck, stood a rose-quartz and silver finial. The Arch-priest stepped out upon the highest platform and, holding his arms high, he spoke to the refugees in a voice amplified by six great spiral shells.

"To victims and unfortunates, we extend twenty profound solaces! However, if your hopes include entry into this sacred place, they must be abandoned. We have neither food to feed hunger nor drink to slake thirst!

"Furthermore, I can extend no fair portents! The glory of the world is gone; it will never return until a hundred dreary centuries have run their course! Then hope and splendor will revivify the land, in a culmination of all that is good! This era will then persist until the earth finally rolls beyond Gwennart the Soft Curtain.

"To prepare for the ultimate age we will now select a quota of the choicest and the best, to the number of five thousand six hundred and forty-two, which is a Holy and Mysterious Number heavy with secrets.

"Half of this company will be the noble 'Best of the Best': heroes of ancient lineage! Half will be chosen from 'Nephryne's Foam': maidens of virtue and beauty no less brave and gallant than their masculine counterparts. Together they are the 'Paragons': the highest excellence of the kingdom, and the flower of the race!

"By the Spell of a Hundred Centuries we will bind them, and they shall sleep through the Dark Epoch which lies ahead. Then, when the Spell is done and the Age of Glory has come, the Paragons will march forth to institute the Kingdom of Light!

"To all others I give this instruction: continue on your way. Go south to the Lands of Cabanola and Eio, or — should you find there no respite — onward to the Land of Farwan, or — should you so elect — across the Lutic Ocean to the Scanduc Isles.

"Time presses upon us! We must take our Paragons. Let the King's Companions and their families come forward, and the surviving Knights, and the maidens from the Institute of Gleyen and the Flower Songs, as well as Nephryne's Foam, and all others who in pride and dignity must be considered Paragons!

"To expedite matters, all those of the lowest castes: the twittlers, public entertainers and buffoons; the stupid and ill-bred; the criminals and night-runners; those with short ears and long toenails: let them continue on their journey.

"The same suggestion applies to the somewhat more worthy castes, who, despite their rectitude, will not be included among the 'Paragons'.

"All aspiring to the Golden Age: let them step forward! We will choose with all possible facility."

Rhialto again tried to position himself directly below the sky-spot, hoping by some means to identify that person who carried the Perciplex, but found no success.

Either through vanity or desperate hope, few indeed heeded the strictures of the Arch-priest, so that those who pressed forward declaring themselves 'Paragons' included not only the noble and well-formed, but also the toothless and corpulent; the hydrocephalics, victims of chronic hiccup, notorious criminals, singers of popular songs and several persons on their death-beds.

The confusion tended to impede the process of selection, and so the day passed. Toward the end of the afternoon, some of the more realistic individuals gave up hope of finding sanctuary in Luid Shug and began to trudge off across the plain. Rhialto watched the sky-spot attentively, but it hung in the sky as before, until at last it faded into the murk of evening. Rhialto somberly returned to the inn at Vils of the Ten Steeples, and passed another restless night.

In the morning he again coursed north to Luid Shug, to discover that the selectors had worked the whole night through, so that all of the 'Paragons' had been selected and taken into the city. The gates were now sealed.

A pair of Bohul armies, moving slowly across the Joheim Valley, converged upon Luid Shug, and all those refugees still encamped near the crater departed in haste.

The dark blue sky-spot now hung over Luid Shug. Rhialto, descending to the ground, approached a postern beside the west gate. He was denied admittance. A voice from the shadows said: "Go your way, stranger; a hundred centuries will pass before Luid Shug again opens its gates. The Spell of Distended Time is on us; go, therefore, and do not bother to look back, since you will see only dreaming gods."

The Bohul armies were close at hand. Rhialto took to the air and climbed to the tumble of a low white cumulus cloud.

A strange silence muffled the valley. The city showed no movement. With a deliberation more menacing than haste the war-wagons rolled toward the eastern gates of Luid Shug. The Bohul veterans, grumbling and walking as if their feet hurt, came behind.

From the spiral voice-horns above the city came amplified words: "Warriors, turn away! Make no molestation upon us. Luid Shug is now lost to your control."

Paying no heed, the commanders prepared to strike down the gates with blast-bolts. Five of the stone effigies moved in their niches and raised their arms. The air quivered; the war-wagons shriveled to small tumbles of char. The peevish veterans became like the husks of dead insects. The Joheim Valley was once again quiet.

Rhialto turned away, and strode thoughtfully from cloud to cloud into the south. Where the hills began to rise, some twenty or thirty miles west of Fader's Waft, he stepped down upon a hummock covered with dry grass and, seeking the shade of a solitary tree, sat leaning against the bole.

The time was close on noon. The fragrance of dry grass came

pleasantly on puffs of warm wind. Far to the north-east a coil of smoke rose above the corpse of Vasques Tohor.

Chewing a straw, Rhialto sat reflecting upon his condition. Circumstances were not at the optimum, even though the Perciplex had been more or less precisely located. Osherl must be considered a weak reed, sullen and indifferent. Ildefonse? His interests comported more with those of Rhialto than those of the treacherous Hache-Moncour. Still, Ildefonse was known for his tendencies toward flexibility and expedience. As Preceptor, Ildefonse, even lacking the chug, might be able to compel Sarsem to correct conduct; in the main, however, and all taken with all, Sarsem must be reckoned even less dependable than Osherl.

Rhialto put the pleurmalion to his eye, and as before took note of the dark blue sky-spot over Luid Shug. Rhialto put aside the pleurmalion and called Osherl out from his walnut-shell.

Osherl showed himself as a wefkin four feet high with blue skin and green hair. He spoke in a voice meticulously polite. "My best regards, Rhialto! As I look about, I discover a fine warm day of the sixteenth aeon! The air tingles at one's skin with characteristic zest. You are chewing grass like an idle farm-boy; I am happy to perceive your enjoyment of time and place."

Rhialto ignored the pleasantries. "I still lack the Perciplex, and for this failure, you and Sarsem share the blame."

The wefkin, laughing soundlessly, combed its green silk hair between blue fingers. "My dear fellow! This style of expression becomes you not at all!"

"No matter," said Rhialto. "Go now to yonder city, and bring me back the Perciplex."

The wefkin uttered a gay laugh. "Dear Rhialto, your witticisms are superb! The concept of poor Osherl trapped, dragged, pounded, stamped upon, dissected and maltreated by twenty vicious gods is a masterpiece of absurd imagery!"

"I intended no joke," said Rhialto. "Yonder lies the Perciplex; the Perciplex I must have."

Osherl himself plucked a blade of grass and waved it in the air to emphasize his remarks. "Perhaps you should recast your goals. In many ways the sixteenth aeon is more kindly than the twenty-first. You chew grass like one born to it. This time is yours, Rhialto! So it has been ordained by stronger voices than either yours or mine!"

"My voice is adequately strong," said Rhialto. "Also I am friend to the chug and I distribute indenture points with lavish prodigality."

"Such humor is mordant," growled Osherl.

"You refuse to enter Luid Shug for the Perciplex?"

"Impossible while the gods stand guard."

"Then you must take us forward exactly a hundred centuries, so that when Luid Shug awakens to the Age of Gold, we will be on hand to claim our property."

Osherl wished to discuss the onerous quality of his indenture, but Rhialto would not listen. "All in good time, when we are once more in Boumergarth, Perciplex in hand!"

"The Perciplex? Is that all you want?" asked Osherl with patently false heartiness. "Why did you not say so in the first place? Are you prepared?"

"I am indeed. Work with accuracy."

13

The hillock and the solitary tree were gone. Rhialto stood on the slope of a stony valley, with a river wandering sluggishly below.

The time seemed to be morning, although a heavy overcast concealed the sky. The air felt raw and damp against his skin; to the east dark wisps of rain drifted down into a black forest.

Rhialto looked about the landscape, but found no evidences of human habitancy: neither fence, farm-house, road, track or path. Rhialto seemed to be alone. Where was Osherl? Rhialto looked here and there in annoyance, then called out: "Osherl! Make yourself known!"

Osherl stepped forward, still the blue-skinned wefkin. "I am here."

Rhialto indicated the dour landscape. "This does not seem the Age of Gold. Have we come exactly one hundred centuries? Where is Luid Shug?"

Osherl pointed to the north. "Luid Shug is yonder, at the edge of the forest."

Rhialto brought out the pleurmalion, but the dark blue sky-spot could not be seen for the overcast. "Let us make a closer approach."

The two coursed north to the site of the sacred city, to discover only a tumble of ruins. Rhialto spoke in perplexity: "This is a most dreary prospect! Where have the gods gone?"

"I will go to Gray Dene and there make inquiry," said Osherl. "Wait here; in due course I will return with all information."

"Stop! Hold up!" cried Rhialto. "My question was casual. First find the Perciplex; then you can seek after the gods as long as you like."

Osherl grumbled under his breath: "You have dawdled away a hundred centuries, yet if I spent a single year in Gray Dene I would still hear threats and abuse on my return. It dulls the edge of one's initiative."

"Enough!" said Rhialto. "I am interested only in the Perciplex."

The two approached the ruins. Wind and weather had worked at the old crater walls so that only traces remained. The temples were rubble; the twenty gods, carved from marble, had likewise eroded to a few toppled fragments, with all their force seeped into the mire.

Rhialto and Osherl walked slowly around the edge of the old city, testing the pleurmalion from time to time, without result.

To the north the forest grew close to the old parapets, and at this point they caught the scent of wood smoke on the wind. Looking here and there, they discovered a crude village of twenty huts just inside the edge of the forest.

"We will make inquiries," said Rhialto. "I suggest that you change your appearance; otherwise they will think us a queer pair indeed."

"You should also make alterations. Your hat, for instance, is the shape of an inverted soup-pot, and purple to boot. I doubt if this is the current fashion."

"There is something in what you say," admitted Rhialto.

Using the semblance of Lavrentine Redoubtables in glistening armor, barbed and spiked, and with helmets crested with tongues of blue fire, Rhialto and Osherl approached the village, which lacked all charm and smelled poorly.

Rhialto reinforced himself with his glossolary and called out: "Villagers, attention! Two Lavrentine grandees stand nearby; come perform the proper ceremonies of welcome."

One by one the villagers appeared from their huts, yawning and scratching: folk of a squat long-armed race with liver-colored skins and long lank hair. Their garments were fashioned from bird-skins and the village showed few civilized amenities; still they seemed sleekly well-fed. At the sight of Rhialto and Osherl, certain of the men called out in pleasure, and taking up long-handled nets advanced upon the two with sinister purpose.

Rhialto called out: "Stand back! We are magicians! Your first sneer of menace will bring down a spell of great distress; be warned!"

The men refused to heed and raised high their nets. Rhialto made a sign to Osherl. The nets folded over backwards to enclose and clench into tight balls those who had thought to use them. Osherl jerked his thumb to whisk these balls away, into the northern sky, through the overcast and out of sight.

Rhialto looked around the group and spoke to a flat-faced woman: "Who is the chieftain of this repulsive group?"

The woman pointed. "There is Doulka who is butcher and trundle-man. We need no chieftain; such folk eat more than their share."

A big-bellied old man with gray wattles sidled a few steps forward. He spoke in a wheedling nasal voice: "Must your disgust be so blatant? True: we are anthropophages. True: we put strangers to succulent use. Is this truly good cause for hostility? The world is as it is and each of us must hope in some fashion to be of service to his fellows, even if only in the form of a soup."

"Our talents lie elsewhere," said Rhialto. "If I see any more nets, you will be first to fly the sky."

"No fear, now that we know your preferences," declared Doulka. "What are your needs? Are you hungry?"

"We are curious in regard to Luid Shug, which at this time should be awakening to the Age of Gold. Instead we find only rubble, slime and the stink from your village. Why have events gone in this unhappy fashion?"

Doulka had recovered his confidence and blinked at his visitors with torpid complacence. Idly, as if through the force of habit, he began to twist and interweave his fingers with a dexterity which Rhialto found interesting, even fascinating. He spoke in a droning nasal monotone:

"The mystery surrounding the ruins is more apparent than real." As Doulka spoke, he wove his fingers slowly back and forth. "Centuries passed by, one upon the other, and the gods stood steadfast, by day and by night. At last they succumbed to the grind of wind and rain. They became dust and their power was gone."

Doulka worked his fingers in and out. "The land was empty and the ruins lay quiet. The 'Paragons' slept their long sleep in alabaster eggs. Youths and maidens of prime quality ripened on their silken couches, unknown to all!"

Doulka's fingers created odd patterns. Rhialto began to feel a pleasant lassitude, which he ascribed to his efforts of the day.

"My dear fellow, I see that you are weary!" said Doulka. "I reproach myself!" Three ceremonial chairs of woven withe were brought out, their backs carved to represent contorted human faces.

"Sit," said Doulka in a soothing voice. "Rest yourself."

Doulka ponderously placed his own fat buttocks upon the creaking withe of a chair. Rhialto also seated himself, to ease his tired limbs. He turned to Osherl and spoke in the language of the twenty-first aeon: "What is this sly old devil doing to me, that I feel such torpor?"

Osherl responded in an offhand manner: "He commands four sandestins of an inferior sort: the type we call 'madlings'. They are building patterns of lassitude in and out of your eyes, which are now somewhat skewed. Doulka has already given orders to prepare for a feast."

Rhialto spoke indignantly: "Why did you not prevent this trickery? Where is your loyalty?"

Osherl merely coughed in discomfiture.

Rhialto told Osherl: "Order the madlings to pull Doulka's nose out to a length of two feet, to impose an ulcerous cyst at the tip, and also a large painful carbuncle on each buttock."

"As you wish."

The work was done to his satisfaction. "Now," he told Osherl, "and this should go without saying, order the madlings to desist from all further nuisances upon my person."

"Yes, true. We would not want Doulka to retaliate in kind."

"Then you will accord the madlings their freedom, and send them on their way, with instructions never again to serve Doulka."

"A generous thought!" declared Osherl. "Does the same instruction apply to me?"

"Osherl, do not distract me. I must question Doulka, despite his new preoccupations." Rhialto turned back to the agitated trundleman and spoke in the language of the village: "You have learned the penalty of bad faith. All in all, I consider myself merciful, so be grateful and rejoice in this fact! Now then: shall we continue our conversation?"

Doulka said sulkily: "You are an irritable man! I intended no great harm! What more can I tell you?"

"You have explored the ruins thoroughly?"

"We are not interested in the ruins, except as they yield alabaster eggs for our delectation."

"I see. How many eggs have you devoured?"

"Over the years they number five thousand six hundred and forty one. Few remain."

Rhialto said: "'Few'? Unless you have miscounted, a single Paragon remains to institute the Age of Gold. You have eaten all the others."

Doulka momentarily forgot his nose and buttocks. "Only one remaining? This is bad news! Our feasts are at an end!"

"What of treasure?" asked Rhialto. "Have you taken gems and crystals from the vaults of the city?"

"We have indeed, since we take pleasure in fine things: notably all red, pink and yellow gems. Those which are blue and green induce bad luck and we use them for our amusement."

"How so?"

"We tie them to the tails of bogadils, or ursial lopers or even manks, which prompts them to absolutely comical acts of worry and shame, so that they run pell-mell through the forest."

"Hmmf. And what of a luminous blue crystal in the form of a prism, thus and so? Has such an object come to your attention?"

Doulka ruefully felt the length of his nose. "I seem to recall such an item, in the not too distant past."

Rhialto, all kindliness, asked: "Does your nose truly cause you such distress?"

"Oh indeed, indeed!"

"And your buttocks?"

Fader's Waft

"They are exquisitely painful."

"When you bring me the blue crystal I seek, your sores will be healed."

Doulka gave a surly grunt. "That is no easy task."

Rhialto had no more to say and with Osherl moved somewhat away from the village, where Osherl established a comfortable pavilion of dark blue silk. On a heavy red and blue rug of intricate pattern Osherl arranged a massive table of carved dark timber surrounded by four low chairs with dark red velvet cushions. Outside the structure he laid down a similar rug and a second table, for occasions when the day was fine. Above he arranged a canopy and at each corner placed a tall black iron pedestal with a lamp of many facets.

Leaving Osherl sitting at the interior table, Rhialto climbed into the sky, up through the overcast and out into a glare of vermilion sunlight charged with an acrid blue overtone.

The time was middle afternoon; the sun hung half-way down the sky. The cloud-cover extended without break for as far as Rhialto could see in all directions. He looked through the pleurmalion, and to his pleasure discovered the dark spot hanging in the sky somewhat to the north and east of where he stood.

Rhialto ran at speed above the clouds and ranged himself immediately below the spot, then dropped down through the overcast and toward the forest below. Finally he reached the forest floor, where he made a quick and superficial search, finding nothing.

Returning to the pavilion, Rhialto found Osherl sitting as before. Rhialto described his activities. "My search definitely lacked accuracy. Tomorrow you shall mount as high as possible with the pleurmalion and post yourself precisely under the spot. From this point you will lower a weighted cord until it dangles close to the forest, where we can hope to find the Perciplex...What is that savage hooting and yelping sound?"

Osherl looked out through the silken flap at the front of the pavilion. "The villagers are excited; they are calling out in enthusiasm."

"Curious," said Rhialto. "Perhaps Doulka, rather than cooperate, has seen fit to cut off his nose...Otherwise they would seem to have little reason to rejoice. Now then, another thought has occurred to me: why does the blue spot fly so high in the air?"

"No mystery there: for reasons of far visibility."

"All very well, but surely another signal could have served more efficiently: for instance, a rod of blue light, conspicuous from afar, but also accurate at its lower end."

"In candour, I do not understand Sarsem's motives, unless he truly took Hache-Moncour's injunctions to heart."

"Oh? What injunctions were these?"

"Just idle badinage, or so I suppose. Hache-Moncour ordered that the sky-spot be made to perform so rudely that you would never truly strike home to the crystal, but would forever be chasing it back and forth like some mad fool chasing the will o' the wisp."

"I see. And why did you not tell me this before? No matter; the day will come when you learn who controls your indenture points: me or Hache-Moncour…That howling and whooping is incessant! Doulka must be cutting off his nose an inch at a time. Osherl, order them to quiet."

"It seems a harmless jollity; they are merely preparing a feast."

Rhialto looked up alertly. "A feast? Of what sort?"

"The last of the Paragons: a maiden who has only just emerged from the alabaster egg. After ingestion is under way, the noise no doubt will abate."

Rhialto leapt to his feet. "Osherl, words fail me. Come along, on the double-quick."

Striding back to the village, Rhialto found Doulka sitting before his hut on a pair of enormous down pillows, his nose tied in a poultice. Preparations for a feast were under way, with women of the village cutting and slicing roots, vegetables, and seasonings to the specifications of their recipe. In a pen to the side stood the last of the Paragons: a maiden whom a butcher might classify in the 'slightly smaller than medium' range, of 'choice quality', 'tender if lacking in excessive fat'. Her garments had disintegrated during her long sleep; she wore nothing but a necklace of copper and turquoise. Haggard with fear she looked through the bars of the pen as a pair of hulking apprentice butchers arranged a work table and began to sharpen their implements.

Doulka the Trundleman saw the approach of Rhialto and Osherl with a scowl. "What is it this time? We are preparing to indulge ourselves in a last feast of quality. Your business must wait, unless you have come to relieve me of my pain."

Rhialto said: "There will be no feast, unless you yourself wish to climb into the pot. Osherl, bring the lady from the pen and provide her suitable garments."

Osherl split the pen into a million motes, and draped the girl's body in a pale blue robe. Doulka cried out in grief and the villagers went so far as to take up weapons. For distraction, Osherl evoked four blue goblins eight feet tall. Hopping forward and gnashing their fangs, they sent the villagers fleeing with high heels into the forest.

Rhialto, Osherl and the dazed maiden returned to the pavilion, where Rhialto served her a cordial, and explained the circumstances in a gentle voice. She listened with a blank gaze and perhaps understood something of what Rhialto told her, for presently she wept tears of grief. Rhialto had mixed an anodyne into the cordial, and her grief became a languid dream-state in which the disasters of her life were without emotive force, and she was content to sit close beside Rhialto and take comfort from his presence.

Osherl looked on with cynicism. "Rhialto, you are a curious creature, one of an obstinate and enigmatic race."

"How so?"

"Poor Doulka is desolate; his folk creep through the forest, afraid to go home for fear of goblins; meanwhile you console and flatter this mindless female."

Rhialto responded with quiet dignity: "I am motivated by gallantry, which is a sentiment beyond your understanding."

"Bah!" said Osherl. "You are as vain as a jay-cock and already you are planning fine postures to strike in front of this pubescent little creature, with whom you will presently attempt a set of amorous pastimes. Meanwhile Doulka goes hungry and my indenture is as irksome as ever."

Rhialto reflected a moment. "Osherl, you are clever but not clever enough. I am not so easily distracted as you would hope. Therefore, let us now resume our conversation. What else have you concealed from me in connection with Sarsem and Hache-Moncour?"

"I gave little attention to their strategies. You should have specified the topics in which you were interested."

RHIALTO THE MARVELLOUS

Osherl split the pen into a million motes...

"Before the fact? I can not know whether I am interested or not until the plans are made."

"In truth, I know little more than you. Hache-Moncour hopes to advance his own cause, with Sarsem's help, but this is no surprise."

"Sarsem is playing a dangerous game. Ultimately he will suffer the penalties of duplicity! Let all others learn from Sarsem's despicable example!"

"Ah well, who knows how the game will go?" said Osherl airily.

"And what do you mean by that?"

Osherl would say no more, and Rhialto with pointed displeasure sent him out into the night to guard the pavilion. Osherl eased his task by setting up four large goblin's heads glowing with a ghastly blue luminosity, which startled Rhialto himself when he stepped out to see how went the night.

Returning within, Rhialto arranged a couch for the maiden, where she presently slept the sleep of emotional exhaustion. A short time later Rhialto also took his repose.

In the morning the maiden awoke composed but listless. Rhialto arranged a bath of perfumed water in the lavatory, while Osherl, using the guise of a serving woman, laid out for her use a crisp outfit of white duck trousers, a scarlet coat trimmed with golden buttons and black frogging, and black ankle-boots trimmed with red floss. She bathed, dressed, ordered her ear-length black hair, and came tentatively out into the main chamber where Rhialto joined her at breakfast.

Through the power of the glossolary, he spoke to her in her own tongue: "You have suffered a terrible tragedy, and I offer you my sympathy. My name is Rhialto; like yourself I am not native to this dreary epoch. May I inquire your name?"

At first the maiden seemed indisposed to respond, then said in a resigned voice: "My secrets are no longer of consequence. In my personal thought-language I have named myself 'Furud Dawn-stuff' or 'Exquisite Dawn-thing'. At my school I won a credential as 'Shalukhe' or 'Expert Water-Swimmer' and this was used as my friend-name."

"That seems a good name, and it is the name I will use, unless you prefer otherwise."

The maiden showed him a dreary smile. "I no longer have the status to command the luxury of preference."

Rhialto found the concept complex but comprehensible. "It is true that 'innate quality' and 'merit derived from bold assertion' must be the source of your self-esteem. You shall be known as Shalukhe the Survivor; is not that a prideful condition?"

"Not particularly, since your help alone saved my life."

Osherl, overhearing the remark, ventured a comment: "Nevertheless, your tactics are instinctively correct. To deal with Rhialto the Marvellous, and here I allude to your host and the conservator of my indenture, you must fuel the fires of his bloated vanity. Exclaim upon his handsome countenance; feign awe at his wisdom; he will be putty in your hands."

Rhialto said in a measured voice: "Osherl's mood is often acerb; despite his sarcasm, I will be happy to earn your good opinion."

Shalukhe the Swimmer could not restrain her amusement. "You have already gained it, Sir Rhialto! I am also grateful to Osherl for his assistance."

"Bah!" said Rhialto. "He felt greater concern for the hunger of poor Doulka."

"Not so!" cried Osherl. "That was just my little joke!"

"In any event, and if you will forgive me the presumption of asking: what is to become of me now?"

"When our business here is done, we shall return to Almery, and talk further of the matter. As for now, you may regard yourself as my subaltern, and you are assigned to the supervision of Osherl. See that he is at all times neat, alert and courteous!"

Again half-smiling, Shalukhe appraised Osherl. "How can I supervise someone so clever?"

"Simplicity itself! If he shirks, speak only two words: 'indenture points'."

Osherl uttered a hollow laugh. "Already Rhialto the Marvellous works his supple wiles."

Rhialto paid no heed. He reached down, took her hands and pulled her erect. "And now: to work! Are you less distraught than before?"

"Very much so! Rhialto, I thank you for your kindness."

"Shalukhe the Swimmer, or Dawn-thing, or however you will be called: a shadow still hangs over you, but it is a pleasure to see you smile."

Fader's Waft

Osherl spoke in the language of the twenty-first aeon: "Physical contact has been made, and the program now enters its second phase... Such a poor torn little wretch, how could she resist Rhialto?"

"Your experience is limited," said Rhialto. "It is more a case of 'How could Rhialto resist such a poor torn little wretch?'"

The girl looked from one to the other, hoping to divine the sense of the interchange. Rhialto spoke out: "Now, to our business! Osherl, take the pleurmalion —" he handed the object to Osherl "— then climb above the clouds to locate the sky-spot. From a point directly below, lower a heavy flashing red lantern on a long cord until it hangs close above the Perciplex. The day is windless and accuracy should be fine."

Osherl, for reasons of caprice, now took upon himself the guise of a middle-aged Walvoon shopkeeper dressed in baggy black breeches, a mustard-ocher vest and a wide-brimmed black hat. He took the pleurmalion in a pudgy hand, mounted the sky on three lunging strides.

"With any luck," Rhialto told Shalukhe, "my irksome task is close to its end, whereupon we will return to the relative calm of the twenty-first aeon...What's this? Osherl back so soon?"

Osherl jumped down from the sky to the rug before the pavilion. He made a negative signal and Rhialto uttered a poignant cry. "Why have you not located the Perciplex?"

Osherl gave his fat shop-keeper's face a doleful shake. "The sky-spot is absorbed in the mists and cannot be seen. The pleurmalion is useless."

Rhialto snatched the device and sprang high through the air, into the clouds and out, to stand in the acrid vermilion radiance. He put the pleurmalion to his eye, but, as Osherl had asserted, the sky-spot no longer could be seen.

For a period Rhialto stood on the white expanse, casting a long pale blue shadow. With frowning attention he examined the pleurmalion, then again looked around the sky, to no avail.

Something was amiss. Staring thoughtfully off across the white cloud-waste, Rhialto pondered the conceivable cases. Had the Perciplex been moved? Perhaps the pleurmalion had lost its force?...Rhialto returned to the pavilion.

Osherl stood to the side, gazing vacantly toward the mouldering ruins. Rhialto called out: "Osherl! A moment of your time, if you please."

Osherl approached without haste, to stand with hands thrust into the pockets of his striped pantaloons. Rhialto stood waiting, tossing the pleurmalion from one hand to the other, and watching Osherl with a pensive gaze.

"Well then, Rhialto: what now?" asked Osherl, with an attempt at ease of manner.

"Osherl, who suggested to you that the projection of the Perciplex might be captured by the overcast?"

Osherl waved one of his hands in a debonair flourish. "To an astute intellect, so much is apparent."

"But you lack an astute intellect. Who provided this insight?"

"I learn from a multitude of sources," muttered Osherl. "I cannot annotate or codify each iota of information which comes my way."

"Let me imagine a sequence of events," said Rhialto. "Osherl, are you paying close attention?"

Osherl, standing disconsolate with hanging jowls and moist gaze, muttered: "Where is my choice?"

"Then consider these imagined events. You climb above the overcast where Sarsem greets you. A conversation ensues, in this fashion:

Sarsem: 'What now, Osherl? What is your task?'

Osherl: 'That stone-hearted Rhialto wants me to search about the sky for signs of the Perciplex, using this pleurmalion.'

Sarsem: 'Indeed? Let me look … I see nothing.'

Osherl: 'No? Most singular! What shall I tell Rhialto?'

Sarsem: 'He is easily confused. Tell him that the image is trapped in the clouds. This pleurmalion is now worthless. Take it back.'

Osherl: 'But this is a different pleurmalion from the one I gave you! It is only a trifle of ordinary glass!'

Sarsem: 'What then? Both are now equally useless. Take it back and give it to that mooncalf Rhialto; he will never know the difference.'

Fader's Waft

Osherl: 'Hm. Rhialto is a mooncalf, but a cunning mooncalf.'

Sarsem: 'He is very troublesome to our friend Hache-Moncour, who has promised us so many indulgences... My advice is this: by some subterfuge induce him to cancel your indenture; then leave him to cool his heels here in this dank and tiresome epoch.'

Osherl: 'The concept has much to recommend it.'

"So saying, the two of you chuckled together, then you took leave of your crony and descended with the false pleurmalion and the news that the sky showed no projection, owing to the overcast."

Osherl cried out with quivering jowls: "Is this not plausible? You have no reason to believe either that the new pleurmalion is false, or that Sarsem's views are incorrect!"

"First of all: why did you not report your conversation with Sarsem?"

Osherl shrugged. "You failed to ask."

"Explain, if you will, why the sky-spot was clear and evident last night, through this self-same overcast?"

"I am mystified."

"Would you not say that either the Perciplex was moved or that the true pleurmalion was exchanged for a falsity?"

"I suppose that a case could be made along these lines."

"Precisely so. Osherl, the game is up! I here and now fine you three indenture points for faulty and faithless conduct."

Osherl uttered a wild cry of emotion. Rhialto raised his hand to induce quiet. "Further, I will now put to you a most earnest question, which you must answer with truth and any elaboration necessary to provide me a practical and accurate picture of the situation. Sarsem took from you the pleurmalion. Did he also take, touch, hide, move, alter, destroy, make temporal transfer of, or any other sort of transfer, or in any other way disturb or influence the condition of the Perciplex? Here I refer to that true Perciplex he guarded at Fader's Waft. I dislike verbosity, but it must be used in dealing with you."

"No."

"'No'? No what? I myself have become confused."

"Sarsem, despite the urgings of Hache-Moncour, does not dare to touch the Perciplex."

"Bring Sarsem here."

After another interchange of acrimony Sarsem, as usual in the form of the lavender-scaled youth, appeared before the pavilion.

"Sarsem, return to me the pleurmalion," said Rhialto evenly.

"Impossible! By order of the new Preceptor I destroyed it."

"Who is the new Preceptor?"

"Hache-Moncour, of course."

"And how do you know this for a fact?"

"He so assured me from his own mouth, or at least implied that this would shortly be the case."

"He told you incorrectly. You should have ascertained the facts from Ildefonse. I fine you three indenture points!"

Like Osherl, Sarsem set up an outcry. "You have no such authority!"

"Hache-Moncour's lack of authority worried you not at all."

"That is different."

"I now order you and Osherl to search the forest and find the Perciplex, and then immediately bring it here to me."

"I cannot do so. I am working to other orders. Let Osherl search. He has been assigned to your service."

"Sarsem, listen carefully! Osherl, you must be my witness! I hesitate to call out that Great Name on such small affairs, but I am becoming ever more annoyed by your tricks. If you interfere once again in my recovery of the Perciplex, I will call upon —"

Both Osherl and Sarsem set up a fearful outcry. "Do not so much as mention the Name; he might hear!"

"Sarsem, is my meaning clear?"

"Most clear," muttered the youth.

"And how will you guide your conduct now?"

"Hmmf… I must use evasive tactics in the service of Hache-Moncour so as to satisfy both him and you."

"I warn you that I am henceforth highly sensitive. Your three points have been justly earned; already you have caused me far too much travail."

Sarsem made an inarticulate sound and was gone.

14

Rhialto turned his attention to Osherl. "Yesterday I thought to locate the Perciplex near that tall button-top. Now there is work to be done!"

"By me, no doubt," gloomed Osherl.

"Had you been faithful, the work would have been done, we would be at Boumergarth arranging Hache-Moncour's well-earned penalties; you would have earned probably two points instead of being fined three: a difference of five indenture points!"

"It is a tragedy over which I, alas! have little control!"

Rhialto ignored the implicit insolence. "So then: shoulders to the wheel! A scrupulous search must be made!"

"And I must work alone? The task is large."

"Exactly so. Range around the forest and assemble here, in order and discipline, all bogadils, ursial lopers, manks and flantics, and any other creatures of sentience."

Osherl licked the ropy lips of his shop-keeper face. "Do you include the anthropophages?"

"Why not? Let tolerance rule our conduct! But first, elevate the pavilion upon a pedestal twenty feet high so that we need not be subjected to the crush. Instruct all these creatures to civil conduct."

In due course Osherl assembled the specified creatures before the pavilion. Stepping forward, Rhialto addressed the group: remarks which his glossolary, working at speed, rendered into terms of general comprehension.

"Creatures, men, half-men and things! I extend to you my good wishes, and my deep sympathy that you are forced to live so intimately in the company of each other.

"Since your intellects are, in the main, of no great complexity, I will be terse. Somewhere in the forest, not too far from yonder tall button-top, is a blue crystal, thus and so, which I wish to possess. All of you are now ordered to search for this crystal. He who finds it and brings it here will be greatly rewarded. To stimulate zeal and expedite the search, I now visit upon each of you a burning sensation, which will be repeated at ever shorter intervals until the blue crystal is in my possession. Search everywhere: in the rubbish, among the forest detritus, in the branches and foliage. The anthropophages originally tied this crystal to the person of someone present, so let that be a clue. Each should search his memory and go to the spot where he might have discarded or scraped off the object. Go now to the button-top tree, which will be the center of your effort. Search well, since the pangs will only intensify until I hold the blue crystal in my hand. Osherl, inflict the first pang, if you will."

The creatures cried out in pain and departed on the run.

Only moments passed before an ursial loper returned with a fragment of blue porcelain, and demanded the reward. Rhialto bestowed upon him a collar woven of red feathers and sent him out once again.

During the morning a variety of blue objects were laid hopefully before Rhialto, who rejected all and increased both the frequency and force of the stimulating pangs.

Somewhat before noon Rhialto noticed unusual conduct on the part of Osherl, and instantly made inquiry: "Well then, Osherl: what now?"

Osherl said stiffly: "It is actually none of my affair, but if I kept my own counsel, you would never let me hear the end of it. There might even be spiteful talk of indenture points —"

Rhialto cried: "What do you have to tell me?"

"It is in connection with the Perciplex, and since you have made certain efforts to secure this crystal —"

"Osherl, I command you! Get to the point! What of the Perciplex?"

"To make a long story short, I tend to believe that it has been discovered by a flantic*, who at first thought to bring it to you, and then was diverted by a counter-offer from someone who shall go nameless, but the flantic now swoops here and there in indecision…There! See him now! He is coming in this direction. The Perciplex is clutched in his dextral claw…No! He wavers…He has changed his mind; no doubt he has heard more persuasive terms."

"Quick then! After him! Strike him with pervulsions! Turn him back, or wrest away the Perciplex! Osherl, will you make haste?"

---

* flantic: winged creature with grotesque man-like head; precursor of the pelgrane.

Fader's Waft

Osherl stood back. "This is a matter between you and Hache-Moncour; I am not allowed to enter such contests, and here Ildefonse will support me."

Rhialto roared furious curses. "Then come; I will chase down the creature! He will learn more of sorrow than even he cares to know! Put a full charge of speed into my air-boots!"

Rhialto sprang into the air and ran on great lunging strides after the flapping black flantic, which, swinging its gray head about and observing Rhialto, only flew the faster.

The chase led to the south and west: over a range of mountains and a forest of ocher and gray palmatics, then across a swamp of slime-puddles, trickling watercourses and tufts of black rushes. In the distance the Santune Sea reflected a leaden gleam from the overcast.

The flantic began to tire; its wings beat down with ever less force, and Rhialto, leaping across chasms of air, began to overtake the creature.

With the sea below and no haven in sight, the flantic turned suddenly to attack Rhialto with claws and battering wings, and Rhialto was almost taken unawares. He dodged the furious lunge, but by so close a margin that the wing-edge struck his shoulder. He reeled and toppled; the flantic dived upon him, but Rhialto desperately twisted away. Osherl, standing to the side, uttered a compliment: "You are more agile than I expected. That was a deft contortion."

Rhialto jerked aside a third time, and the flantic's claws tore his cloak and sent Rhialto whirling away. He managed to scream a spell of effectiveness and threw a handful of Blue Havoc towards the swooping hulk, and the dazzling slivers penetrated the torso and slashed holes in the wings. The flantic threw back its head and vented a scream of fear and agony. "Manling, you have killed me; you have taken my one precious life, and I have no other! I curse you and I take your blue crystal with me where you can never recover it: to the Kingdom of Death!"

The flantic became a limp tangle of arms, wings, torso and long awkward neck, and toppled into the sea, where it sank quickly from sight.

Rhialto cried out in vexation. "Osherl! Down with you; into the sea! Recover the Perciplex!"

Osherl descended to look diffidently into the water. "Where did the creature fall?"

"Precisely where you stand. Dive deep, Osherl; it is by your negligence that we are here today."

Osherl hissed between his teeth and lowered a special member into the water. Presently he said: "There is nothing to be found. The bottom is deep and dark. I discover only slime."

"I will hear no excuses!" cried Rhialto. "Dive and grope, and do not show yourself until you have found the Perciplex!"

Osherl uttered a hollow moan and disappeared below the surface. At last he returned.

Rhialto cried: "You have retrieved it? Give it to me, at once!"

"All is not so simple," stated Osherl. "The gem is lost in slime. It shows no radiance, and it has no resonance. In short, the Perciplex must be considered lost."

"I am more sanguine than you," said Rhialto. "Anchor yourself on this site, and on no account allow either Hache-Moncour or Sarsem to interfere. I will consult with you shortly."

"Make haste," called Osherl. "The water is deep, dark and cold, and unknown creatures toy with my member."

"Be patient! Most important: do not shift your position by so much as an inch; since you are now like a buoy marking the location of the Perciplex."

Rhialto returned to the pavilion beside the ruins of Luid Shug. He terminated the search and allowed the stimulations to lapse, to the relief of the company.

Rhialto flung himself wearily into a chair and gave his attention to Shalukhe, the Paragon of Vasques Tohor, where she sat pensively on the couch. She had recovered much of her self-possession, and watched Rhialto with eyes dark and brooding. Rhialto thought: "She has had time to reflect on her plight. She sees nothing optimistic in her future."

Rhialto spoke aloud: "Our first concern is to leave this dismal place forever. And then —"

"And then?"

"We will study the options open to you. They are not entirely cheerless, as you will presently learn."

Shalukhe gave her head a shake of perplexity. "Why do you trouble yourself for me? I have no wealth; my status is now gone. I have few skills and no great diligence. I can climb hyllas trees for pods and squeeze hyssop; I can recite the *Naughty Girls' Dream of Impropriety*; these are skills of specialized value. Still —" she shrugged and smiled "— we are strangers and you owe me not even caste-duty."

Rhialto, happy in the absence of Osherl's cynical gaze, went to sit beside her. He took her hands in his. "Would you not rescue a helpless civilized person from a cannibal's cutting-table if you were able?"

"Yes, naturally."

"I did the same. Then, with so much accomplished, I became aware of you as a person, or rather, a combination of persons: first a lost and forlorn waif; then as Shalukhe the Swimmer, a maiden of remarkable charm and urgent physical attributes. This combination, for a vain and pompous person like myself, exerts an irresistible appeal. Still, as a man of perhaps inordinate self-esteem, I would not think it proper to intrude unwelcome intimacies upon you; so, whatever your fears in this regard, you may put them aside. I am first and last a gentleman of honour."

Shalukhe the Swimmer's mouth twitched at the corners. "And also a master of extravagant sentiments, some of which perhaps I should not take seriously."

Rhialto rose to his feet. "My dear young lady, here you must trust to the accuracy of your instincts. Still, you may look to me for both comfort and protection, and whatever may be your other needs."

Shalukhe laughed. "At the very least, Rhialto, you are able to amuse me."

Rhialto sighed and turned away. "Now we must go off to deal with Osherl. I suspect that he is acting in concert with my enemies, if only passively. This of course is intolerable. We will now fly this pavilion south, across the Mag Mountains, over the Santune Sea, to where Osherl has stationed himself. There we will make further plans."

Rhialto uttered a cantrap of material transfer, to convey the pavilion across the land and over the sea to where the flantic had sunk beneath the waves. Osherl, for the sake of convenience, had assumed the form of a buoy, painted red and black to conform with maritime regulations. A human head wrought in iron protruded from the top, with a navigation light above.

"Rhialto, you have returned!" cried Osherl in a metallic voice. "Not a moment too soon! I have no taste for a life at sea."

"No more have I! As soon as we recover the Perciplex, our work is done."

Osherl gave a harsh melancholy cry, in the tones of a sea-bird. "Have I not explained that the Perciplex is lost in the depths? You must give up this obsession and accept the inevitable!"

"It is you who must accept the inevitable," said Rhialto. "Until the Perciplex is in my hands, you must remain here to mark and certify this spot."

Osherl tolled his warning bell in agitation. "Why not exercise your magic and move the sea aside? Then we may search in convenience!"

"I no longer command such magic; my best power was stolen by Hache-Moncour and others. Still, you have supplied me with the germ of an idea…What is the name of this particular sea?"

"That is an irrelevant item of trivia!"

"Not at all! I am never irrelevant, nor yet trivial."

Osherl produced a heavy moaning curse. "During this epoch, it is an inland arm of the Accic Ocean: the Santune Sea. During the Seventeenth Aeon, a land-bridge rises across the Straits of Garch; the sea slowly dries and becomes extinct. During the last epoch of the Seventeenth Aeon the old sea-bed is known as the Tchaxmatar Steppe. In the second epoch of the Eighteenth Aeon, Baltanque of the Tall Towers rises five miles to the north of our present station, and persists until its capture by Isil Skilte the archveult. Later in the Eighteenth Aeon the sea returns. I hope that your sudden fascination with Middle-Earth geography has been satiated?"

"Quite so," said Rhialto. "I now issue the following orders, which must be implemented in most minute detail. Without stirring from your position, you will transfer me and my subaltern, Shalukhe the Swimmer, to a convenient moment during the latter Seventeenth Aeon when the bed of the erstwhile Santune Sea is dry and ready to be searched for the Perciplex.

"Meanwhile you are explicitly ordered not to move from your present anchorage by so much as one inch, nor may you appoint substitute guardians, specifically and particularly Sarsem, to maintain the vigil while you deal with other business."

Osherl set up a weird moaning sound, which Rhialto ignored. "The Perciplex is under your foot at this moment; if it is not there when we return in the Seventeenth Aeon, there can be only one party at fault: yourself. Therefore, guard well, with all obduracy. Allow neither Sarsem nor Hache-Moncour, nor any other, to hoodwink you and seduce you from your duty!

"We are now disposed to the transfer. Let there be no errors! The recovery of the true and original Perciplex, and its delivery to me, has become your responsibility! Many, many indenture points ride on the outcome of your work! So then: to the Seventeenth Aeon!"

15

The pavilion now stood in the blaze of geranium-red sunlight. The sky was clear of clouds and overcast; the air felt warm, dry and carried a smoky-tart odor exhaled by a low-growing black bush. To the west the gleam of the retreating Santune Sea was yet visible, with a village of white cottages among low trees a half-mile away. In other directions the steppe spread away over the horizon.

At a distance of a hundred feet stood a small white cottage, with a massive black shairo tree rising high to each side. On the porch sat Osherl, in the guise of a low-caste vagabond, or lack-wit, with blinking eyes, sandy hair and upper teeth hanging foolishly over a receding chin. Osherl wore a soiled gown of coarse white cloth and a low flap-brimmed hat.

Taking note of Rhialto, Osherl waved a limp-fingered hand. "Ah Rhialto! After so long a vigil, even your face is welcome!"

Rhialto responded in a manner somewhat more cool. He surveyed the cottage. "You seem to have made yourself thoroughly comfortable. I hope that, in your ease, you have not neglected the security of the Perciplex?"

Osherl responded evenly: "My 'comfort', as you put it, is primordial, and is basically designed to protect me from night-prowling beasts. I lack both silken couches and attentive subalterns."

"And the Perciplex?"

Osherl jerked his thumb toward a rusty iron post fifty yards away. "Directly under that post, at some unknown depth, lies the Perciplex."

Rhialto, surveying the area, noticed racks of empty flagons to the side of the cottage. "Mind you, I intend neither criticism nor scorn, but is it possible that you have taken to drink?"

"And if so, what then?" grumbled Osherl. "The vigil has been long. To vary the tedium, I compound tonics of various flavors which I sell to the villagers."

"Why did you not start an exploratory tunnel towards the Perciplex?"

"Need I explain? I feared that if I did so and found nothing, I would be forced to endure your reproaches. I decided to take no initiatives."

"What of, let us say, competing entities?"

"I have not been molested."

Rhialto's keen ear detected an almost imperceptible nicety of phrasing. He asked sharply: "Have either Sarsem or Hache-Moncour made their presence known?"

"To no significant degree, if any. They understand the importance of our work, and would not think to interfere."

"Just so. Might they have sunk a shaft at a distance, let us say, of ten miles, and driven a tunnel so that they came upon the Perciplex in a manner beyond your knowledge?"

"Impossible. I am not easily fooled. I arranged devices to signal all illicit incursions, either temporal, torsional, squalmaceous, or dimensional. The Perciplex is as before."

"Excellent. You may commence your excavation at once."

Osherl only made himself more comfortable in his chair. "First things first! This acreage is owned by a certain Um-Foad, resident at the village Az-Khaf, which you see yonder. He must be consulted before a single shovelful of dirt is turned. I suggest that you visit him at his home and make the arrangements. But first! Dress in garments like my own, to avoid ridicule."

Dressed in accordance with Osherl's recommendations, Rhialto and Shalukhe sauntered off to Az-Khaf.

They discovered a neat village of stark white houses in gardens of enormous red sun-flowers.

Rhialto made inquiries and the two were directed to a house with windows of blue glass and a roof of blue tile. Standing in the street Rhialto called across the garden, until Um-Foad at last came out upon his porch: a man small and white-haired with a shrewd darting gaze and

Fader's Waft

a fine mustache with sharply upturned points. He called out sharply: "Who calls the name 'Um-Foad' and for what purpose? He may or may not be at home."

"I am Rhialto, a student of antiquities. This is my assistant Shalukhe the Swimmer. Will you come here, or shall we go there, so that we need not shout?"

"Shout as loud as you like. I am only here to listen."

Rhialto spoke in a quiet voice: "I wish to speak of money."

Um-Foad came bounding forward, mustache a-bristle. "Speak up, sir! Did you mention money?"

"Perhaps you mis-heard me. We want to dig a hole on your land."

"For what purpose, and how much will you pay?"

"More to the point: what will you pay us?" demanded Rhialto. "We are enhancing the value of your land."

Um-Foad laughed scornfully. "So that when I walk out by night, I fall in the hole and break my head? If you dig, you must pay! And you must pay once again for the refill! That is the first stipulation."

"And the second?"

Um-Foad chuckled wisely and tapped the side of his nose. "Do you take me for a fool? I know full well that valuable objects are buried on my land. If treasure is found, all belongs to me. If you dig, you acquire rights only in the hole."

"Unreasonable! Is there a third stipulation?"

"There is indeed! The excavation contract must be tendered to my brother Um-Zuic. I will personally act as project supervisor. Further, all payments must be made in gold zikkos of recent mintage."

Rhialto tried to argue, but Um-Foad proved to be a negotiator of great skill and in every important essential had his way with Rhialto.

As Rhialto and Shalukhe returned to the pavilion, she said: "You are most generous in your dealings, or so it seems to me. Um-Foad is obsessively avaricious."

Rhialto agreed. "In the presence of money, Um-Foad is like a hunger-maddened shark. Still, why not allow the fellow his hour of pleasure? It is as easy to promise two hundred gold zikkos as a hundred."

"Rhialto, you are a kindly man!" said Shalukhe.

※

Um-Foad and his brother Um-Zuic brought a gang of labourers to Osherl's hut and commenced to dig a hole fifty feet in diameter at the spot designated by Osherl. The dirt excavated was sifted through a screen before the attentive scrutiny of Osherl, Rhialto, and Um-Foad.

Inch by inch, foot by foot, the hole sank into the old sea-bed, but not at a rate to suit Rhialto. At last he complained to Um-Foad: "What is wrong with the work-force? They saunter here and there; they laugh and gossip at the water-barrel; they stare into space for long periods. That old gaffer yonder, he moves so seldom that twice I have feared for his life."

Um-Foad made an easy response: "Come now, Rhialto! Do not forever be carping and chiding! These men are being paid handsomely by the hour. They are in no hurry to see the end of so noble an enterprise. As for the old man, he is my uncle Yaa-Yimpe, who suffers severe back pains, and is also deaf. Must he be penalized on this account? Let him enjoy the same perquisites as the others!"

Rhialto shrugged. "As you wish. Our contract encompasses situations of this sort."

"Eh? How so?"

"I refer to the section: 'Rhialto at his option may pay all charges on the basis of cubic footage removed from the hole. The amount of said payment shall be determined by the speed at which Rhialto, standing beside a pile of soft dirt with a stout shovel, can transfer ten cubic feet of said dirt to a new pile immediately adjacent.'"

Um-Foad cried out in consternation, and consulted the contract. "I do not remember including any such provision!"

"I added it as an afterthought," said Rhialto. "Perhaps you failed to notice."

Um-Foad darted away to exhort the workers. Grudgingly they bent to their shovels, and even old Yaa-Yimpe shifted his position from time to time.

As the hole grew deeper, the soil began to yield articles lost into the ancient sea from passing ships. Each of these items Um-Foad seized upon with quick fingers, then tried to sell them to Rhialto.

"Look now, Rhialto! We have here a true treasure, this earthenware mug, despite its broken handle! It represents the culmination of a free and unself-conscious art no longer practiced in the crass world of today."

Rhialto agreed. "A fine piece! It will grace the mantle-piece of your home and bring you hours of pleasure."

Um-Foad clicked his tongue in vexation. "Then this is not the object you are seeking?"

"Definitely not. Still, put it with the other articles you have salvaged and perhaps someday I will take the lot off your hands."

"Please, then, define for me exactly what you are seeking!" demanded Um-Foad. "If we knew, we could use a keener eye at the sifting table."

"And you could also put an exorbitant value upon this object if and when it comes to light."

Um-Foad showed Rhialto an unpleasantly avaricious grin. "My recourse is clear. I shall set large values on everything discovered."

Rhialto reflected a moment. "In that case, I too must alter my tactics."

During the noon-time rest-period, Rhialto addressed the workers. "I am pleased to see that the hole is sinking apace. The object I seek must now be near at hand. I will now describe it, so that all may work alertly, inasmuch as the man who finds this object will earn a bonus of ten golden zikkos in addition to his pay."

Um-Foad interjected a quick remark. "These gold zikkos, needless to say, are to be paid by Rhialto."

"Just so," said Rhialto. "Listen then! Are all attentive?" He glanced around the group and even deaf old Yaa-Yimpe seemed to sense the importance of the occasion. "We are seeking the Sacred Lantern which at one time graced the bow of the Cloud-king's Pleasure-barge. During a terrible storm, it was dislodged by a dart of blue lightning-ice, and toppled into the sea. So then: to whomever finds the lantern, ten golden zikkos! To whomever finds a fragment, a shatter, or even so much as a small prism of the blue lightning-ice I will pay a bonus of one gold zikko, in true coin; such a fragment will indicate to me that the Sacred Lantern is close at hand. Such a fragment, or shard, or prism, is recognizable by its blue lightning-like color, and must instantly be brought to me for inspection. So now, to work, and with utmost vigilance for the blue lightning-ice, as this will lead us to our goal!"

Um-Foad gave the signal to return to work. "All hands to the shovels; let the work go at double-quick time! Heed well the words of Rhialto!"

A moment later Um-Foad took Rhialto aside. "Since the subject has come up, you may now pay me an instalment of ten gold zikkos against my costs to date, along with another five zikkos in settlement of licensing fees. Let us say twenty gold zikkos in all."

"Five must suffice."

Um-Foad at last accepted the coins. "I am puzzled by one of your phrases. You spoke to the workmen of 'one gold zikko, in true coin'. What, precisely, do you imply by use of the word 'true'?"

Rhialto made a negligent gesture. "Merely a mode of speaking — a touch of hyperbole, if you will — to express our reverence for such a gold coin."

"An interesting usage," said Um-Foad. "Nevertheless, quite clear and commendable… Now then! Who is this odd fellow, who comes sauntering across my property like Pululias, Friend of the Oak Trees?"

Rhialto looked around to where a tall handsome man with chestnut curls and graceful mannerisms stood casually inspecting the excavation. Rhialto said shortly: "I know the gentleman slightly; he has probably come to pay his respects. Hache-Moncour! Are you not far from your usual haunts?"

"Yes, in some degree." Hache-Moncour turned away from the hole and approached. "The excellent Sarsem mentioned that you were indulging your fancies in these parts and since I had a trifle of other business along the way, I decided to pay my respects. You have dug a fine hole yonder, though I cannot divine its purpose here in this reprehensible landscape."

Um-Foad retorted sharply: "Rhialto is a famous savant and student of antiquities; this landscape, of which you are making salutary use, is a parcel of my private acreage."

"You must forgive me my trespass. I envy you a property so notable! Rhialto is indeed a scholar of wide fame… I will be moving along. It has been pleasant chatting with you both."

Hache-Moncour strolled off behind Osherl's cottage and disappeared from view.

"A most curious fellow!" declared Um-Foad. "Surely you do not number him among your intimates?"

"An acquaintance, only."

From behind the shairo trees flanking Osherl's cottage floated an almost invisible bubble. Rhialto watched with a frown as the bubble drifted over the hole and hung motionless.

"Still," said Rhialto, "Hache-Moncour is a man of sensitive perceptions and many extraordinary talents."

"He was notably fast on his feet when I hinted at a fee for his trespass. Yes, what have we here?" This to one of the diggers who had approached with an earthenware bowl. "Rhialto, here is the lantern! I claim your reward."

Rhialto examined the object. "This is no lantern; it is a child's porridge bowl, no doubt flung overboard during a tantrum. Notice the quaint scenes depicted in the base of the bowl. Here we have a flantic flying to its lair with a baby gripped in its claws. Here a pouncing langomir devours a somewhat older child, while here, aboard this ship, a small girl is being dragged overboard by a parrot-headed sea-monster. An interesting find, but neither lightning-ice nor lantern."

Rhialto handed the bowl to Um-Foad, then, glancing casually about, took note that the bubble had drifted directly overhead.

An hour after sunset, with an afterglow the color of persimmon still rimming the sky, Rhialto took Osherl aside. "Who watches from the floating bubble? Is it Sarsem?"

"It is a madling, no more, with an eye illuminating a section of Hache-Moncour's vision, so that he may watch all that transpires."

"Catch it in a net and put it into a box, so that Hache-Moncour may enjoy a good night's rest."

"As you wish... It is done."

"And who watches us now, and who listens to us?"

"No one. We are alone."

"Osherl, I wonder why you persist in your deceptions?"

Osherl spoke in a startled tone: "What is it this time?"

"Today a bowl was brought from the hole. It had been thrown into the Santune Sea an epoch before the Perciplex was lost: so much I infer from the style of the ship and the nature of its rigging, and also from the animal species depicted in the decorations. Therefore, the stratum containing the Perciplex has already been mined. Still I lack the Perciplex! How do you explain this?"

"A curious situation, I readily admit," said Osherl in hearty tones. "Let us examine the pit."

"Bring light."

Osherl and Rhialto went to the excavation and peered over the edge, with their lights illuminating the bottom. Osherl said: "See there?" With a beam of light he indicated an area to the side, near the circumference, which had been dug two feet deeper than the area at the center. "That is the spot where the bowl was found: in a deeper section of the hole. Are you now satisfied?"

"Not yet. If that level predated the Perciplex, and all other levels have yielded nothing, then the Perciplex must now reside in that small hummock of dirt at the very center of the hole."

"So it would seem."

"Well then, Osherl, why are you waiting? Descend into the hole, take up shovel and dig, while I hold the light."

A figure came briskly out of the dusk. "Osherl? Rhialto? Why are you shining lights into my hole? Is this act not in default of our contract? Why, tonight of all nights, do you take these steps?"

"One night is much like another," said Rhialto. "Do you begrudge us our evening stroll, that we may breathe the cool fresh air?"

"Certainly not! Still, why do you equip yourselves with strong and vibrant lights?"

"Obviously, to avoid stumbling into holes and excavations! Already, as you have noted, the lights have served us well. Careful there, Osherl! Shine your light behind you! That is a thorn-bush into which you were backing."

"One cannot be too careful," said Osherl. "Rhialto, have you taken enough of the evening air?"

"Quite enough. Good night, Um-Foad."

"One moment! I want another instalment paid on your debt."

"Um-Foad, do you always work to such narrow margins? Here is another five gold zikkos. Be content for a period."

In the morning Rhialto was early at the sifting box, and scrutinized each load of dirt brought from the hole with special care. Um-Foad, taking note of Rhialto's attentiveness, became even more officious, often pushing Rhialto aside so that he might be first to inspect the siftings. The workmen, observing Um-Foad's distraction, relaxed their efforts to such an extent that dirt arrived to the screen at ever longer intervals. Um-Foad at last took note of the situation and, running to the edge of the hole, set matters right. The workers, however, had lost the edge of their zeal. Yaa-Yimpe, complaining both of ague and lumbar spasms, refused to work under what he felt to be Rhialto's niggardly dispositions. Climbing from the hole, he returned to the village.

Somewhat later, a young man came running out from the village and accosted Rhialto. "Yaa-Yimpe is somewhat deaf; he did not understand that you had offered gold coins in exchange for blue lightning-ice. He now wishes to inform you that he found a fragment of the stuff today. You may entrust the reward to me, his grandson; Yaa-Yimpe is too tired to come out himself, and also he is planning a feast." The grandson, brisk and eager, with bright round eyes and a toothy grin, extended his hand.

Rhialto spoke crisply. "I must inspect this lightning-ice, to test its quality. Come, take me to Yaa-Yimpe."

The young man scowled. "He does not wish to be irked with details; give me the gold coins now, as well as my gratuity."

"Not another word!" thundered Rhialto. "At once! To the village!"

The young man sulkily led Rhialto to a house where festivities congratulating Yaa-Yimpe on the occasion of his reward were already in progress. Joints of meat turned on the spit and casks of wine had been broached. On a platform to the side six musicians played tankles, jigs and tyreens for the pleasure of the guests.

As Rhialto approached, Yaa-Yimpe himself, wearing only a pair of short loose pantaloons, emerged from the house. The company called out plaudits and the musicians struck up a lively quickstep. Yaa-Yimpe darted forward to dance a high-kicking saltarello, entailing quick rushing lunges back and forth, with thrust-forward belly shaking in double-time.

In his fervor Yaa-Yimpe jumped on the table, to perform a stamping arm-swinging hornpipe. Around his neck the Perciplex swung by a thong tied around its middle.

Yaa-Yimpe suddenly took note of Rhialto and jumped to the ground.

Rhialto spoke politely: "I am happy to find that your sufferings have been eased."

"True! Notice the lightning-ice! You may now give me the twenty gold zikkos."

Rhialto held out his hand. "Immediately, but let me inspect the prism!"

Hache-Moncour jumped forward from the side. "One moment! It is more appropriate that I take custody of this object! Here, sir! Your twenty gold zikkos!" Hache-Moncour flung the coins into Yaa-Yimpe's ready hand, snatched the Perciplex and strode to the side.

Rhialto made a convulsive motion forward but Hache-Moncour cried out: "Stand back, Rhialto! I must study the authenticity of this object!" He held the prism up to the light. "As I expected: a shameless hoax! Rhialto, we have been misled!" Hache-Moncour flung the prism to the ground, pointed his finger; the object broke into a hundred gouts of blue fire and was gone.

Rhialto stared numbly at the scorched ground. Hache-Moncour spoke in a kindly voice: "Seek elsewhere, Rhialto, if you are so minded; your work is truly useful! If you discover another arrant forgery, or even if you suspect as much, call on me again for advice. I bid you good-day." Hache-Moncour was gone as quickly as he had come, leaving Yaa-Yimpe and his guests staring open-mouthed.

Rhialto slowly returned to the excavation. Osherl stood in front of his hut, looking pensively off into the sky. Shalukhe the Swimmer sat cross-legged on a rug before the pavilion, eating grapes. Um-Foad came at the run from the excavation. "Rhialto, what are all these rumors?"

"I have no time for rumors," said Rhialto. "Still, you may now halt the digging."

"So soon? What of the Cloud-king's lantern?"

"I begin to think it a myth. I must return to study my references."

"In that case, I demand the full balance of what you owe."

"Certainly," said Rhialto. "Where is your invoice?"

"I have prepared no formal document. The due amount, however, is fifty-two golden zikkos."

"Highly exorbitant!" cried Rhialto. "Have you not miscalculated?"

Fader's Waft

"I include the use and enjoyment of my land, by day and by night; labor costs, in both digging and refilling the hole; re-landscaping and re-planting the site; my own fees, both as supervisor and consultant; certain honorariums due the civic functionaries; imposts and —"

Rhialto held up his hand. "You have already told me more than I care to hear. For my part, I want only the porridge bowl, for a souvenir."

Um-Foad's mustaches bristled anew. "Can you be serious? That is a valuable antique, worth at least ten zikkos!"

"Whatever you say."

Um-Foad found the porridge bowl and tendered it to Rhialto. "Now then, my money, and let there be no mistakes in the tally."

Rhialto passed over a satchel. Um-Foad counted the contents with satisfaction. He rose to his feet. "I take it that you are now vacating the premises?"

"Almost immediately."

"My fees resume at Midnight." Um-Foad gave a crisp signal of farewell, then, striding to the pit, called up the workers and the group returned to the village.

The geranium-red sun floated down the western sky. With the cessation of activity the site seemed unnaturally quiet. Rhialto stood in contemplation of the pit. Shalukhe the Swimmer lazed on the rug before the pavilion. Osherl stood in the entrance to his cottage, looking off across the landscape with a somewhat moony expression.

Rhialto heaved a deep sigh and turned to Osherl: "Well then, I am waiting to hear what you have to say."

Osherl's eyes went unfocused. "Ah yes...I am happy to hear that Yaa-Yimpe has recovered his health."

"Is that all? You are curiously placid. Have you no word in regard to the Perciplex?"

Osherl scratched his cheek. "Did you not come to agreement with Yaa-Yimpe?"

"Why should I bother, when he held a patently false version of the Perciplex?"

"Indeed? How could even Rhialto make so definite a finding, when he never so much as laid hands on the object?"

Rhialto shook his head sadly. "My dear fellow, you yourself certified the object as brummagem when you allowed it to be found in the same stratum as the porridge bowl."

"Not at all! You yourself saw how the area of the porridge bowl was well below the central knob which yielded the Perciplex."

"Exactly so: the same levels, when they should have been six feet or more apart."

"Hmmf," said Osherl. "Somewhere you have made errors. One cannot judge important matters on the basis of porridge bowls."

"In sheer point of fact, you and Sarsem were careless, though I am sure you enjoyed your trick, chuckling and nudging each other in the ribs as you envisioned poor Rhialto's distress."

Osherl, stung, cried out: "Error once again! The arrangements were made in all dignity! Also, your theories lack proof. The bowl may imitate the early style, or it might have been preserved exactly one epoch and then thrown into the sea!"

"Osherl, you walk the very brink of absurdity. My so-called 'theories' stand on two legs: first, logical deduction; and second, simple observation. The object which you allowed Yaa-Yimpe to find admittedly resembled the Perciplex — in fact enough to deceive Hache-Moncour. But not me."

Osherl blinked in puzzlement. "How are your eyes so keen and Hache-Moncour's so dull?"

"I am not only wise and just; I am intelligent. Hache-Moncour boasts only a low animal cunning scarcely superior to your own."

"You are still telling me nothing."

"Have you no eyes? The false object dangled on a thong around Yaa-Yimpe's neck — at the horizontal. The true Perciplex holds itself forever upright, so that its sacred text may never be misread. Hache-Moncour paid no heed, and I am grateful for his vulgar haste. So now, what have you to say?"

"I must give the matter thought."

"Two questions remain. First: who has the Perciplex, you or Sarsem? Second: how will you and Sarsem be at once rewarded for your services and punished for your faithlessness?"

"The former far outweigh the latter, at least in my case," said Osherl.

"As for Sarsem, who was so adroitly gulled by Hache-Moncour, I will make no recommendations."

"And the Perciplex?"

"Ah! That is a delicate subject, which I am not free to discuss before unauthorized ears."

"What?" cried Rhialto in outrage. "You include me in this category, when Ildefonse specifically placed you under my orders?"

"Subject to the limits of common sense."

"Very well! We will lay the facts before Ildefonse at Boumergarth, and I hope that I may restrain all prejudice in my report. Still, I must take note of your sullen obduracy, which can only add aeons to your indenture."

Osherl blinked and winced. "Is it truly so important? Well then, I can offer a hint. Hache-Moncour and Sarsem devised the plan as a joke. I instantly pointed out the serious nature of this matter, and gave Yaa-Yimpe a false crystal." Osherl uttered a nervous laugh. "Sarsem of course retained possession of the true Perciplex, and his guilt far outweighs mine."

At the pavilion Shalukhe the Swimmer jumped to her feet. "I hear a great tumult from the village... It sounds like men shouting in rage, and it seems to be growing louder."

Rhialto listened. "I expect that Hache-Moncour's gold zikkos have become bull-frogs or acorns, or perhaps my payments to Um-Foad have altered prematurely... In any event, it is time we were moving on. Osherl, we will now return to Boumergarth, at a time one minute subsequent to our departure."

16

In response to Ildefonse's urgent summons, the magicians assembled in the Great Hall at Boumergarth. Only Rhialto appeared to be absent from the conclave, but no one mentioned his name.

Ildefonse sat silently in his massive chair behind the podium, head bowed so that his yellow beard rested on his folded arms. The other magicians conversed in subdued voices, glancing from time to time toward Ildefonse and discussing the purported purpose of the meeting.

The moments passed, one by one, and still Ildefonse sat in silence. Other small conversations around the room gradually quieted, and all sat looking towards Ildefonse wondering at his reason for delay... At last Ildefonse, perhaps at the receipt of a signal, stirred himself and spoke, in a voice of gravity.

"Noble magicians: the occasion today is momentous! In full panoply of reason and wisdom we must consider issues of importance.

"Our business is unusual, even unprecedented. To forestall any intrusions, I have arranged a web of impermeability around Boumergarth. There is a consequential inconvenience, to the effect that, while no one can enter to disturb us, neither can anyone depart, neither forward nor backward, nor thither nor yon."

Hurtiancz, with his usual asperity, called out: "Why these unique precautions? I am not one for stays and restrictions; I must inquire the reason why I should be thus pent!"

"I have already explained my motives," said Ildefonse. "In short, I wish neither entries nor exits during our discussions."

"Proceed," said Hurtiancz in clipped tones. "I will restrain my impatience as best I can."

"To establish a basis for my remarks, I advert to the authority of Phandaal, the Grand Master of our art. His admonitions are stern and direct, and form the theoretical background to the protocol by which we rule our conduct. Here, naturally, I refer to the Blue Principles."

Hache-Moncour called out: "Truly, Ildefonse, your periods, while resonant, are somewhat protracted. I suggest that you get on with the business of the day. I believe you mentioned that new discoveries compel a redistribution of Rhialto's properties. May I ask, then, what new articles have appeared, and what may be their quality?"

"You anticipate me!" rumbled Ildefonse. "Still, since the subject has been broached, I trust that everyone has brought with him the full tally of those effects awarded him and distributed after Rhialto's trial? Has everyone done so? No? In all candour, I expected not much else... Well then — where was I? I believe that I had just paid my respects to Phandaal."

"True," said Hache-Moncour. "Now, describe the new findings, if you will. Where, for instance, were they secreted?"

Fader's Waft

Ildefonse held up his hand. "Patience, Hache-Moncour! Do you recall the chain of events which stemmed from the impulsive conduct of Hurtiancz at Falu? He tore Rhialto's copy of the Blue Principles, thus prompting Rhialto to take legal action."

"I recall the situation perfectly: a tempest in a tea-pot, or so it seems to me."

A tall figure wearing black trousers, a loose black blouse and a loose black cap pulled low, moved forward from the shadows. "It does not seem so to me," said the man in black and moved back into the shadows.

Ildefonse paid him no heed. "If only from a theoretical point of view, this case absorbs our interest. Rhialto was the plaintiff; the group now assembled are the defendants. As Rhialto stated his case, the issues were simple. The Blue, so he claimed, declared that any purposeful alteration or destruction of the Monstrament or obvious and ostensible copy thereof, constituted a crime, punishable at minimum by a fine equal to three times the value of any wrongful losses sustained; at maximum, total confiscation. Such was Rhialto's contention, and he brought forward the torn copy both as evidence of the crime and as his documentation of the law itself.

"The defendants, led by Hache-Moncour, Hurtiancz, Gilgad and others, decried the charges as not only artificial but also a wrongful act in themselves. Rhialto's action, so they claim, formed the substance of a counteraction. To support this position, Hache-Moncour and the others took us to Fader's Waft, where we examined the Monstrament there projected, and where Hache-Moncour asserted, and now I paraphrase, that any attempt to present a damaged, mutilated or purposefully altered copy of the Monstrament is in itself a crime of major consequence.

"Hache-Moncour and his group argue, therefore, that in presenting the damaged copy of the Blue as evidence, Rhialto committed a crime which must be adjudicated even before his own charges can be considered. They argue that Rhialto is clearly guilty, and that not only are his charges moot, but that the only real issue becomes the degree of Rhialto's punishment."

Ildefonse here paused and looked from face to face. "Have I fairly stated the case?"

"Quite so," said Gilgad. "I doubt if you will find dissent anywhere. Rhialto has long been a thorn in our side."

Vermoulian spoke. "I do not favor Forlorn Encystment* for Rhialto; I say, let him live out his days as a salamander, or a Gangue River lizard."

Ildefonse cleared his throat. "Before passing sentence — or, for that matter, before arriving at a judgment — there are certain odd facts to be considered. First of all, let me ask this question: how many here have consulted their own copies of the Blue Principles in connection with this case?…What? No one?"

Dulce-Lolo gave a light laugh. "It is hardly necessary; am I not right? After all, we made that chilly and inconvenient visit to Fader's Waft for that very purpose."

"Just so," said Ildefonse. "Peculiarly, my recollection of the passage accorded with Rhialto's torn copy, rather than that at Fader's Waft."

"The mind plays peculiar tricks," said Hache-Moncour. "Now then, Ildefonse, in order to accelerate a possibly tedious —"

"In a moment," said Ildefonse. "First, let me add that I referred to my personal copy of the Blue, and discovered that the text duplicated that placed in evidence by Rhialto."

The room became silent, with the stillness of bewilderment. Then Hurtiancz made a vehement gesture. "Bah! Why ensnare ourselves in subtleties? Rhialto irrefutably committed the crime, as defined by the Perciplex. What more is there to be said?"

"Only this! As our esteemed colleague Hache-Moncour has pointed out, the mind plays strange tricks. Is it possible that the other night we were all victims of mass hallucination? If you recall, we found the projection unaccountably turned upside-down, which had a very confusing effect, certainly upon me."

Once more the figure in black stepped forward from the shadows. "Most especially when the Perciplex will not allow itself to be altered from the upright position, for fear of just such a consequence."

The dark shape returned to the shadows, and as before both he and his words were ignored as if non-existent.

---

* The Spell of Forlorn Encystment operates to bury that luckless individual subject to the spell in a capsule forty-five miles below the surface of the earth.

Hache-Moncour said weightily: "Could this entire group, all keen observers, have witnessed the same hallucination? I tend to scout such a possibility."

"I also!" cried Hurtiancz. "I have never hallucinated!"

Ildefonse said: "Nevertheless, in my capacity as Preceptor, I hereby rule that we now transfer ourselves into my whirlaway, which is also enwebbed to protect us from nuisance, and visit Fader's Waft, so that we may settle the matter once and for all."

"As you like," said Dulce-Lolo peevishly. "But why this elaborate system of webs and screens? If no one can molest us, neither can any of us go off about his business should, for instance, a sudden emergency develop at his manse."

"True," said Ildefonse. "Precisely so. This way then, if you please."

Only the man in black who sat in the shadows remained behind.

17

The whirlaway flew high through the red light of afternoon: south across Ascolais to a set of soft swelling hills and at last settled upon Fader's Waft.

From the whirlaway to the six-sided fane extended an arch of web: "—lest archveults seize upon this opportunity to expunge all of us together!" So Ildefonse explained the precaution.

Into the enclosure filed the group, with Ildefonse bringing up the rear. As always, the Perciplex rested upon its cushion of black satin. In a chair to the side sat a man-shaped creature white of skin and white of eye, with a soft fluff of pink feathers for hair.

"Ah Sarsem," said Ildefonse in a hearty voice. "How goes the vigil?"

"All is well," said Sarsem in a glum voice.

"No difficulties? Neither incursions nor excursions since I saw you last? All is in order?"

"The vigil proceeds unmarred by incident."

"Good!" declared Ildefonse. "Now let us examine the projection. Possibly it confused us before, and this time we will all look closely and make no mistakes. Sarsem, the projection!"

Upon the wall flashed the Blue Principles. Ildefonse chortled with delight. "Precisely so! As I declared, we were all confused together — even the redoubtable Hurtiancz, who now reads the Monstrament for a third and decisive time. Hurtiancz! Be kind enough to read the passage aloud!"

Tonelessly Hurtiancz read: "Any person who knowingly and purposefully alters, mutilates, destroys or secretes the Blue Principles or any copy thereof is guilty of a crime, and likewise in equal measure his conspirators, punishable by the measures described in Schedule D. If said acts are committed in the progress of an unlawful act, or for unlawful purposes, the penalties shall be those described in Schedule G."

Ildefonse turned to Hache-Moncour, who stood with bulging eyes and sagging jaw. "So there you are, Hache-Moncour! I was right after all and now you must acknowledge as much."

Hache-Moncour muttered abstractedly: "Yes, yes; so it seems." He turned a long frowning glance towards Sarsem, who avoided his gaze.

"So much is now settled!" declared Ildefonse. "Let us return to Boumergarth and proceed with our inquiry."

Hache-Moncour said sulkily: "I am not well. Raise your web so that I may return to my manse."

"Impossible!" said Ildefonse. "All must be present during the deliberations. If you recall, we are trying a case against Rhialto."

"But there is no longer a case against Rhialto!" bleated Byzant the Necrope. "The proceedings are now devoid of interest! We must go home to look to our properties!"

"To Boumergarth, all!" thundered Ildefonse. "I will brook no further reluctance!"

With poor grace the magicians trooped to the whirlaway and sat in silence during the return flight. Three times Hache-Moncour raised a finger as if to address Ildefonse, but each time caught himself and held his tongue.

At Boumergarth the magicians filed glumly into the Great Hall and took their places. In the shadows stood the man in black, as if he had never moved.

Ildefonse spoke: "We now resume consideration of the action brought by Rhialto and its counter-action. Are there any opinions to be heard?"

Fader's Waft

The chamber was silent.

Ildefonse turned to the man in black. "Rhialto, what have you to say?"

"I have stated my case against Hurtiancz and his conspirators. I now await resolution of the action."

Ildefonse said: "The persons present are divided into two categories: Rhialto, the plaintiff, and the defendants who number all the rest of us. In such a case we can only go for guidance to the Blue, and there can be no question as to the findings. Rhialto, as Preceptor, I declare that you have fairly proved your case. I declare that you are entitled to recover your sequestered goods and a stipulated penalty."

Rhialto came forward to lounge against the lectern. "I have won a sad and profitless victory, against persons whom I deemed my lesser or greater friends."

Rhialto looked around the room. Few returned his gaze. In a flat voice Rhialto continued: "The victory has not been easy. I have known toil, fear, and disappointment. Nevertheless, I do not intend to grind home my advantage. I make the same demand upon each of you, save in one case only: return all my sequestered property to Falu, with the addition of a single IOUN stone from each as penalty."

Ao of the Opals said: "Rhialto, your act is both generous and wise. Naturally you have won little popularity with your victory; in fact, I notice both Hurtiancz and Zilifant grinding their teeth. Still, you have incurred no new enmity. I admit my mistake; I accept the penalty and will pay you an IOUN stone with humility. I urge my fellows to do the same."

Eshmiel cried out: "Well spoken, Ao! I share your sentiments. Rhialto, who is the one person whom you except from the penalty and why do you do so?"

"I except Hache-Moncour, whose actions cannot be excused. By his attack upon our law he attacked us all: you are his victims no less than I, though your sufferings would be yet to come.

"Hache-Moncour must lose all his magic, and all his capacity for magic. This effect was worked upon him by Ildefonse as I spoke to you. The Hache-Moncour you see yonder is not the same man who stood here an hour ago, and even now Ildefonse is calling his servants. They will take him down to the local tannery, where he will be afforded suitable employment.

"As for me, tomorrow I return to Falu, where my life will continue more or less as before, or so I hope."

18

Shalukhe the Swimmer sat beside the River Ts under the blue aspens which grew along the banks and partly screened Falu from sight. Rhialto, with his household restored to order, came out to join her. She turned her head, took note of his approach, then returned to her contemplation of the river.

Rhialto seated himself nearby and, leaning back, watched the shiver of dark sunlight along the moving water. Presently he turned his head and studied first the delicate profile, then the graceful disposition of her body. Today she wore sand-colored trousers fitted close at the ankles, loose around the hips, black slippers, a white shirt and a black sash. A red ribbon confined her dark hair. In her own time, reflected Rhialto, she had been a Paragon of Excellence, the Best of the Best, and now who would ever know?

She became aware of his inspection and turned him a questioning glance.

Rhialto spoke. "Shalukhe the Swimmer, Furud Dawn-thing: what shall be done with you?"

The Paragon returned to her contemplation of the river. "I too wonder what to do with myself."

Rhialto raised his eyebrows. "Admittedly this era, the last to be known on the world Earth, is in many ways dark and disturbing. Still, you want nothing; you are irked by no enemies; you are free to come and go as you wish. What then troubles you?"

Shalukhe the Swimmer shrugged. "I would seem captious were I to complain. Your conduct has been courteous; you have treated me with both dignity and generosity. But I am alone. I have watched you at your colloquy, and I was minded of a group of crocodiles basking on a Kuyike River mud-bank."

Rhialto winced. "I as well?"

Shalukhe, preoccupied with her own musings, ignored the remark. "At the Court of the East-Rising Moon I was Paragon, the Best of the Best! Gentlemen of rank came eagerly to touch my hand; when I passed, my perfume evoked sighs of wistful passion and sometimes, after I passed, I heard muffled exclamations, which I took to signify admiration. Here I am shunned as if I were the Worst of the Worst; no one cares whether I leave a perfume in my wake or the odor of a pig-sty. I have become gloomy and full of doubts. Am I so bland, dull and tiresome that I instill apathy everywhere I go?"

Rhialto leaned back in his seat and stared towards the sky. "Absurdity! Mirage! Dream-madness!"

Shalukhe smiled a tremulous bitter-sweet smile. "If you had treated me shamefully, and ravished me to your desires, at least I would have been left with my pride. Your courteous detachment leaves me with nothing."

Rhialto at last found his voice. "You are the most perverse of all maidens! How often my hands have tingled and twitched to seize you; always I have held back so that you might feel secure and easy! And now you accuse me of cold blood and call me a crocodile! My graceful and poetic restraint you choose to regard as senile disability. It is I who should feel the pangs!"

Jumping to his feet, Rhialto went to sit beside her; he took her hands. "The most beautiful maidens are also the most cruel! Even now you use a subtle means to rack my emotions!"

"Oh? Tell me, so that I may do it again."

"You are troubled because I seemed to ignore your presence. But, by this reasoning, you would feel equally diminished in your pride had the man been Dulce-Lolo with his expressive feet, or Zilifant, or even Byzant the Necrope. That it was I, Rhialto, who treated you so shabbily seems to be incidental! My own vanity now torments me; am I then so unappealing? Do you feel not the slightest regard for me?"

Shalukhe the Swimmer at last smiled. "Rhialto, I will say this: were you Dulce-Lolo, or Zilifant, or Byzant, or any other than Rhialto, I would not be sitting here holding your hands so tightly in my own."

Rhialto sighed in relief. He drew her close; their faces met. "Confusions and cross-purposes: they are now resolved; perhaps the Twenty-first Aeon now seems a less dismal time."

Shalukhe looked sidelong towards the sun where it hung low over the River Ts. "To a certain extent. Still, what if the sun goes out even while we sit here: what then?"

Rhialto rose to his feet and pulled her up after him; he kissed the upturned face. "Who knows? The sun may totter and lurch still another hundred years!"

The maiden sighed and pointed. "Ah! Notice how it blinks! It seems tired and troubled! But perhaps it will enjoy a restful night."

Rhialto whispered a comment in her ear, to the effect that she should not expect the same. She gave his arm a tug, and the two, close together, walked slowly back to Falu.

III: Morreion

1

The archveult Xexamedes, digging gentian roots in Were Wood, became warm with exertion. He doffed his cloak and returned to work, but the glint of blue scales was noticed by Herark the Harbinger and the diabolist Shrue. Approaching by stealth they leapt forth to confront the creature. Then, flinging a pair of nooses about the supple neck, they held him where he could do no mischief.

After great effort, a hundred threats and as many lunges, twists and charges on the part of Xexamedes, the magicians dragged him to the castle of Ildefonse, where other magicians of the region gathered in high excitement.

In times past Ildefonse had served the magicians as preceptor and he now took charge of the proceedings. He first inquired the archveult's name.

"I am Xexamedes, as well you know, old Ildefonse!"

"Yes," said Ildefonse, "I recognize you now, though my last view was your backside, as we sent you fleeting back to Jangk. Do you realize that you have incurred death by returning?"

"Not so, Ildefonse, since I am no longer an archveult of Jangk. I am an immigrant of Earth; I declare myself reverted to the estate of a man. Even my fellows hold me in low esteem."

"Well and good," said Ildefonse. "However, the ban was and is explicit. Where do you now house yourself?" The question was casual, and Xexamedes made an equally bland response.

"I come, I go; I savor the sweet airs of Earth, so different from the chemical vapors of Jangk."

Ildefonse was not to be put off. "What appurtenances did you bring: specifically, how many IOUN stones?"

"Let us talk of other matters," suggested Xexamedes. "I now wish to join your local coterie, and, as a future comrade to all present, I find these nooses humiliating."

The short-tempered Hurtiancz bellowed, "Enough impudence! What of the IOUN stones?"

"I carry a few such trinkets," replied Xexamedes with dignity.

"Where are they?"

Xexamedes addressed himself to Ildefonse. "Before I respond, may I inquire your ultimate intentions?"

Ildefonse pulled at his white beard and raised his eyes to the chandelier. "Your fate will hinge upon many factors. I suggest that you produce the IOUN stones."

"They are hidden under the floorboards of my cottage," said Xexamedes in a sulky voice.

"Which is situated where?"

"At the far edge of Were Wood."

Rhialto the Marvellous leapt to his feet. "All wait here! I will verify the truth of the statement!"

The sorcerer Gilgad held up both arms. "Not so fast! I know the region exactly! I will go!"

Ildefonse spoke in a neutral voice. "I hereby appoint a committee to consist of Rhialto, Gilgad, Mune the Mage, Hurtiancz, Kilgas, Ao of the Opals, and Barbanikos. This group will go to the cottage and bring back all contraband. The proceedings are adjourned until your return."

2

The adjuncts of Xexamedes were in due course set forth on a sideboard in Ildefonse's great hall, including thirty-two IOUN stones: spheres, ellipsoids, spindles, each approximately the size of a small plum, each displaying inner curtains of pale fire. A net prevented them from drifting off like dream-bubbles.

"We now have a basis for further investigation," said Ildefonse. "Xexamedes, exactly what is the source of these potent adjuncts?"

Haze of Wheary Water held one rope, Barbanikos the other...

Xexamedes jerked his tall black plumes in surprise, either real or simulated. He was yet constrained by the two nooses. Haze of Wheary Water held one rope, Barbanikos the other, to ensure that Xexamedes could touch neither. Xexamedes inquired, "What of the indomitable Morreion? Did he not reveal his knowledge?"

Ildefonse frowned in puzzlement. "'Morreion'? I had almost forgotten the name…What were the circumstances?"

Herark the Harbinger, who knew lore of twenty aeons, stated: "After the archveults were defeated, a contract was made. The archveults were given their lives, and in turn agreed to divulge the source of the IOUN stones. The noble Morreion was ordered forth to learn the secret and was never heard from since."

"He was instructed in all the procedures," declared Xexamedes. "If you wish to learn — seek out Morreion!"

Ildefonse asked, "Why did he not return?"

"I cannot say. Does anyone else wish to learn the source of the stones? I will gladly demonstrate the procedure once again."

For a moment no one spoke. Then Ildefonse suggested, "Gilgad, what of you? Xexamedes has made an interesting proposal."

Gilgad licked his thin brown lips. "First, I wish a verbal description of the process."

"By all means," said Xexamedes. "Allow me to consult a document." He stepped toward the sideboard, drawing Haze and Barbanikos together; then he leaped back. With the slack thus engendered he grasped Barbanikos and exuded a galvanic impulse. Sparks flew from Barbanikos' ears; he jumped into the air and fell down in a faint. Xexamedes snatched the rope from Haze and before anyone could prevent him, he fled from the great hall.

"After him!" bawled Ildefonse. "He must not escape!"

The magicians gave chase to the fleet archveult. Across the Scaum hills, past Were Wood ran Xexamedes; like hounds after a fox came the magicians. Xexamedes entered Were Wood and doubled back, but the magicians suspected a trick and were not deceived.

Leaving the forest Xexamedes approached Rhialto's manse and took cover beside the aviary. The bird-women set up an alarm and old Funk, Rhialto's servitor, hobbled forth to investigate.

The bird-women set up an alarm...

Gilgad now spied Xexamedes and exerted his Instantaneous Electric Effort — a tremendous many-pronged dazzle which not only shivered Xexamedes but destroyed Rhialto's aviary, shattered his antique way-post and sent poor old Funk dancing across the sward on stilts of crackling blue light.

3

A linden leaf clung to the front door of Rhialto's manse, pinned by a thorn. A prank of the wind, thought Rhialto, and brushed it aside. His new servant Puiras, however, picked it up and, in a hoarse grumbling voice, read:

NOTHING THREATENS MORREION

"What is this regarding Morreion?" demanded Rhialto. Taking the leaf he inspected the minute silver characters. "A gratuitous reassurance." A second time he discarded the leaf and gave Puiras his final instructions. "At midday prepare a meal for the Minuscules — gruel and tea will suffice. At sunset serve out the thrush pâté. Next, I wish you to scour the tile of the great hall. Use no sand, which grinds at the luster of the glaze. Thereafter, clear the south sward of debris; you may use the aeolus, but take care; blow only down the yellow reed; the black reed summons a gale, and we have had devastation enough. Set about the aviary; salvage all useful material. If you find corpses, deal with them appropriately. Is so much clear?"

Puiras, a man spare and loose-jointed, with a bony face and lank black hair, gave a dour nod. "Except for a single matter. When I have accomplished all this, what else?"

Rhialto, drawing on his cloth-of-gold gauntlets, glanced sidewise at his servant. Stupidity? Zeal? Churlish sarcasm? Puiras' visage offered no clue. Rhialto spoke in an even voice. "Upon completion of these tasks, your time is your own. Do not tamper with the magical engines; do not, for your life, consult the portfolios, the librams or the compendiary. In due course, I may instruct you in a few minor dints; until then, be cautious!"

"I will indeed."

Rhialto adjusted his six-tiered black satin hat, donned his cloak with that flourish which had earned him his soubriquet 'the Marvellous'. "I go to visit Ildefonse. When I pass the outer gate impose the boundary curse; under no circumstances lift it until I signal. Expect me at sunset: sooner, if all goes well."

Making no effort to interpret Puiras' grunt, Rhialto sauntered to the north portal, averting his eyes from the wreckage of his wonderful aviary. Barely had he passed the portal by, when Puiras activated the curse, prompting Rhialto to jump hastily forward. Rhialto adjusted the set of his hat. The ineptitude of Puiras was but one in a series of misfortunes, all attributable to the archveult Xexamedes. His aviary destroyed, the way-post shattered, old Funk dead! From some source compensation must be derived!

4

Ildefonse lived in a castle above the River Scaum: a vast and complex structure of a hundred turrets, balconies, elevated pavilions and pleasaunces. During the final ages of the 21st Aeon, when Ildefonse had served as preceptor, the castle had seethed with activity. Now only a single wing of this monstrous edifice was in use, with the rest abandoned to dust, owls and archaic ghosts.

Ildefonse met Rhialto at the bronze portal. "My dear colleague, splendid as usual! Even on an occasion like that of today! You put me to shame!" Ildefonse stood back the better to admire Rhialto's austerely handsome visage, his fine blue cloak and trousers of rose velvet, his glossy boots. Ildefonse himself, for reasons obscure, presented himself in the guise of a jovial sage, with bald pate, a lined countenance, pale blue eyes, an irregular white beard — conceivably a natural condition which vanity would not let him discard.

"Come in, then," cried Ildefonse. "As always, with your sense of drama, you are last to arrive!"

They proceeded to the great hall. On hand were fourteen sorcerers: Zilifant, Perdustin, Herark the Harbinger, Haze of Wheary Water, Ao of the Opals, Eshmiel, Kilgas, Byzant the Necrope, Gilgad, Vermoulian the Dream-walker, Barbanikos, the diabolist Shrue, Mune the Mage,

Hurtiancz. Ildefonse called out, "The last of our cabal has arrived: Rhialto the Marvellous, at whose manse the culminating stroke occurred!"

Rhialto doffed his hat to the group. Some returned the salute; others, Gilgad, Byzant the Necrope, Mune the Mage, Kilgas, merely cast cool glances over their shoulders.

Ildefonse took Rhialto by the arm and led him to the buffet. Rhialto accepted a goblet of wine, which he tested with his amulet.

In mock chagrin Ildefonse protested: "The wine is sound; have you yet been poisoned at my board?"

"No. But never have circumstances been as they are today."

Ildefonse made a sign of wonder. "The circumstances are favorable! We have vanquished our enemy; his IOUN stones are under our control!"

"True," said Rhialto. "But remember the damages I have suffered! I claim corresponding benefits, of which my enemies would be pleased to deprive me."

"Tush," scolded Ildefonse. "Let us talk on a more cheerful note. How goes the renewal of your way-post? The Minuscules carve with zest?"

"The work proceeds," Rhialto replied. "Their tastes are by no means coarse. For this single week their steward has required two ounces of honey, a gill of Misericord, a dram and a half of malt spirits, all in addition to biscuit, oil and a daily ration of my best thrush pâté."

Ildefonse shook his head in disapproval. "They become ever more splendid, and who must pay the score? You and I. So the world goes." He turned away to refill the goblet of the burly Hurtiancz.

"I have made investigation," said Hurtiancz ponderously, "and I find that Xexamedes had gone among us for years. He seems to have been a renegade, as unwelcome on Jangk as on Earth."

"He may still be the same," Ildefonse pointed out. "Who found his corpse? No one! Haze here declares that electricity to an archveult is like water to a fish."

"This is the case," declared Haze of Wheary Water, a hot-eyed wisp of a man.

"In that event, the damage done to my property becomes more irresponsible than ever!" cried Rhialto. "I demand compensation before any other general adjustments are made."

Hurtiancz frowned. "I fail to comprehend your meaning."

"It is elegantly simple," said Rhialto. "I suffered serious damage; the balance must be restored. I intend to claim the IOUN stones."

"You will find yourself one among many," said Hurtiancz.

Haze of Wheary Water gave a sardonic snort. "Claim as you please."

Mune the Mage came forward. "The archveult is barely dead; must we bicker so quickly?"

Eshmiel asked, "Is he dead after all? Observe this!" He displayed a linden leaf. "I found it on my blue tile kurtivan. It reads, 'NOTHING THREATENS MORREION'."

"I also found such a leaf!" declared Haze.

"And I!" said Hurtiancz.

"How the centuries roll, one past the other!" mused Ildefonse. "Those were the days of glory, when we sent the archveults flitting like a band of giant bats! Poor Morreion! I have often puzzled as to his fate."

Eshmiel frowned down at his leaf. "'NOTHING THREATENS MORREION' — so we are assured. If such is the case, the notice would seem superfluous and over-helpful."

"It is quite clear," Gilgad grumbled. "Morreion went forth to learn the source of the IOUN stones; he did so, and now is threatened by nothing."

"A possible interpretation," said Ildefonse in a pontifical voice. "There is certainly more here than meets the eye."

"It need not trouble us now," said Rhialto. "To the IOUN stones in present custody, however, I now put forward a formal claim, as compensation for the damage I took in the common cause."

"The statement has a specious plausibility," remarked Gilgad. "Essentially, however, each must benefit in proportion to his contribution. I do not say this merely because it was my Instantaneous Electric Effort which blasted the archveult."

Ao of the Opals said sharply, "Another casuistic assumption which must be rejected out-of-hand, especially since the providential energy allowed Xexamedes to escape!"

The argument continued an hour. Finally a formula proposed by Ildefonse was put to vote and approved by a count of fifteen to one. The goods formerly owned by the archveult Xexamedes were to be set out for inspection. Each magician would list the items in order of choice; Ildefonse would collate the lists. Where conflict occurred determination must be made by lot. Rhialto, in recognition of his loss, was granted a free selection after Choice five had been determined; Gilgad was accorded the same privilege after Choice ten.

Rhialto made a final expostulation: "What value to me is Choice five? The archveult owned nothing but the stones, a few banal adjuncts and these roots, herbs and elixirs."

His views carried no weight. Ildefonse distributed sheets of paper; each magician listed the articles he desired; Ildefonse examined each list in turn. "It appears," he said, "that all present declare their first choice to be the IOUN stones."

Everyone glanced towards the stones; they winked and twinkled with pale white fire.

"Such being the case," said Ildefonse, "determination must be made by chance."

He set forth a crockery pot and sixteen ivory disks. "Each will indite his sign upon one of the chips and place it into the pot, in this fashion." Ildefonse marked one of the chips, dropped it into the pot. "When all have done so, I will call in a servant, who will bring forth a single chip."

"A moment!" exclaimed Byzant. "I apprehend mischief; it walks somewhere near."

Ildefonse turned the sensitive Necrope a glance of cold inquiry. "To what mischief do you refer?"

"I detect a contradiction, a discord; something strange walks among us; there is someone here who should not be here."

"Someone moves unseen!" cried Mune the Mage. "Ildefonse, guard the stones!"

Ildefonse peered here and there through the shadowy old hall. He made a secret signal and pointed to a far corner: "Ghost! Are you on hand?"

A soft sad whisper said, "I am here."

"Respond: who walks unseen among us?"

"Stagnant eddies of the past. I see faces: the less-than-ghosts, the ghosts of dead ghosts…They glimmer and glimpse, they look and go."

"What of living things?"

"No harsh blood, no pulsing flesh, no strident hearts."

"Guard and watch." Ildefonse returned to Byzant the Necrope. "What now?"

"I feel a strange flavor."

"What do you suggest then?"

Byzant spoke softly, to express the exquisite delicacy of his concepts. "Among all here, I alone am sufficiently responsive to the subtlety of the IOUN stones. They should be placed in my custody."

"Let the drawing proceed!" Hurtiancz called out. "Byzant's plan will never succeed."

"Be warned!" cried Byzant. With a black glance towards Hurtiancz, he moved to the rear of the group.

Ildefonse summoned one of his maidens. "Do not be alarmed. You must reach into the pot, thoroughly stir the chips, and bring forth one, which you will then lay upon the table. Do you understand?"

"Yes, Lord Magician."

"Do as I bid."

The girl went to the pot. She reached forth her hand. At this precise instant Rhialto activated a spell of Temporal Stasis, with which, in anticipation of some such emergency, he had come prepared.

Time stood still for all but Rhialto. He glanced around the chamber, at the magicians in their frozen attitudes, at the servant girl with one hand over the pot, at Ildefonse staring at the girl's elbow.

Rhialto leisurely sauntered over to the IOUN stones. He could now take possession, but such an act would arouse a tremendous outcry and all would league themselves against him. A less provocative system was in order. He was startled by a soft sound from the corner of the room, when there should be no sound in still air.

"Who moves?" called Rhialto.

"I move," came the soft voice of the ghost.

"Time is at a standstill. You must not move, or speak, or watch, or know."

"Time, no-time — it is all one. I know each instant over and over."

Rhialto shrugged and turned to the urn. He brought out the chips. To his wonder each was indited 'Ildefonse'.

"Aha!" exclaimed Rhialto. "Some crafty rascal selected a previous

The girl went to the pot. She reached forth her hand.

Morreion

instant for his mischief! Is it not always the case? At the end of this, he and I will know each other the better!" Rhialto rubbed out Ildefonse's signs and substituted his own. Then he replaced all in the pot.

Resuming his former position, he revoked the spell.

Noise softly filled the room. The girl reached into the pot. She stirred the chips, brought forth one of them which she placed upon the table. Rhialto leaned over the chip, as did Ildefonse. It gave a small jerk. The sign quivered and changed before their eyes.

Ildefonse lifted it and in a puzzled voice read, "Gilgad!"

Rhialto glanced furiously at Gilgad, who gave back a bland stare. Gilgad had also halted time, but Gilgad had waited until the chip was actually upon the table.

Ildefonse said in a muffled voice, "That is all. You may go." The girl departed. Ildefonse poured the chips on the table. They were correctly indited; each bore the sign or the signature of one of the magicians present. Ildefonse pulled at his white beard. He said, "It seems that Gilgad has availed himself of the IOUN stones."

Gilgad strode to the table. He emitted a terrible cry. "The stones! What has been done to them?" He held up the net, which now sagged under the weight of its contents. The brooding translucence was gone; the objects in the net shone with a vulgar vitreous glitter. Gilgad took one and dashed it to the floor, where it shattered into splinters. "These are not the IOUN stones! Knavery is afoot!"

"Indeed!" declared Ildefonse. "So much is clear."

"I demand my stones," raved Gilgad. "Give them to me at once or I loose a spell of anguish against all present!"

"One moment," growled Hurtiancz. "Delay your spell. Ildefonse, bring forth your ghost; learn what transpired."

Ildefonse gave his beard a dubious tug, then raised his finger towards the far corner. "Ghost! Are you at hand?"

"I am."

"What occurred while we drew chips from the pot?"

"There was motion. Some moved, some stayed. When the chip at last was laid on the table, a strange shape passed into the room. It took the stones and was gone."

"What manner of strange shape?"

"It wore a skin of blue scales; black plumes rose from its head, still it carried a soul of man."

"Archveult!" muttered Hurtiancz. "I suspect Xexamedes!"

Gilgad cried, "So then, what of my stones, my wonderful stones? How will I regain my property? Must I always be stripped of my valued possessions?"

"Cease your keening!" snapped the diabolist Shrue. "The remaining items must be distributed. Ildefonse, be so good as to consult the lists."

Ildefonse took up the papers. "Since Gilgad won the first draw, his list will now be withdrawn. For second choice —"

He was interrupted by Gilgad's furious complaint. "I protest this intolerable injustice! I won nothing but a handful of glass gewgaws!"

Ildefonse shrugged. "It is the robber-archveult to whom you must complain, especially when the drawing was attended by certain temporal irregularities, to which I need make no further reference."

Gilgad raised his arms in the air; his saturnine face knotted to the surge and counter-surge of his passions. His colleagues watched with dispassionate faces. "Proceed, Ildefonse," said Vermoulian the Dream-walker.

Ildefonse spread out the papers. "It appears that among the group only Rhialto has selected, for second choice, this curiously shaped device, which appears to be one of Houlart's Preterite Recordiums. I therefore make this award and place Rhialto's list with Gilgad's. Perdustin, Barbanikos, Ao of the Opals, and I myself have evinced a desire for this Casque of Sixty Directions, and we must therefore undertake a trial by lot. The jar, four chips —"

"On this occasion," said Perdustin, "let the maid be brought here now. She will put her hand over the mouth of the pot; we will insert the chips between her fingers; thus we ensure against a disruption of the laws of chance."

Ildefonse pulled at his white whiskers, but Perdustin had his way. In this fashion all succeeding lots were drawn. Presently it became Rhialto's turn to make a free choice.

"Well then, Rhialto," said Ildefonse. "What do you select?"

Rhialto's resentment boiled up in his throat. "As restitution for my seventeen exquisite bird-women, my ten-thousand-year-old way-post, I am supposed to be gratified with this packet of Stupefying Dust?"

Ildefonse spoke soothingly. "Human interactions, stimulated as they are by disequilibrium, never achieve balance. In even the most favorable transaction, one party — whether he realizes it or not — must always come out the worse."

"The proposition is not unknown to me," said Rhialto in a more reasonable voice. "However —"

Zilifant uttered a sudden startled cry. "Look!" He pointed to the great mantel-piece; here, camouflaged by the carving, hung a linden leaf. With trembling fingers Ildefonse plucked it down. Silver characters read:

MORREION LIVES A DREAM.
NOTHING IS IMMINENT!

"Ever more confusing," muttered Hurtiancz. "Xexamedes persists in reassuring us that all is well with Morreion: an enigmatic exercise!"

"It must be remembered," the ever cautious Haze pointed out, "that Xexamedes, a renegade, is enemy to all."

Herark the Harbinger held up a black-enameled forefinger. "My habit is to make each problem declare its obverse. The first message, 'NOTHING THREATENS MORREION', becomes 'SOMETHING DOES NOT THREATEN MORREION'; and again, 'NOTHING DOES THREATEN MORREION'."

"Verbiage, prolixity!" grumbled the practical Hurtiancz.

"Not so fast!" said Zilifant. "Herark is notoriously profound! 'NOTHING' might be intended as a delicate reference to death; a niceness of phrase, so to speak."

"Was Xexamedes famous for his exquisite good taste?" asked Hurtiancz with heavy sarcasm. "I think not. Like myself, when he meant 'death' he said 'death'."

"My point exactly!" cried Herark. "I ask myself: What is the 'Nothing', which threatens Morreion? Shrue, what or where is 'Nothing'?"

Shrue hunched his thin shoulders. "It is not to be found among the demon-lands."

"Vermoulian, in your peregrine palace you have traveled far. Where or what is 'Nothing'?"

Vermoulian the Dream-walker declared his perplexity. "I have never discovered such a place."

"Mune the Mage: What or where is 'Nothing'?"

"Somewhere," reflected Mune the Mage, "I have seen a reference to 'Nothing', but I cannot recall the connection."

"The key word is 'reference'," stated Herark. "Ildefonse, be so good as to consult the Great Gloss."

Ildefonse selected a volume from a shelf, threw back the broad covers. "'Nothing'. Various topical references…a metaphysical description…a place? *'Nothing: the nonregion beyond the end of the cosmos.'*"

Hurtiancz suggested, "For good measure, why not consult the entry 'Morreion'?"

Somewhat reluctantly Ildefonse found the reference. He read: "*'Morreion: A legendary hero of the 21st Aeon, who vanquished the archveults and drove them, aghast, to Jangk. Thereupon they took him as far as the mind can reach, to the shining fields where they win their IOUN stones. His erstwhile comrades, who had vowed their protection, put him out of mind, and thereafter nought can be said.'* A biased and inaccurate statement, but interesting nonetheless."

Vermoulian the Dream-walker rose to his feet. "I have been planning an extended journey in my palace; this being the case I will take it upon myself to seek Morreion."

Gilgad gave a croak of fury and dismay. "You think to explore the 'shining fields'! It is I who has earned the right, not you!"

Vermoulian, a large man, sleek as a seal, with a pallid inscrutable face, declared: "My exclusive purpose is to rescue the hero Morreion; the IOUN stones to me are no more than an idle afterthought."

Ildefonse spoke: "Well said! But you will work more efficaciously with a very few trusted colleagues; perhaps myself alone."

"Precisely correct!" asserted Rhialto. "But a third person of proved resource is necessary in the event of danger. I also will share the hardships; otherwise I would think ill of myself."

Hurtiancz spoke with truculent fervor. "I never have been one to hold back! You may rely on me."

"The presence of a Necrope is indispensable," stated Byzant. "I must therefore accompany the group."

Vermoulian asserted his preference for traveling alone, but no one would listen. Vermoulian at last capitulated, with a peevish droop to his usually complacent countenance. "I leave at once. If any are not at the palace within the hour I will understand that they have changed their minds."

"Come, come!" chided Ildefonse. "I need three-and-a-half hours simply to instruct my staff! We require more time."

"The message declared, 'Nothing is imminent'," said Vermoulian. "Haste is of the essence!"

"We must take the word in its context," said Ildefonse. "Morreion has known his present condition several aeons; the word 'imminent' may well designate a period of five hundred years."

With poor grace Vermoulian agreed to delay his departure until the following morning.

5

The ancient sun sank behind the Scaum hills; thin black clouds hung across the maroon afterlight. Rhialto arrived at the outer portal to his domain. He gave a signal and waited confidently for Puiras to lift the boundary curse.

The manse showed no responsive sign.

Rhialto made another signal, stamping impatiently. From the nearby forest of sprawling kang trees came the moaning of a grue, arousing the hairs at the back of Rhialto's neck. He flashed his finger-beams once more: where was Puiras? The white jade tiles of the roof loomed pale through the twilight. He saw no lights. From the forest the grue moaned again and in a plaintive voice called out for solace. Rhialto tested the boundary with a branch, to discover no curse, no protection whatever.

Flinging down the branch, he strode to the manse. All seemed to be in order, though Puiras was nowhere to be found. If he had scoured the hall the effort was not noticeable. Shaking his head in deprecation, Rhialto went to examine the way-post, which was being repaired by his Minuscules. The superintendent flew up on a mosquito to render his report; it seemed that Puiras had neglected to set out the evening victuals. Rhialto did so now and added half an ounce of jellied eel at his own expense.

With a dram of Blue Ruin at his elbow, Rhialto examined the convoluted tubes of bronze which he had brought from the castle of Ildefonse: the so-called Preterite Recordium. He tried to trace the course of the tubes but they wound in and out in a most confusing fashion. He gingerly pressed one of the valves, to evoke a sibilant whispering from the horn. He touched another, and now he heard a far-off guttural song. The sound came not from the horn, but from the pathway, and a moment later Puiras lurched through the door. He turned a vacuous leer toward Rhialto and staggered off toward his quarters.

Rhialto called sharply: "Puiras!"

The servitor lurched about. "What then?"

"You have taken too much to drink; in consequence you are drunk."

Puiras ventured a knowing smirk. "Your perspicacity is keen, your language is exact. I take no exception to either remark."

Rhialto said, "I have no place for an irresponsible or bibulous servant. You are hereby discharged."

"No, you don't!" cried Puiras in a coarse voice, and emphasized the statement with a belch. "They told me I'd have a good post if I stole no more than old Funk and praised your noble airs. Well then! Tonight I stole only moderately, and from me the lack of insult is high praise. So there's the good post and what's a good post without a walk to the village?"

"Puiras, you are dangerously intoxicated," said Rhialto. "What a disgusting sight you are indeed!"

"No compliments!" roared Puiras. "We can't all be fine magicians with fancy clothes at the snap of a finger."

In outrage Rhialto rose to his feet. "Enough! Be off to your quarters before I inflict a torment upon you!"

"That's where I was going when you called me back," replied Puiras sulkily.

Rhialto conceived a further rejoinder to be beneath his dignity. Puiras stumbled away, muttering under his breath.

6

At rest upon the ground, Vermoulian's wonderful peregrine palace, together with its loggias, formal gardens and entrance pavilion, occupied an octagonal site some three acres in extent. The plan of the palace proper was that of a four-pointed star, with a crystal spire at each apex and a spire, somewhat taller, at the center, in which Vermoulian maintained his private chambers. A marble balustrade enclosed the forward pavilion. At the center a fountain raised a hundred jets of water; to either side grew lime trees with silver blossoms and silver fruit. The quadrangles to the right and left were laid out as formal gardens; the area at the rear was planted with herbs and salads for the palace kitchen.

Vermoulian's guests occupied suites in the wings; under the central spire were the various salons, the morning and afternoon rooms, the library, the music chamber, the formal dining room and the lounge.

An hour after sunrise the magicians began to arrive, with Gilgad first on the scene and Ildefonse the last. Vermoulian, his nonchalance restored, greeted each magician with carefully measured affability. After inspecting their suites the magicians gathered in the grand salon. Vermoulian addressed the group. "It is my great pleasure to entertain so distinguished a company! Our goal: the rescue of the hero Morreion! All present are keen and dedicated — but do all understand that we must wander far regions?" Vermoulian turned his placid gaze from face to face. "Are all prepared for tedium, discomfort and danger? Such may well eventuate, and if any have doubts or if any pursue subsidiary goals, such as a search for IOUN stones, now is the time for these persons to return to their respective manses, castles, caves, and eyries. Are any so inclined? No? We depart."

Vermoulian bowed to his now uneasy guests. He mounted to the control belvedere where he cast a spell of buoyancy upon the palace; it rose to drift on the morning breeze like a pinnacled cloud. Vermoulian consulted his Celestial Almanac and made note of certain symbols; these he inscribed upon the carnelian mandate-wheel, which he set into rotation; the signs were spun off into the interflux, to elucidate a route across the universe. Vermoulian fired a taper and held it to the

...it rose to drift on the morning breeze like a pinnacled cloud.

speed-incense; the palace departed; ancient Earth and the waning sun were left behind.

Beside the marble balustrade stood Rhialto. Ildefonse came to join him; the two watched Earth dwindle to a rosy-pink crescent. Ildefonse spoke in a melancholy voice: "When one undertakes a journey of this sort, where the event is unknown, long thoughts come of their own accord. I trust that you left your affairs in order?"

"My household is not yet settled," said Rhialto. "Puiras has proved unsatisfactory; when drunk he sings and performs grotesque capers; when sober he is as surly as a leech on a corpse. This morning I demoted him to Minuscule."

Ildefonse nodded absently. "I am troubled by what I fear to be cross-purposes among our colleagues, worthy fellows though they may be."

"You refer to the 'shining fields' of IOUN stones?" Rhialto put forward delicately.

"I do. As Vermoulian categorically declared, we fare forth to the rescue of Morreion. The IOUN stones can only prove a distraction. Even if a supply were discovered, I suspect that the interests of all might best be served by a highly selective distribution, the venal Gilgad's complaints notwithstanding."

"There is much to be said for this point of view," Rhialto admitted. "It is just as well to have a prior understanding upon a matter so inherently controversial. Vermoulian of course must be allotted a share."

"This goes without saying."

At this moment Vermoulian descended to the pavilion where he was approached by Mune the Mage, Hurtiancz and the others. Mune raised a question regarding their destination. "The question of ultimates becomes important. How, Vermoulian, can you know that this precise direction will take us to Morreion?"

"A question well put," said Vermoulian. "To respond, I must cite an intrinsic condition of the universe. We set forth in any direction which seems convenient; each leads to the same place: the end of the universe."

"Interesting!" declared Zilifant. "In this case, we must inevitably find Morreion; an encouraging prospect!"

Gilgad was not completely satisfied. "What of the 'shining fields' in the reference? Where are these located?"

"A matter of secondary or even tertiary concern," Ildefonse reminded him. "We must think only of the hero Morreion."

"Your solicitude is late by several aeons," said Gilgad waspishly. "Morreion may well have grown impatient."

"Other circumstances intervened," said Ildefonse with a frown of annoyance. "Morreion will certainly understand the situation."

Zilifant remarked. "The conduct of Xexamedes becomes ever more puzzling! As a renegade archveult, he has no ostensible reason to oblige either Morreion, the archveults, or ourselves."

"The mystery in due course will be resolved," said Herark the Harbinger.

7

So went the voyage. The palace drifted through the stars, under and over clouds of flaming gas, across gulfs of deep black space. The magicians meditated in the pergolas, exchanged opinions in the salons over goblets of liquor, lounged upon the marble benches of the pavilion, leaned on the balustrade to look down at the galaxies passing below. Breakfasts were served in the individual suites, luncheons were usually set forth al fresco on the pavilion, the dinners were sumptuous and formal and extended far into the night. To enliven these evenings Vermoulian called forth the most charming, witty and beautiful women of all the past eras, in their quaint and splendid costumes. They found the peregrine palace no less remarkable than the fact of their own presence aboard. Some thought themselves dreaming; others conjectured their own deaths; a few of the more sophisticated made the correct presumption. To facilitate social intercourse Vermoulian gave them command of contemporary language, and the evenings frequently became merry affairs. Rhialto became enamored of a certain Mersei from the land of Mith, long since foundered under the waters of the Shan Ocean. Mersei's charm resided in her slight body, her grave pale face behind which thoughts could be felt but not seen. Rhialto plied her with all gallantry, but she failed to respond, merely looking at him in disinterested silence, until Rhialto wondered if she were slack-witted, or possibly more subtle than himself. Either case made him uncomfortable, and he was not sorry when Vermoulian returned this particular group to oblivion.

Through clouds and constellations they moved, past bursting galaxies and meandering star-streams; through a region where the stars showed a peculiar soft violet and hung in clouds of pale green gas; across a desolation where nothing whatever was seen save a few far luminous clouds. Then presently they came to a new region, where blazing white giants seemed to control whirlpools of pink, blue and white gas, and the magicians lined the balustrade looking out at the spectacle.

At last the stars thinned; the great star-streams were lost in the distance. Space seemed darker and heavier, and finally there came a time when all the stars were behind and nothing lay ahead but darkness. Vermoulian made a grave announcement. "We are now close to the end of the universe! We must go with care. 'Nothing' lies ahead."

"Where then is Morreion?" demanded Hurtiancz. "Surely he is not to be found wandering vacant space."

"Space is not yet vacant," stated Vermoulian. "Here there and roundabout are dead stars and wandering star-hulks; in a sense, we traverse the refuse-heap of the universe, where the dead stars come to await a final destiny; and notice, yonder, far ahead, a single star, the last in the universe. We must approach with caution; beyond lies 'Nothing'."

" 'Nothing' is not yet visible," remarked Ao of the Opals.

"Look more closely!" said Vermoulian. "Do you see that dark wall? That is 'Nothing'."

"Again," said Perdustin, "the question arises: where is Morreion? Back at Ildefonse's castle, when we formed conjectures, the end of the universe seemed a definite spot. Now that we are here, we find a considerable latitude of choice."

Gilgad muttered, half to himself, "The expedition is a farce. I see no 'fields', shining or otherwise."

Vermoulian said, "The solitary star would seem an initial object of investigation. We approach at a rash pace; I must slake the speed-incense."

The magicians stood by the balustrade watching as the far star waxed in brightness. Vermoulian called down from the belvedere to announce a lone planet in orbit around the sun.

"A possibility thereby exists," stated Mune the Mage, "that on this very planet we may find Morreion."

8

The palace moved down to the solitary star and the lone planet became a disk the color of moth-wing. Beyond, clearly visible in the wan sunlight, stood the ominous black wall. Hurtiancz said, "Xexamedes' warning now becomes clear — assuming, of course, that Morreion inhabits this drab and isolated place."

The world gradually expanded, to show a landscape dreary and worn. A few decayed hills rose from the plains; as many ponds gleamed sullenly in the sunlight. The only other features of note were the ruins of once-extensive cities; a very few buildings had defied the ravages of time sufficiently to display a squat and distorted architecture.

The palace settled close above one of the ruins; a band of small weasel-like rodents bounded away into the scrub; no other sign of life was evident. The palace continued west around the planet. Vermoulian presently called down from the belvedere: "Notice the cairn; it marks an ancient thoroughfare."

Other cairns at three-mile intervals appeared, mounds of carefully fitted stones six feet high; they marked a way around the planet.

At the next tumble of ruins Vermoulian, observing a level area, allowed the palace to settle so that the ancient city and its cluster of surviving structures might be explored.

The magicians set off in various directions, the better to pursue their investigations. Gilgad went towards the desolate plaza, Perdustin and Zilifant to the civic amphitheatre, Hurtiancz into a nearby tumble of sandstone blocks. Ildefonse, Rhialto, Mune the Mage and Herark the Harbinger wandered at random, until a raucous chanting brought them up short.

"Peculiar!" exclaimed Herark. "It sounds like the voice of Hurtiancz, the most dignified of men!"

The group entered a cranny through the ruins, which opened into a large chamber, protected from sifting sand by massive blocks of rock. Light filtered through various chinks and apertures; down the middle ran a line of six long slabs. At the far end sat Hurtiancz, watching the entry of the magicians with an imperturbable gaze. On the slab in front of him stood a globe of dark brown glass, or glazed stone. A rack behind him held other similar bottles.

"It appears," said Ildefonse, "that Hurtiancz has stumbled upon the site of the ancient tavern."

"Hurtiancz!" Rhialto called out. "We heard your song and came to investigate. What have you discovered?"

Hurtiancz hawked and spat on the ground. "Hurtiancz!" cried Rhialto. "Do you hear me? Or have you taken too much of this ancient tipple to be sensible?"

Hurtiancz replied in a clear voice, "In one sense I have taken too much: in another, not enough."

Mune the Mage picked up the brown glass bottle and smelled the contents. "Astringent, tart, herbal." He tasted the liquid. "It is quite refreshing."

Ildefonse and Herark the Harbinger each took a brown glass globe from the rack and broke open the bung; they were joined by Rhialto and Mune the Mage.

Ildefonse, as he drank, became garrulous, and presently he fell to speculating in regard to the ancient city: "Just as from one bone the skilled palaeontologist deduces an entire skeleton, so from a single artifact the qualified scholar reconstructs every aspect of the responsible race. As I taste this liquor, as I examine this bottle, I ask myself, What do the dimensions, textures, colors and flavors betoken? No intelligent act is without symbolic significance."

Hurtiancz, upon taking drink, tended to become gruff and surly. Now he stated in an uncompromising voice, "The subject is of small import."

Ildefonse was not to be deterred. "Here the pragmatic Hurtiancz and I, the man of many parts, are at variance. I was about to carry my argument a step farther, and in fact I will do so, stimulated as I am by this elixir of a vanished race. I therefore suggest that in the style of the previous examples, a natural scientist, examining a single atom, might well be able to asseverate the structure and history of the entire universe!"

"Bah!" muttered Hurtiancz. "By the same token, a sensible man need listen to but a single word in order to recognize the whole for egregious nonsense."

Ildefonse, absorbed in his theories, paid no heed. Herark took occasion to state that in his opinion not one, but at least two, even better, three of any class of objects was essential to understanding. "I cite the discipline of mathematics, where a series may not be determined by less than three terms."

"I willingly grant the scientist his three atoms," said Ildefonse, "though in the strictest sense, two of these are supererogatory."

Rhialto, rising from his slab, went to look into a dirt-choked aperture, to discover a passage descending by broad steps into the ground. He caused an illumination to proceed before him and descended the steps. The passage turned once, turned twice, then opened into a large chamber paved with brown stone. The walls held a number of niches, six feet long, two feet high, three feet deep; peering into one of these Rhialto discovered a skeleton of most curious structure, so fragile that the impact of Rhialto's gaze caused it to collapse into dust.

Rhialto rubbed his chin. He looked into a second niche to discover a similar skeleton. He backed away, and stood musing a moment or two. Then he returned up the steps, the drone of Ildefonse's voice growing progressively louder: "— in the same manner to the question: Why does the universe end here and not a mile farther? Of all questions, *why?* is the least pertinent. It begs the question: it assumes the larger part of its own response; to wit, that a sensible response exists." Ildefonse paused to refresh himself, and Rhialto took occasion to relate his discoveries in the chamber below.

"It appears to be a crypt," said Rhialto. "The walls are lined with niches, and each contains the veriest wraith of a dead corpse."

"Indeed, indeed!" muttered Hurtiancz. He lifted the brown glass bottle and at once put it down.

"Perhaps we are mistaken in assuming this place a tavern," Rhialto continued. "The liquid in the bottles, rather than tipple, I believe to be embalming fluid."

Ildefonse was not so easily diverted. "I now propound the basic and elemental verity: What is IS. Here you have heard the basic proposition of magic. What magician asks *Why?* He asks *How? Why* leads to stultification; each response generates at least one other question, in this fashion:

"Question: Why does Rhialto wear a black hat with gold tassels and a scarlet plume?

"Answer: Because he hopes to improve his semblance.

"Question: Why does he want to improve his semblance?

"Answer: Because he craves the admiration and envy of his fellows.

"Question: Why does he crave admiration?

"Answer: Because, as a man, he is a social animal.

"Question: Why is Man a social animal?

"So go the questions and responses, expanding to infinity. Therefore —"

In a passion Hurtiancz leapt to his feet. Raising the brown glass pot above his head he dashed it to the floor. "Enough of this intolerable inanity! I propose that such loquacity passes beyond the scope of nuisance and over the verge of turpitude."

"It is a fine point," said Herark. "Ildefonse, what have you to say on this score?"

"I am more inclined to punish Hurtiancz for his crassness," said Ildefonse. "But now he simulates a swinish stupidity to escape my anger."

"Absolute falsity!" roared Hurtiancz. "I simulate nothing!"

Ildefonse shrugged. "For all his deficiencies as polemicist and magician, Hurtiancz at least is candid."

Hurtiancz controlled his fury. He said, "Who could defeat your volubility? As a magician, however, I outmatch your bumbling skills as Rhialto the Marvellous exceeds your rheumy decrepitude."

Ildefonse in his turn became angry. "A test!" He flung up his hand; the massive blocks scattered in all directions; they stood on a vacant floor in the full glare of sunlight. "What of that?"

"Trivial," said Hurtiancz. "Match this!" He held up his two hands; from each finger issued a jet of vivid smoke in ten different colors.

"The pretty prank of a charlatan," declared Ildefonse. "Now watch! I utter a word: 'Roof!'" The word leaving his lips hesitated in the air, in the form of symbol, then moved out in a wide circle, to impinge upon the roof of one of the strangely styled structures still extant. The symbol disappeared; the roof glowed a vivid orange and melted to spawn a

He flung up his hand; the massive blocks scattered in all directions...

thousand symbols like the word Ildefonse had sent forth. These darted high in the sky, stopped short, disappeared. From above, like a great clap of thunder, came Ildefonse's voice: "ROOF!"

"No great matter," stated Hurtiancz. "Now—"

"Hist!" said Mune the Mage. "Cease your drunken quarrel. Look yonder!"

From the structure whose roof Ildefonse had demolished came a man.

9

The man stood in the doorway. He was impressively tall. A long white beard hung down his chest; white hair covered his ears; his eyes glittered black. He wore an elegant caftan woven in patterns of dark red, brown, black and blue. Now he stepped forward, and it could be seen that he trailed a cloud of glowing objects. Gilgad, who had returned from the plaza, instantly set up a shout: "The IOUN stones!"

The man came forward. His face showed an expression of calm inquiry. Ildefonse muttered, "It is Morreion! Of this there can be no doubt. The stature, the stance — they are unmistakable!"

"It is Morreion," Rhialto agreed. "But why is he so calm, as if each week he received visitors who took off his roof, as if 'Nothing' loomed over someone else?"

"His perceptions may have become somewhat dulled," Herark suggested. "Notice: he evinces no signal of human recognition."

Morreion came slowly forward, the IOUN stones swirling in his wake. The magicians gathered before the marble steps of the palace. Vermoulian stepped forth and raised his hand. "Hail, Morreion! We have come to take you from this intolerable isolation!"

Morreion looked from one face to the other. He made a guttural sound, then a rasping croak, as if trying organs whose use he had long forgotten.

Ildefonse now presented himself. "Morreion, my comrade! It is I, Ildefonse; do you not remember the old days at Kammerbrand? Speak then!"

"I hear," croaked Morreion. "I speak, but I do not remember."

Morreion came slowly forward, the IOUN stones swirling in his wake.

Morreion

Vermoulian indicated the marble stairs. "Step aboard, if you will; we depart this dreary world at once."

Morreion made no move. He examined the palace with a frown of vexation. "You have placed your flying hut upon the area where I dry my skeins."

Ildefonse pointed toward the black wall, which through the haze of the atmosphere showed only as a portentous shadow. "'Nothing' looms close. It is about to impinge upon this world, whereupon you will be no more; in short, you will be dead."

"I am not clear as to your meaning," said Morreion. "If you will excuse me, I must be away and about my affairs."

"A quick question before you go," spoke Gilgad. "Where does one find IOUN stones?"

Morreion looked at him without comprehension. At last he gave his attention to the stones, which swirled with a swifter motion. In comparison, those of the archveult Xexamedes were listless and dull. These danced and curveted, and sparkled with different colors. Closest to Morreion's head moved the lavender and the pale green stones, as if they thought themselves the most loved and most privileged. Somewhat more wayward were the stones glowing pink and green together; then came stones of a proud pure pink, then the royal carmine stones, then the red and blue; and finally, at the outer periphery, a number of stones glittering with intense blue lights.

As Morreion cogitated, the magicians noted a peculiar circumstance: certain of the innermost lavender stones lost their glow and became as dull as the stones of Xexamedes.

Morreion gave a slow thoughtful nod. "Curious! So much which I seem to have forgotten... I did not always live here," he said in a voice of surprise. "There was at one time another place. The memory is dim and remote."

Vermoulian said, "That place is Earth! It is where we will take you."

Morreion smilingly shook his head. "I am just about to start on an important journey."

"Is the trip absolutely necessary?" inquired Mune the Mage. "Our time is limited, and even more to the point, we do not care to be engulfed in 'Nothing'."

"I must see to my cairns," said Morreion in a mild but definite manner.

For a moment there was silence. Then Ildefonse asked, "What is the purpose of these cairns?"

Morreion used the even voice of one speaking to a child. "They indicate the most expeditious route around my world. Without the cairns it is possible to go astray."

"But remember, there is no longer need for such landmarks," said Ao of the Opals. "You will be returning to Earth with us!"

Morreion could not restrain a small laugh at the obtuse persistence of his visitors. "Who would look after my properties? How could I fare if my cairns toppled, if my looms broke, if my kilns crumbled, if my other enterprises dissolved, and all for the lack of methodical care?"

Vermoulian said blandly, "At least come aboard the palace to share our evening banquet."

"It will be my pleasure," replied Morreion. He mounted the marble steps, to gaze with pleasure around the pavilion. "Charming. I must consider something of this nature as a forecourt for my new mansion."

"There will be insufficient time," Rhialto told him.

"'Time'?" Morreion frowned as if the word were unfamiliar to him. Other of the lavender stones suddenly went pale. "Time indeed! But time is required to do a proper job! This gown for instance." He indicated his gorgeously patterned caftan. "The weaving required four years. Before that I gathered beast-fur for ten years; then for another two years I bleached and dyed and spun. My cairns were built a stone at a time, each time I wandered around the world. My wanderlust has waned somewhat, but I occasionally make the journey, to rebuild where necessary, and to note the changes of the landscape."

Rhialto pointed to the sun. "Do you recognize the nature of that object?"

Morreion frowned. "I call it 'the sun' — though why I have chosen this particular term escapes me."

"There are many such suns," said Rhialto. "Around one of them swings that ancient and remarkable world which gave you birth. Do you remember Earth?"

Morreion looked dubiously up into the sky. "I have seen none of these other suns you describe. At night my sky is quite dark; there is no other light the world over save the glow of my fires. It is a peaceful world indeed... I seem to recall more eventful times." The last of the lavender stones and certain of the green stones lost their color. Morreion's eyes became momentarily intent. He went to inspect the tame water-nymphs which sported in the central fountain. "And what might be these glossy little creatures? They are most appealing."

"They are quite fragile, and useful only as show," said Vermoulian. "Come, Morreion, my valet will help you prepare for the banquet."

"You are most gracious," said Morreion.

10

The magicians awaited their guest in the grand salon. Each had his own opinion of the circumstances. Rhialto said, "Best that we raise the palace now and so be off and away. Morreion may be agitated for a period, but when all the facts are laid before him he must surely see reason."

The cautious Perdustin demurred. "There is power in the man! At one time, his magic was a source of awe and wonder; what if in a fit of pique he wreaks a harm upon all of us?"

Gilgad endorsed Perdustin's view. "Everyone has noted Morreion's IOUN stones. Where did he acquire them? Can this world be the source?"

"Such a possibility should not automatically be dismissed," admitted Ildefonse. "Tomorrow, when the imminence of 'Nothing' is described, Morreion will surely depart without resentment."

So the matter rested. The magicians turned their discussion to other aspects of this dismal world.

Herark the Harbinger, who had skill as a cognizancer, attempted to divine the nature of the race which had left ruins across the planet, without notable success. "They have been gone too long; their influence has waned. I seem to discern creatures with thin white legs and large green eyes... I hear a whisper of their music: a jingling, a tinkle, to a rather plaintive obbligato of pipes... I sense no magic. I doubt if they recognized the IOUN stones, if in fact such exist on this planet."

"Where else could they originate?" demanded Gilgad.

"The 'shining fields' are nowhere evident," remarked Haze of Wheary Water.

Morreion entered the hall. His appearance had undergone a dramatic change. The great white beard had been shaved away; his bush of hair had been cropped to a more modish style. In the place of his gorgeous caftan he wore a garment of ivory silk with a blue sash and a pair of scarlet slippers. Morreion now stood revealed as a tall spare man, attentive and alert. Glittering black eyes dominated his face, which was taut, harsh at chin and jaw, massive of forehead, disciplined in the even lines of the mouth. The lethargy and boredom of so many aeons were nowhere evident; he moved with easy command, and behind him, darting and circling, swarmed the IOUN stones.

Morreion greeted the assembled magicians with an inclination of the head, and gave his attention to the appointments of the salon. "Magnificent and luxurious! But I will be forced to use quartz in the place of this splendid marble, and there is little silver to be found; the Sahars plundered all the surface ores. When I need metal I must tunnel deep underground."

"You have led a busy existence," declared Ildefonse. "And who were the Sahars?"

"The race whose ruins mar the landscape. A frivolous and irresponsible folk, though I admit that I find their poetic conundrums amusing."

"The Sahars still exist?"

"Indeed not! They became extinct long ages ago. But they left numerous records etched on bronze, which I have taken occasion to translate."

"A tedious job, surely!" exclaimed Zilifant. "How did you achieve so complicated a task?"

"By the process of elimination," Morreion explained. "I tested a succession of imaginary languages against the inscriptions, and in due course I found a correspondence. As you say, the task was time-consuming; still I have had much entertainment from the Sahar chronicles. I want to orchestrate their musical revelries; but this is a task for the future, perhaps after I complete the palace I now intend."

Ildefonse spoke in a grave voice. "Morreion, it becomes necessary to impress certain important matters upon you. You state that you have not studied the heavens?"

"Not extensively," admitted Morreion. "There is little to be seen save the sun, and under favorable conditions a great wall of impenetrable blackness."

"That wall of blackness," said Ildefonse, "is 'Nothing', toward which your world is inexorably drifting. Any further work here is futile."

Morreion's black eyes glittered with doubt and suspicion. "Can you prove this assertion?"

"Certainly. Indeed we came here from Earth to rescue you."

Morreion frowned. Certain of the green stones abruptly lost their color. "Why did you delay so long?"

Ao of the Opals gave a bray of nervous laughter, which he quickly stifled. Ildefonse turned him a furious glare.

"Only recently were we made aware of your plight," explained Rhialto. "Upon that instant we prevailed upon Vermoulian to bring us hither in his peregrine palace."

Vermoulian's bland face creased in displeasure. "'Prevailed' is not correct!" he stated. "I was already on my way when the others insisted on coming along. And now, if you will excuse us for a few moments, Morreion and I have certain important matters to discuss."

"Not so fast," Gilgad cried out. "I am equally anxious to learn the source of the stones."

Ildefonse said, "I will put the question in the presence of us all. Morreion, where did you acquire your IOUN stones?"

Morreion looked around at the stones. "To be candid, the facts are somewhat vague. I seem to recall a vast shining surface...But why do you ask? They have no great usefulness. So many ideas throng upon me. It seems that I had enemies at one time, and false friends. I must try to remember."

Ildefonse said, "At the moment you are among your faithful friends, the magicians of Earth. And if I am not mistaken, the noble Vermoulian is about to set before us the noblest repast in any of our memories!"

Morreion said with a sour smile, "You must think my life that of a savage. Not so! I have studied the Sahar cuisine and improved upon it! The lichen which covers the plain may be prepared in at least one hundred seventy fashions. The turf beneath is the home of succulent helminths. For all its drab monotony, this world provides a bounty. If what you say is true, I shall be sorry indeed to leave."

"The facts cannot be ignored," said Ildefonse. "The IOUN stones, so I suppose, derive from the northern part of this world?"

"I believe not."

"The southern area, then?"

"I rarely visit this section; the lichen is thin; the helminths are all gristle."

A gong-stroke sounded; Vermoulian ushered the company into the dining room, where the great table glittered with silver and crystal. The magicians seated themselves under the five chandeliers; in deference to his guest who had lived so long in solitude, Vermoulian refrained from calling forth the beautiful women of ancient eras.

Morreion ate with caution, tasting all set before him, comparing the dishes to the various guises of lichen upon which he usually subsisted. "I had almost forgotten the existence of such food," he said at last. "I am reminded, dimly, of other such feasts — so long ago, so long… Where have the years gone? Which is the dream?" As he mused, some of the pink and green stones lost their color. Morreion sighed. "There is much to be learned, much to be remembered. Certain faces here arouse flickering recollections; have I known them before?"

"You will recall all in due course," said the diabolist Shrue. "And now, if we are certain that the IOUN stones are not to be found on this planet —"

"But we are not sure!" snapped Gilgad. "We must seek, we must search; no effort is too arduous!"

"The first to be found necessarily will go to satisfy my claims," declared Rhialto. "This must be a definite understanding."

Gilgad thrust his vulpine face forward. "What nonsense is this? Your claims were satisfied by a choice from the effects of the archveult Xexamedes!"

Morreion jerked around. "The archveult Xexamedes! I know this name… How? Where? Long ago I knew an archveult Xexamedes; he was my foe, or so it seems… Ah, the ideas which roil my mind!" The pink and green stones all had lost their color. Morreion groaned and put his hands to his head. "Before you came my life was placid; you have brought me doubt and wonder."

"Doubt and wonder are the lot of all men," said Ildefonse. "Magicians are not excluded. Are you ready to leave Sahar Planet?"

Morreion sat looking into a goblet of wine. "I must collect my books. They are all I wish to take away."

11

Morreion conducted the magicians about his premises. The structures which had seemed miraculous survivals had in fact been built by Morreion, after one or another mode of the Sahar architecture. He displayed his three looms: the first for fine weaves, linens and silks; the second where he contrived patterned cloths; the third where his heavy rugs were woven. The same structure housed vats, dyes, bleaches and mordants. Another building contained the glass cauldron, as well as the kilns where Morreion produced earthenware pots, plates, lamps and tiles. His forge in the same building showed little use. "The Sahars scoured the planet clean of ores. I mine only what I consider indispensable, which is not a great deal."

Morreion took the group to his library, in which were housed many Sahar originals as well as books Morreion had written and illuminated with his own hand: translations of the Sahar classics, an encyclopedia of natural history, ruminations and speculations, a descriptive geography of the planet with appended maps. Vermoulian ordered his staff to transfer the articles to the palace.

Morreion turned a last look around the landscape he had known so long and had come to love. Then without a word he went to the palace and climbed the marble steps. In a subdued mood the magicians followed. Vermoulian went at once to the control belvedere where he performed rites of buoyancy. The palace floated up from the final planet.

Ildefonse gave an exclamation of shock. "'Nothing' is close at hand — more imminent than we had suspected!"

The black wall loomed startlingly near; the last star and its single world drifted at the very brink.

"The perspectives are by no means clear," said Ildefonse. "There is no sure way of judging but it seems that we left not an hour too soon."

"Let us wait and watch," suggested Herark. "Morreion can learn our good faith for himself."

So the palace hung in space, with the pallid light of the doomed sun playing upon the five crystal spires, projecting long shadows behind the magicians where they stood by the balustrade.

The Sahar world was first to encounter 'Nothing'. It grazed against the enigmatic nonsubstance, then urged by a component of orbital motion, a quarter of the original sphere moved out clear and free: a moundlike object with a precisely flat base, where the hitherto secret strata, zones, folds, intrusions and core were displayed to sight. The sun reached 'Nothing'; it touched, advanced. It became a half-orange on a black mirror, then sank away from reality. Darkness shrouded the palace.

In the belvedere Vermoulian indited symbols on the mandate-wheel. He struck them off, then put double fire to the speed-incense. The palace glided away, back towards the star-clouds.

Morreion turned away from the balustrade and went into the great hall, where he sat deep in thought.

Gilgad presently approached him. "Perhaps you have recalled the source of the IOUN stones?"

Morreion rose to his feet. He turned his level black eyes upon Gilgad, who stepped back a pace. The pink and green stones had long become pallid, and many of the pink as well.

Morreion's face was stern and cold. "I recall much! There was a cabal of enemies who tricked me — but all is as dim as the film of stars which hangs across far space. In some fashion, the stones are part and parcel of the matter. Why do you evince so large an interest in stones? Were you one of my former enemies? Is this the case with all of you? If so, beware! I am a mild man until I encounter antagonism."

The diabolist Shrue spoke soothingly. "We are not your enemies! Had we not lifted you from Sahar Planet, you would now be with 'Nothing'. Is that not proof?"

Morreion gave a grim nod; but he no longer seemed the mild and affable man they had first encountered.

To restore the previous amiability, Vermoulian hastened to the room of faded mirrors where he maintained his vast collection of beautiful women in the form of matrices. These could be activated into corporeality by a simple antinegative incantation; and presently from the room, one after the other, stepped those delightful confections of the past which Vermoulian had seen fit to revivify. On each occasion they came forth fresh, without recollection of previous manifestations; each appearance was new, no matter how affairs had gone before.

Among those whom Vermoulian had called forth was the graceful Mersei. She stepped into the grand salon, blinking in the bewilderment common to those evoked from the past. She stopped short in amazement, then with quick steps ran forward. "Morreion! What do you do here? They told us you had gone against the archveults, that you had been killed! By the Sacred Ray, you are sound and whole!"

Morreion looked down at the young woman in perplexity. The pink and red stones wheeled around his head. "Somewhere I have seen you; somewhere I have known you."

"I am Mersei! Do you not remember? You brought me a red rose growing in a porcelain vase. Oh, what have I done with it? I always keep it near… But where am I? Where is the rose? No matter. I am here and you are here."

Ildefonse muttered to Vermoulian, "An irresponsible act, in my judgment; why were you not more cautious?"

Vermoulian pursed his lips in vexation. "She stems from the waning of the 21st Aeon but I had not anticipated anything like this!"

"I suggest that you call her back into your room of matrices and there reduce her. Morreion seems to be undergoing a period of instability; he needs peace and quietude; best not to introduce stimulations so unpredictable."

Vermoulian strolled across the room. "Mersei, my dear; would you be good enough to step this way?"

Mersei cast him a dubious look, then beseeched Morreion: "Do you not know me? Something is very strange; I can understand nothing of this — it is like a dream. Morreion, am I dreaming?"

"Come, Mersei," said Vermoulian suavely. "I wish a word with you."

"Stop!" spoke Morreion. "Magician, stand back; this fragrant creature is something which once I loved, at a time far gone."

The girl cried in a poignant voice: "A time far gone? It was no more than yesterday! I tended the sweet red rose, I looked at the sky; they

Among those whom Vermoulian had called forth was the graceful Mersei.

had sent you to Jangk, by the red star Kerkaju, the eye of the Polar Ape. And now you are here, and I am here — what does it mean?"

"Inadvisable, inadvisable," muttered Ildefonse. He called out: "Morreion, this way, if you will. I see a curious concatenation of galaxies. Perhaps here is the new home of the Sahars."

Morreion put his hand to the girl's shoulder. He looked into her face. "The sweet red rose blooms, and forever. We are among magicians and strange events occur." He glanced aside at Vermoulian, then back to Mersei. "At this moment, go with Vermoulian the Dream-walker, who will show you to your chamber."

"Yes, dear Morreion, but when will I see you again? You look so strange, so strained and old, and you speak so peculiarly —"

"Go now, Mersei. I must confer with Ildefonse."

Vermoulian led Mersei back towards the room of matrices. At this door she hesitated and looked back over her shoulder, but Morreion had already turned away. She followed Vermoulian into the room. The door closed behind them.

Morreion walked out on the pavilion, past the dark lime trees with their silver fruit, and leaned upon the balustrade. The sky was still dark, although ahead and below a few vagrant galaxies could now be seen. Morreion put his hand to his head; the pink stones and certain of the red stones lost their color.

Morreion swung around towards Ildefonse and those other magicians who had silently come out on the pavilion. He stepped forward, the IOUN stones tumbling one after the other in their hurry to keep up. Some were yet red, some showed shifting glints of blue and red, some burnt a cold incandescent blue. All the others had become the color of pearl. One of these drifted in front of Morreion's eyes; he caught it, gave it a moment of frowning inspection, then tossed it into the air. Spinning and jerking, with color momentarily restored, it was quick to rejoin the others, like a child embarrassed.

"Memory comes and goes," mused Morreion. "I am unsettled, in mind and heart. Faces drift before my eyes; they fade once more; other events move into a region of clarity. The archveults, the IOUN stones — I know something of these, though much is dim and murky, so best that I hold my tongue —"

"By no means!" declared Ao of the Opals. "We are interested in your experiences."

"To be sure!" said Gilgad.

Morreion's mouth twisted in a smile that was both sardonic and harsh, and also somewhat melancholy. "Very well, I tell this story, then, as if I were telling a dream.

"It seems that I was sent to Jangk on a mission — perhaps to learn the provenance of the IOUN stones? Perhaps. I hear whispers which tell me so much; it well may be... I arrived at Jangk; I recall the landscape well. I remember a remarkable castle hollowed from an enormous pink pearl. In this castle I confronted the archveults. They feared me and stood back, and when I stated my wishes there was no demur. They would indeed take me to gather stones, and so we set out, flying through space in an equipage whose nature I cannot recall. The archveults were silent and watched me from the side of their eyes; then they became affable and I wondered at their mirth. But I felt no fear. I knew all their magic; I carried counter-spells at my fingernails, and at need could fling them off instantly. So we crossed space, with the archveults laughing and joking in what I considered an insane fashion. I ordered them to stop. They halted instantly and sat staring at me.

"We arrived at the edge of the universe, and came down upon a sad cinder of a world; a dreadful place. Here we waited in a region of burnt-out star-hulks, some still hot, some cold, some cinders like the world on which we stood — perhaps it, too, was a dead star. Occasionally we saw the corpses of dwarf stars, glistening balls of stuff so heavy that a speck outweighs an Earthly mountain. I saw such objects no more than ten miles across, containing the matter of a sun like vast Kerkaju. Inside these dead stars, the archveults told me, were to be found the IOUN stones. And how were they to be won? I asked. Must we drive a tunnel into that gleaming surface? They gave mocking calls of laughter at my ignorance; I uttered a sharp reprimand; instantly they fell silent. The spokesman was Xexamedes. From him I learned that no power known to man or magician could mar stuff so dense! We must wait.

"'Nothing' loomed across the distance. Often the derelict hulks swung close in their orbits. The archveults kept close watch; they pointed and calculated, they carped and fretted; at last one of the shining balls struck across 'Nothing', expunging half of itself. When it swung out and away the archveults took their equipage down to the flat surface. All now ventured forth, with most careful precaution; unprotected from gravity a man instantly becomes as no more than an outline upon the surface. With slide-boards immune to gravity we traversed the surface.

"What a wonderful sight! 'Nothing' had wrought a flawless polish; for fifteen miles this mirrored plain extended, marred only at the very center by a number of black pock-marks. Here the IOUN stones were to be found, in nests of black dust.

"To win the stones is no small task. The black dust, like the slide-boards, counters gravity. It is safe to step from the slide-boards to the dust, but a new precaution must be taken. While the dust negates the substance below, other celestial objects suck, so one must use an anchor to hold himself in place. The archveults drive small barbed hooks into the dust, and tie themselves down with a cord, and this I did as well. By means of a special tool the dust is probed — a tedious task! The dust is packed tightly! Nevertheless, with great energy I set to work and in due course won my first IOUN stone. I held it high in exultation, but where were the archveults? They had circled around me; they had returned to the equipage! I sought my slide-boards — in vain! By stealth they had been purloined!

"I staggered, I sagged; I raved a spell at the traitors. They held forward their newly won IOUN stones; the magic was absorbed, as water entering a sponge.

"With no further words, not even signals of triumph — for this is how lightly they regarded me — they entered their equipage and were gone. In this region contiguous with 'Nothing', my doom was certain — so they were assured."

As Morreion spoke the red stones went pale; his voice quavered with a passion he had not hitherto displayed.

"I stood alone," said Morreion hoarsely. "I could not die, with the Spell of Untiring Nourishment upon me, but I could not move a step, not an inch from the cavity of black dust, or I would instantly have been no more than a print upon the surface of the shining field.

"I stood rigid — how long I cannot say. Years? Decades? I cannot

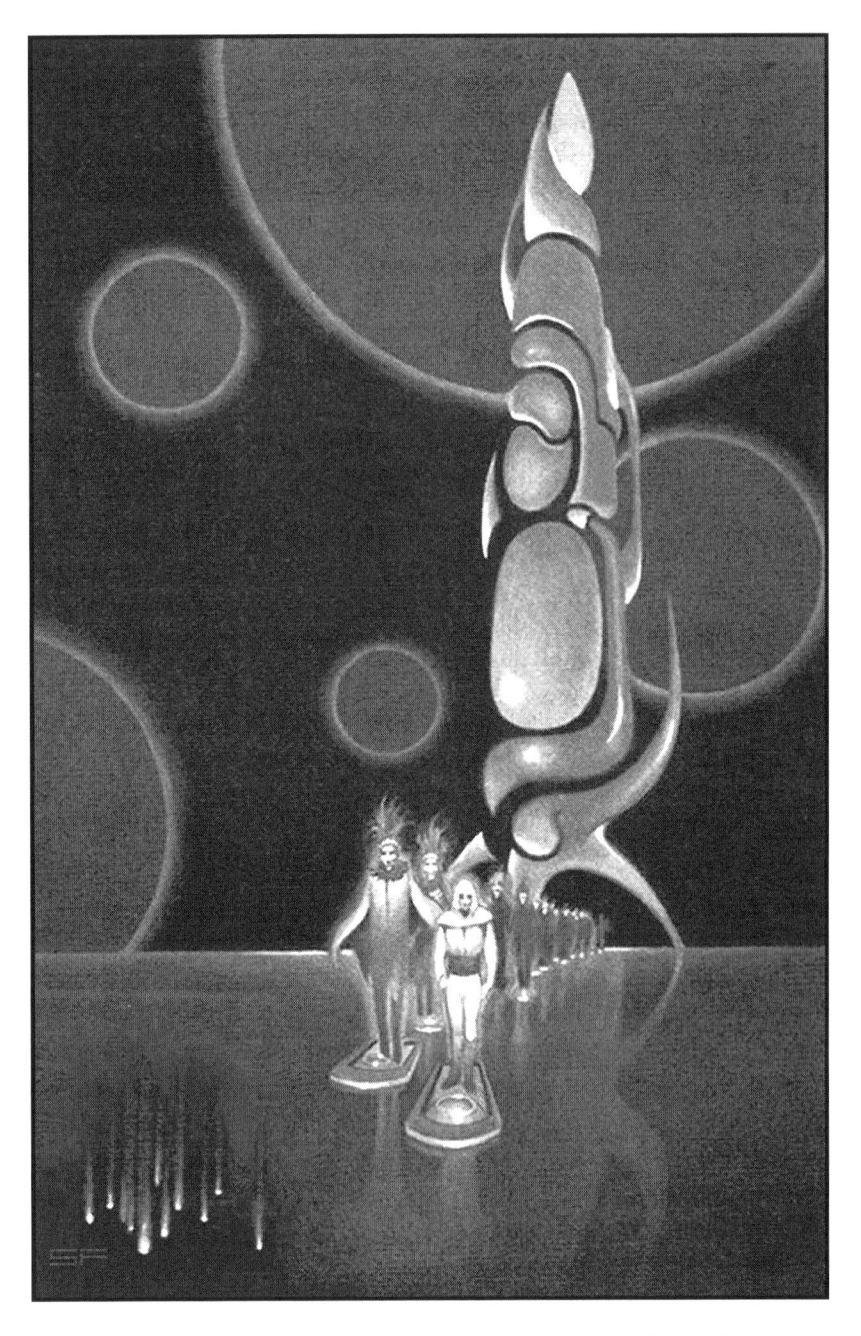

With slide-boards immune to gravity we traversed the surface.

remember. This period seems a time of dull daze. I searched my mind for resources, and I grew bold with despair. I probed for IOUN stones, and I won those which now attend me. They became my friends and gave me solace.

"I embarked then upon a new task, which, had I not been mad with despair, I would never have attempted. I brought up particles of black dust, wet them with blood to make a paste; this paste I molded into a circular plate four feet in diameter.

"It was finished. I stepped aboard; I anchored myself with the barbed pins, and I floated up and away from the half-star.

"I had won free! I stood on my disk in the void! I was free, but I was alone. You cannot know what I felt until you, too, have stood in space, without knowledge of where to go. Far away I saw a single star; a rogue, a wanderer; toward this star I fared.

"How long the voyage required, again I cannot say. When I judged that I had traveled half-way, I turned the disk about and slowed my motion.

"Of this voyage I remember little. I spoke to my stones, I gave them my thoughts. I seemed to become calm from talking, for during the first hundred years of this voyage I felt a prodigious fury that seemed to overwhelm all rational thought; to inflict but a pin prick upon a single one of my adversaries I would have died by torture a hundred times! I plotted delicious vengeance, I became yeasty and exuberant upon the imagined pain I would inflict. Then at times I suffered unutterable melancholy — while others enjoyed the good things of life, the feasts, the comradeship, the caresses of their loved ones, here stood I, alone in the dark. The balance would be restored, I assured myself. My enemies would suffer as I had suffered, and more! But the passion waned, and as my stones grew to know me they assumed their beautiful colors. Each has his name; each is individual; I know each stone by its motion. The archveults consider them the brain-eggs of fire-folk who live within these stars; as to this I cannot say.

"At last I came down upon my world. I had burned away my rage. I was calm and placid, as now you know me. My old lust for revenge I saw to be futility. I turned my mind to a new existence, and over the aeons I built my buildings and my cairns; I lived my new life.

"The Sahars excited my interest. I read their books, I learned their lore…Perhaps I began to live a dream. My old life was far away; a discordant trifle to which I gave ever less importance. I am amazed that the language of Earth returned to me as readily as it has. Perhaps the stones held my knowledge in trust, and extended it as the need came. Ah, my wonderful stones, what would I be without them?

"Now I am back among men. I know how my life has gone. There are still confused areas; in due course I will remember all."

Morreion paused to consider; several of the blue and scarlet stones went quickly dim. Morreion quivered, as if touched by galvanic essence; his cropped white hair seemed to bristle. He took a slow step forward; certain of the magicians made uneasy movements.

Morreion spoke in a new voice, one less reflective and reminiscent, with a harsh grating sound somewhere at its basis. "Now I will confide in you." He turned the glitter of his black eyes upon each face in turn. "I intimated that my rage had waned with the aeons; this is true. The sobs which lacerated my throat, the gnashing which broke my teeth, the fury which caused my brain to shudder and ache: all dwindled; for I had nothing with which to feed my emotions. After bitter reflection came tragic melancholy, then at last peace, which your coming disturbed.

"A new mood has now come upon me! As the past becomes real, so I have returned along the way of the past. There is a difference. I am now a cold cautious man; perhaps I can never experience the extremes of passion which once consumed me. On the other hand, certain periods in my life are still dim." Another of the red and scarlet stones lost its vivid glow; Morreion stiffened, his voice took on a new edge. "The crimes upon my person call out for rebuttal! The archveults of Jangk must pay in the fullest and most onerous measure! Vermoulian the Dream-walker, expunge the present symbols from your mandate-wheel! Our destination now becomes the planet Jangk!"

Vermoulian looked to his colleagues to learn their opinion.

Ildefonse cleared his throat. "I suggest that our host Vermoulian first pause at Earth, to discharge those of us with urgent business. Those others will continue with Vermoulian and Morreion to Jangk; in this way the convenience of all may be served."

Morreion said in a voice ominously quiet: "No business is as urgent as mine, which already has been delayed too long." He spoke to Vermoulian: "Apply more fire to the speed-incense! Proceed directly to Jangk."

Haze of Wheary Water said diffidently, "I would be remiss if I failed to remind you that the archveults are powerful magicians; like yourself they wield IOUN stones."

Morreion made a furious motion; as his hand swept the air, it left a trail of sparks. "Magic derives from personal force! My passion alone will defeat the archveults! I glory in the forthcoming confrontation. Ah, but they will regret their deeds!"

"Forbearance has been termed the noblest of virtues," Ildefonse suggested. "The archveults have long forgotten your very existence; your vengeance will seem an unjust and unnecessary tribulation."

Morreion swung around his glittering black gaze. "I reject the concept. Vermoulian, obey!"

"We fare towards Jangk," said Vermoulian.

12

On a marble bench between a pair of silver-fruited lime trees sat Ildefonse. Rhialto stood beside him, one elegant leg raised to the bench; a posture which displayed his rose satin cape with the white lining to dramatic advantage. They drifted through a cluster of a thousand stars; great lights passed above, below, to each side; the crystal spires of the palace gave back millions of scintillations.

Rhialto had already expressed his concern at the direction of events. Now he spoke again, more emphatically. "It is all very well to point out that the man lacks facility; as he asserts, sheer force can overpower sophistication."

Ildefonse said bluffly, "Morreion's force is that of hysteria, diffuse and undirected."

"Therein lies the danger! What if by some freak his wrath focuses upon us?"

"Bah, what then?" demanded Ildefonse. "Do you doubt my ability, or your own?"

"The prudent man anticipates contingencies," said Rhialto with dignity. "Remember, a certain area of Morreion's life remains clouded."

Ildefonse tugged thoughtfully at his white beard. "The aeons have altered all of us; Morreion not the least of any."

"This is the core of my meaning," said Rhialto. "I might mention that not an hour since I essayed a small experiment. Morreion walked the third balcony, watching the stars pass by. His attention being diverted, I took occasion to project a minor spell of annoyance towards him — Houlart's Visceral Pang — but with no perceptible effect. Next I attempted the diminutive version of Lugwiler's Dismal Itch, again without success. I noted, however, his IOUN stones pulsed bright as they absorbed the magic. I tried my own Green Turmoil; the stones glowed bright and this time Morreion became aware of the attention. By happy chance Byzant the Necrope passed by. Morreion put an accusation upon him, which Byzant denied. I left them engaged in contention. The instruction is this: first, Morreion's stones guard him from hostile magic; second, he is vigilant and suspicious; third, he is not one to shrug aside an offense."

Ildefonse nodded gravely. "We must certainly take these matters into consideration. I now appreciate the scope of Xexamedes's plan: he intended harm to all. But behold in the sky yonder! Is that not the constellation Elektha, seen from obverse? We are in familiar precincts once more. Kerkaju must lie close ahead, and with it that extraordinary planet Jangk."

The two strolled to the forward part of the pavilion. "You are right!" exclaimed Rhialto. He pointed. "There is Kerkaju; I recognize its scarlet empharism!"

The planet Jangk appeared: a world with a curious dull sheen.

At Morreion's direction, Vermoulian directed the palace down to Smokedancers Bluff, at the southern shore of the Quicksilver Ocean. Guarding themselves against the poisonous air, the magicians descended the marble steps and walked out on the bluff, where an inspiring vista spread before them. Monstrous Kerkaju bulged across the green sky, every pore and flocculation distinct, its simulacrum mirrored in the Quicksilver Ocean. Directly below, at the base of the bluff, quicksilver puddled and trickled across flats of black hornblende;

here the Jangk 'dragoons' — purple pansy-shaped creatures six feet in diameter — grazed on tufts of moss. Somewhat to the east the town Kaleshe descended in terraces to the shore.

Morreion, standing at the edge of the bluff, inhaled the noxious vapors which blew in from the ocean, as if they were a tonic. "My memory quickens," he called out. "I remember this scene as if it were yesterday. There have been changes, true. Yonder far peak has eroded to half its height; the bluffs on which we stand have been thrust upwards at least a hundred feet. Has it been so long? While I built my cairns and pored over my books the aeons flitted past. Not to mention the unknown period I rode through space on a disk of blood and star-stuff. Let us proceed to Kaleshe; it was formerly the haunt of the archveult Persain."

"When you encounter your enemies, what then?" asked Rhialto. "Are your spells prepared and ready?"

"What need I for spells?" grated Morreion. "Behold!" He pointed his finger; a flicker of emotion spurted forth to shatter a boulder. He clenched his fists; the constricted passion cracked as if he had crumpled stiff parchment. He strode off toward Kaleshe, the magicians trooping behind.

The Kalsh had seen the palace descend; a number had gathered at the top of the bluff. Like the archveults they were sheathed in pale blue scales. Osmium cords constricted the black plumes of the men; the feathery green plumes of the women, however, waved and swayed as they walked. All stood seven feet tall, and were slim as lizards.

Morreion halted. "Persain, stand forth!" he called.

One of the men spoke: "There is no Persain at Kaleshe."

"What? No archveult Persain?"

"None of this name. The local archveult is a certain Evorix, who departed in haste at the sight of your peregrine palace."

"Who keeps the town records?"

Another Kalsh stepped forth. "I am that functionary."

"Are you acquainted with Persain the archveult?"

"I know by repute a Persain who was swallowed by a harpy towards the end of the 21st Aeon."

Morreion uttered a groan. "Has he evaded me? What of Xexamedes?"

"He is gone from Jangk; no one knows where."

"Djorin?"

He pointed his finger; a flicker of emotion spurted forth…

"He lives, but keeps to a pink pearl castle across the ocean."
"Aha! What of Ospro?"
"Dead."
Morreion gave another abysmal groan. "Vexel?"
"Dead."
Morreion groaned once more. Name by name he ran down the roster of his enemies. Four only survived.

When Morreion turned about his face had become haunted and haggard; he seemed not to see the magicians of Earth. All of his scarlet and blue stones had given up their color. "Four only," he muttered. "Four only to receive the charge of all my force... Not enough, not enough! So many have won free! Not enough, not enough! The balance must adjust!" He made a brusque gesture. "Come! To the castle of Djorin!"

In the palace they drifted across the ocean while the great red globe of Kerkaju kept pace above and below. Cliffs of mottled quartz and cinnabar rose ahead; on a crag jutting over the ocean stood a castle in the shape of a great pink pearl.

The peregrine palace settled upon a level area; Morreion leapt down the steps and advanced toward the castle. A circular door of solid osmium rolled back; an archveult nine feet tall, with black plumes waving three feet over his head, came forth.

Morreion called, "Send forth Djorin; I have dealings with him."

"Djorin is within! We have had a presentiment! You are the land-ape Morreion, from the far past. Be warned; we are prepared for you."

"Djorin!" called Morreion. "Come forth!"

"Djorin will not come forth," stated the archveult, "nor will Arvianid, Ishix, Herclamon, or the other archveults of Jangk who have come to combine their power against yours. If you seek vengeance, turn upon the real culprits; do not annoy us with your peevish complaints." The archveult returned within and the osmium door rolled shut.

Morreion stood stock-still. Mune the Mage came forward, and stated: "I will winkle them out, with Houlart's Blue Extractive." He hurled the spell toward the castle, to no effect. Rhialto attempted a spell of brain pullulations, but the magic was absorbed; Gilgad next brought down his Instantaneous Galvanic Thrust, which spattered harmlessly off the glossy pink surface.

"Useless," said Ildefonse. "Their IOUN stones absorb the magic."

The archveults in their turn became active. Three ports opened; three spells simultaneously issued forth, to be intercepted by Morreion's IOUN stones, which momentarily pulsed the brighter.

Morreion stepped three paces forward. He pointed his finger; force struck at the osmium door. It creaked and rattled, but held firm.

Morreion pointed his finger at the fragile pink nacre; the force slid away and was wasted.

Morreion pointed at the stone posts which supported the castle. They burst apart. The castle lurched, rolled over and down the crags. It bounced from jut to jut, smashing and shattering, and splashed into the Quicksilver Ocean, where a current caught it and carried it out to sea. Through rents in the nacre the archveults crawled forth, to clamber to the top. More followed, until their accumulated weight rolled the pearl over, throwing all on top into the quicksilver sea, where they sank as deep as their thighs. Some tried to walk and leap to the shore, others lay flat on their backs and sculled with their hands. A gust of wind caught the pink bubble and sent it rolling across the sea, tossing off archveults as a turning wheel flings away drops of water. A band of Jangk harpies put out from the shore to envelop and devour the archveults closest at hand; the others allowed themselves to drift on the current and out to sea, where they were lost to view.

Morreion turned slowly toward the magicians of Earth. His face was gray. "A fiasco," he muttered. "It is nothing."

Slowly he walked toward the palace. At the steps he stopped short. "What did they mean: 'The real culprits'?"

"A figure of speech," replied Ildefonse. "Come up on the pavilion; we will refresh ourselves with wine. At last your vengeance is complete. And now…" His voice died as Morreion climbed the steps. One of the bright blue stones lost its color. Morreion stiffened as if at a twinge of pain. He swung around to look from magician to magician. "I remember a certain face: a man with a bald head; black beardlets hung from each of his cheeks. He was a burly man…What was his name?"

"These events are far in the past," said the diabolist Shrue. "Best to put them out of mind."

Morreion

Other blue stones became dull: Morreion's eyes seemed to assume the light they had lost.

"The archveults came to Earth. We conquered them. They begged for their lives. So much I recall... The chief magician demanded the secret of the IOUN stones. Ah! What was his name! He had a habit of pulling on his black beardlets... A handsome man, a great popinjay — I almost see his face — he made a proposal to the chief magician. Ah! Now it begins to come clear!" The blue stones faded one by one. Morreion's face shone with a white fire. The last of the blue stones went pallid.

Morreion spoke in a soft voice, a delicate voice, as if he savored each word. "The chief magician's name was Ildefonse. The popinjay was Rhialto. I remember each detail. Rhialto proposed that I go to learn the secret; Ildefonse vowed to protect me, as if I were his own life. I trusted them; I trusted all the magicians in the chamber: Gilgad was there, and Hurtiancz and Mune the Mage and Perdustin. All my dear friends, who joined in a solemn vow to make the archveults hostage for my safety. Now I know the culprits. The archveults dealt with me as an enemy. My friends sent me forth and never thought of me again. Ildefonse — what have you to say, before you go to wait out twenty aeons in a certain place of which I know?"

Ildefonse said bluffly, "Come now, you must not take matters so seriously. All's well that ends well; we are now happily reunited and the secret of the IOUN stones is ours!"

"For each pang I suffered, you shall suffer twenty," said Morreion. "Rhialto as well, and Gilgad, and Mune, and Herark and all the rest. Vermoulian, lift the palace. Return us the way we have come. Put double fire to the incense."

Rhialto looked at Ildefonse, who shrugged.

"Unavoidable," said Rhialto. He evoked the Spell of Temporal Stasis. Silence fell upon the scene. Each person stood like a monument.

Rhialto bound Morreion's arms to his side with swaths of tape. He strapped Morreion's ankles together, and wrapped bandages into Morreion's mouth, to prevent him uttering a sound. He found a net and, capturing the IOUN stones, drew them down about Morreion's head, in close contact with his scalp. As an afterthought he taped a blindfold over Morreion's eyes.

He could do no more. He dissolved the spell. Ildefonse was already walking across the pavilion. Morreion jerked and thrashed in disbelief. Ildefonse and Rhialto lowered him to the marble floor.

"Vermoulian," said Ildefonse, "be so good as to call forth your staff. Have them bring a trundle and convey Morreion to a dark room. He must rest for a spell."

13

Rhialto found his manse as he had left it, with the exception of the way-post, which was complete. Well satisfied, Rhialto went into one of his back rooms. Here he broke open a hole into subspace and placed therein the netful of IOUN stones which he carried. Some gleamed incandescent blue; others were mingled scarlet and blue; the rest shone deep red, pink, pink and green, pale green, and pale lavender.

Rhialto shook his head ruefully and closed the dimension down upon the stones. Returning to his work-room he located Puiras among the Minuscules and restored him to size.

"Once and for all, Puiras, I find that I no longer need your services. You may join the Minuscules, or you may take your pay and go."

Puiras gave a roar of protest. "I worked my fingers to the bone; is this all the thanks I get?"

"I do not care to argue with you; in fact, I have already engaged your replacement."

Puiras eyed the tall vague-eyed man who had wandered into the work-room. "Is this the fellow? I wish him luck. Give me my money; and none of your magic gold, which goes to sand!"

Puiras took his money and went his way. Rhialto spoke to the new servitor. "For your first task, you may clear up the wreckage of the aviary. If you find corpses, drag them to the side; I will presently dispose of them. Next, the tile of the great hall…"

About the Author

JACK VANCE was born in 1916 to a well-off California family that, as his childhood ended, fell upon hard times. As a young man he worked at a series of unsatisfying jobs before studying mining engineering, physics, journalism and English at the University of California Berkeley. Leaving school as America was going to war, he found a place as an ordinary seaman in the merchant marine. Later he worked as a rigger, surveyor, ceramicist, and carpenter before his steady production of sf, mystery novels, and short stories established him as a full-time writer.

His output over more than sixty years was prodigious and won him three Hugo Awards, a Nebula Award, a World Fantasy Award for lifetime achievement, as well as an Edgar from the Mystery Writers of America. The Science Fiction and Fantasy Writers of America named him a grandmaster and he was inducted into the Science Fiction Hall of Fame.

His works crossed genre boundaries, from dark fantasies (including the highly influential *Dying Earth* cycle of novels) to interstellar space operas, from heroic fantasy (the *Lyonesse* trilogy) to murder mysteries featuring a sheriff (the Joe Bain novels) in a rural California county. A Vance story often centered on a competent male protagonist thrust into a dangerous, evolving situation on a planet where adventure was his daily fare, or featured a young person setting out on a perilous odyssey over difficult terrain populated by entrenched, scheming enemies.

Late in his life, a world-spanning assemblage of Vance aficionados came together to return his works to their original form, restoring material cut by editors whose chief preoccupation was the page count of a pulp magazine. The result was the complete and authoritative *Vance Integral Edition* in 44 hardcover volumes. Spatterlight Press is now publishing the VIE texts as ebooks, and as print-on-demand paperbacks.

Colophon

This book was printed using Adobe Arno Pro as the primary text font, with NeutraFace used on the cover.

This title was created from the digital archive of the Vance Integral Edition, a series of 44 books produced under the aegis of the author by a worldwide group of his readers. The VIE project gratefully acknowledges the editorial guidance of Norma Vance, as well as the cooperation of the Department of Special Collections at Boston University, whose John Holbrook Vance collection has been an important source of textual evidence.

Special thanks to R.C. Lacovara, Patrick Dusoulier, Koen Vyverman, Paul Rhoads, Chuck King, Gregory Hansen, Suan Yong, and Josh Geller for their invaluable assistance preparing final versions of the source files.

Digitize: Erik Arendse, Ian Davies, Joel Hedlund, Andreas Irle, Thomas Rydbeck; Format: John A. Schwab; Diff: Charles King, David Reitsema; Tech Proof: Fred Zoetemeyer; Text Integrity: Rob Friefeld, Jesse Polhemus, Steve Sherman, Tim Stretton; Implement: Donna Adams, David Reitsema; Security: Paul Rhoads; Compose: Joel Anderson, Paul Rhoads; Comp Review: Marcel van Genderen, Brian Gharst, Charles King; Update Verify: Bob Luckin, Paul Rhoads, Steve Sherman; RTF-Diff: Deborah Cohen, Charles King; Proofread: Kjel Anderson, Karl Barrus, Michel Bazin, Mark Bradford, Ursula Brandt, Patrick Dusoulier, Erec Grim, Lucie Jones, Jason Kauffeld, Robert Melson, Mike Myers, Eric Newsom, Steve Sherman

Artwork (maps based on original drawings by Jack and Norma Vance):

Paul Rhoads, Christopher Wood

Book Composition and Typesetting: Joel Anderson

Art Direction and Cover Design: Howard Kistler

Proofing: Steve Sherman, Dave Worden

Jacket Blurb: Matt Hughes

Management: John Vance, Koen Vyverman

Printed in Great Britain
by Amazon